THE
GUTS

C.E. GRIMES

© C. E. Grimes 2025

This book is copyright. Apart from any fair dealing for the purposes of study and research, criticism, review or as otherwise permitted under the Copyright Act, no part may be reproduced by any process without written permission. Inquiries should be made to the publisher.

This is a work of fiction set in the near future. Any resemblance to actual persons, living or dead is purely coincidental.

First published in 2025
Published by Puncher and Wattmann
PO Box 279
Waratah NSW 2298
https://www.puncherandwattmann.com
web@puncherandwattmann.com

ISBN 9781923099609

Edited by Ed Wright
Proofreading by Claudia King
Cover design by Miranda Douglas www.mirandadouglas.com
Typesetting by Miranda Douglas
Printed by Lightning Source International

NATIONAL
LIBRARY OF AUSTRALIA

A catalogue record for this book
is available from the National Library of Australia.

THE
GUTS
C.E. GRIMES

Puncher & Wattmann

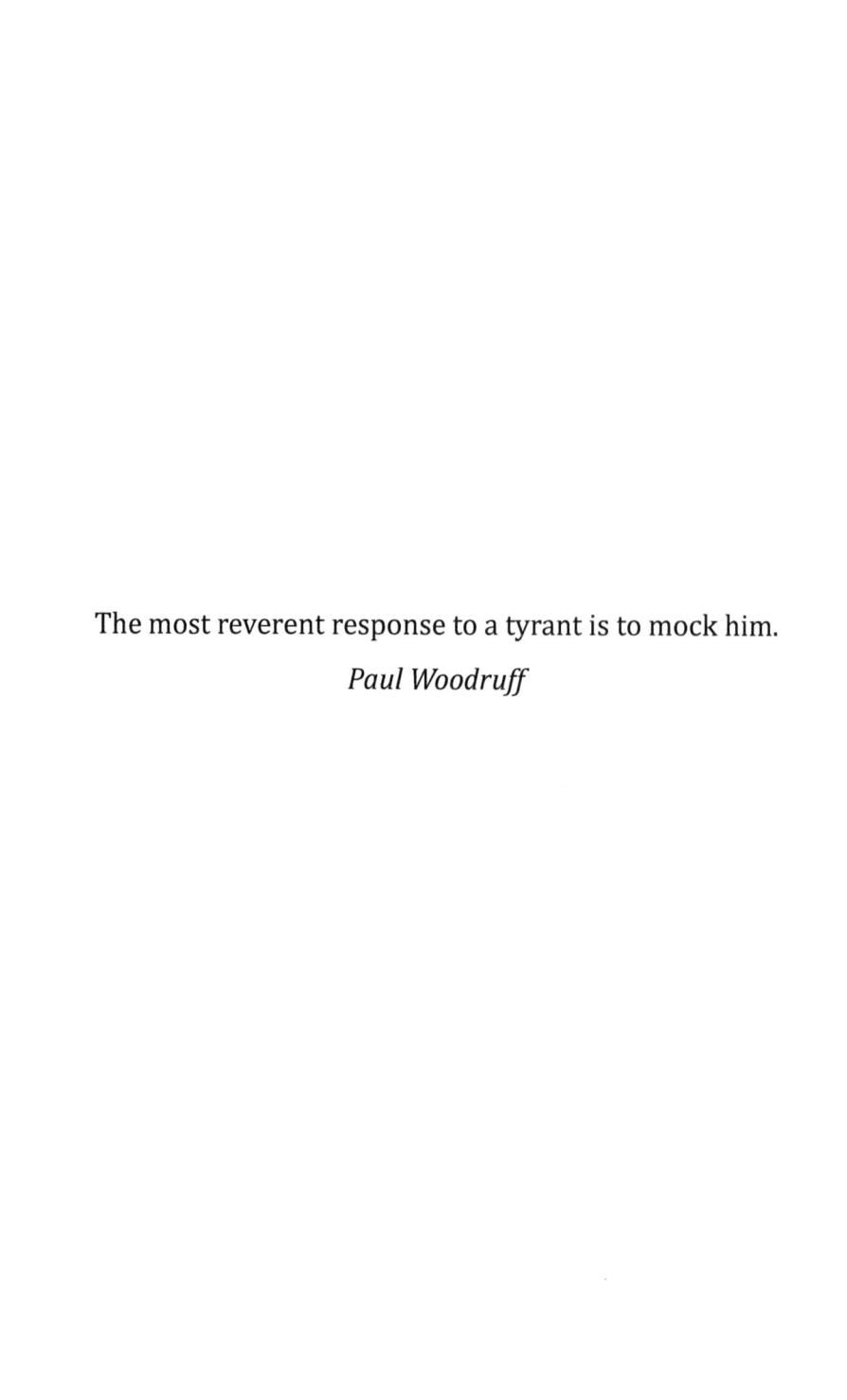

The most reverent response to a tyrant is to mock him.

Paul Woodruff

I

They had come to watch Joe Rosti, the Minister for Ageing, fall on his sword. 'I would like to take this opportunity to say something about my wife Trudie. Trudie is the most amazing person I have ever known. Her sense of justice is powerful, as is her willingness to support the underdog. I have been married to her now for over twenty years and she never ceases to amaze me.'

The Member for Smiles, a first-term MP by the name of John Fowler, passed a note under the Minister for Development's nose. *If he loves her so much, why did he cheat on her?* There was anger in the party room at this latest scandal, the latest in a long line of scandals whose resulting by-elections had left the Sporty Party clinging to a one-seat majority. For MPs like John Fowler, it was looking like their first term might also be their last.

The Minister for Development, Roger Houston, paused for thought. The skin of his face was mottled by years of lunches and his large nose had a pockmarked almost lunar quality. Only his eyes, steely blue, partly concealed by the crinkling of his forehead to a frown and the mess of greying dirty blond curls packed onto the top of his head, gave any indication that his ill-used body was a host for power.

He feigned concentration on the note, delaying his response. Experience told him that Fowler, something of a metrosexual, was nonetheless looking for his approval. Which meant he wanted something. Houston levered a pencil stub from his shirt pocket, wrote *Payback!* then passed the note to his colleague with a wink as if they were schoolboys sharing a secret behind the teacher's back. There was the briefest pause as Fowler took a small double take. The young MP hadn't understood him. But Houston wasn't surprised that he pretended to by nodding his head and giving the Minister a confected conspiratorial smile.

Fowler obviously didn't know the Minister for Ageing's wife. It was sounding like Rosti didn't know his wife either. Politics did keep you away from home a lot. Houston knew her, though. He knew nearly everyone. He'd crossed her a couple of times when she'd been the Mayor of Port Macquarie and had resisted some high-rise developments one of his key contributors had planned. Her price was his support for a seat in the NSW upper house, one of the cushiest part-time jobs in the state, a place where a person could hang out for eight years untroubled by constituents, and perhaps not even have to give a speech beyond the first. Trudie Rosti was ambitious, and not a little fierce, as Houston had discovered when he'd backslid on his promise.

As Rosti continued bleakly in praise of his wife's 'finely honed sense of civic duty,' Houston wondered whether Mrs Rosti had forced the Minister to humiliate himself in this way in revenge for the humiliation his affair with a university student had brought on her. Houston imagined her jackhammering her husband with shrill ferocity: 'Listen here, you dickhead. If you ever want to see the kids again, if you want to see a cent from the house, if you want to keep it a secret that you rigged a secret ballot to get you elected as president of the young Sporty Party, you'll do as I fucking well say.' And with his young mistress already having gone to the press in a huff, all his political allies carefully avoiding him, his career in tatters, who else did he have to turn to? If it weren't for the kids, Rosti conceivably might have killed himself like a disgraced Roman senator, a warm bath and something sharp. But this was Sydney. Behind the apologies, Houston detected a powerful instinct for self-preservation. This self-abasement was a tactic and Rosti was already looking ahead, beyond the years of political purgatory, by showing his willingness to do the bidding of whichever master might emerge to top up his pension with a gig as a consultant, or a lobbyist, or a compliant seat on a board.

It had all been such a terrible beat-up. If the girl's best friend wasn't a journalist, the public may never have known. The sad fact

THE GUTS

was that the Minister of Ageing was one of the few talented members of a mediocre cabinet in a tired government. If sleeping with women you weren't married to was a sacking offense, history would look very different. Paragons of political virtue such as Thomas Jefferson and JFK would have been thrown out of office. France would be in a permanent power vacuum. While Paul Keating might have married a hostie, it was Bob Hawke, architect of the Accord, who had joined the mile high club before he combined modernising the nation with shagging, then marrying his own biographer. The list went on: Clinton, Chifley, Schwarzenegger, Castro, Bolivar, Mao Tse Tung, the great shagging Popes of the magnificent renaissance. Even Nelson Mandela. And he'd spent most of his adult life in jail. For all Houston knew the Dalai Lama was getting his leg over too. It was an unavoidable side effect of charisma. So what if Rosti had used the ministerial car to deliver him to a series of afternoon trysts in the woman's eastern suburbs apartment? In Houston's experience, a post-coital minister was more likely to make good policy. Not that policy, unless it involved helping his business associates win government contracts, had ever been his primary concern.

Having successfully baffled Fowler, Houston looked around and saw far greater travesties than Rosti. There was the Member for befriending young homeless men, feeding them heroin and sodomising them while they were too high to notice. The state of NSW had almost been led by the member for sniffing chairs where women had just been sitting while one junior minister, clearly uncomfortable as he alternated between buttocks on the red leather benches of the house, only ever felt anything like personal equilibrium when he was bent over a table and spanked with a plastic spatula. And this was just sex, an *amuse bouche*. It was scandalous, it was fun, it made people examine their own unacted fantasies. But the entrée, main and dessert were all about the dosh.

Such men and women, spoiled by their own shame, were good for party loyalty Houston had learned during his time as the government's whip. Their weaknesses made their public lives precarious, and they were often forced to seek protection from those higher up in the food chain. In return they fell blindly into line behind the decisions of their protectors, whose interests always pertained to those of the Sporty Party, but not necessarily those of the state. The greater the deviance, the less likely they were to try and cross the floor.

'I'd like to finish by thanking the people of New South Wales for the chance to serve them and to again apologise for the failure of judgement which has brought about my resignation. Politics is a battle, and it is a thrilling but often lonely business; we work long hours separated from those we love. Often by the end of the day there is nothing left in us. And this perhaps makes us more prone than most to these kinds of errors of judgement. This of course is an explanation, but not an excuse. Once again, I would like to apologise to my wife, to my family, to my constituents, and to my party for my poor judgment. I wish my colleagues all the best for the coming election and remain convinced that they are the best possible team in place to prosecute the interests of our wonderful state.'

Embarrassed applause. The former Minister returned to the benches of the Legislative Assembly for the last time, clearly a disappointed man. And that was that.

Thank Christ, thought Houston to himself. He avoided Fowler's eye as the benches emptied and went off in the opposite direction. He had more important business to attend to. There were five voice messages on his mobile phone. An endless chain of meetings to attend. And he was taking his new electoral assistant out to lunch.

2

Adam Osborne was having a fluffy day at the office. There was work to do, but he wasn't doing it. Deadlines were approaching but they were far enough away not to be hitting the panic button, and it was unlikely anything much would be done until it was. His section editor, Ingrid Bright, had asked him to do a story on Sydney's best restaurant toilets. A piss was a piss as far as he was concerned. Unless you had kidney stones. And while there might be something to say as a cautionary note about cockroaches scuttling up the bunched legs of your trousers while a vindaloo stung right through you, that was a story to be vetted by the lawyers and not really the sort of investigative journalism the lifestyle sections of the paper went in for. RUNNING WITH THE ROACHES: SYDNEY'S DIRTIEST DINNER SPOT DUNNIES. It was trashy and tabloid, while the paper was conspicuously broadsheet, or had been. Now it seemed to be getting smaller and more desperate for eyeballs every day.

Adam could remember meals in suburban restaurants where you went through the kitchen down a narrow alleyway and followed your nose while pegging it until you found the john, but he didn't often eat in little suburban restaurants anymore. Since the paper had cut down on cab charges, they were inconvenient to get to, especially if you wanted to drink. The restaurant bathrooms Ingrid was interested in were all in the inner city and they blurred into one: lots of white, porcelain fittings and tiles, slabs of Italian marble, over-sized mirrors, and fancy chrome spouts on the basins. Delicately scented soaps, invisible air fresheners and upmarket toilet lollies that masked their function as well as the smell of the bleach. They were kingdoms of sterile serenity. But why would anyone choose a restaurant for its toilet? There wasn't much point in eating food if you were snorting lots of coke. It was a joke. But Ingrid was full of quirky ideas borrowed from somewhere else. She'd migrated from Adelaide, where her father was a dentist and her mother an opera singer whose diva moment had failed to arrive. And she was sure Sydney was a world-class city. Ignoring the shrinking quality of journalism, where fewer and fewer people were constantly being asked to do more with less, she liked to think and was prone even to saying, usually after a few too many Cosmopolitans, 'I edit a section of a world-class city's world-class metropolitan newspaper.' The toilet story had been done in the *New York Times* and she wanted it for *The Morning Glory* too.

Also on Adam's plate was a bunch of TV cooking shows to preview, but he was saving that for Sunday and the very comfortable couch he and his wife Kate had only just recently bought. There were also interviews to be done with some of Sydney's hottest young chefs on the merits of fusion food. Satay spaghetti, emu burritos, rollmops with ponzu sauce. At first, Adam had thought this story was a bit of a wank too. Mainly he preferred the clean lines of single cuisines with their refined combinations. Yet the more he thought about it, if it wasn't for fusion, the Italians wouldn't have pasta or tomatoes, the Japanese wouldn't have tempura, nor the Indians vindaloo. Worse still, he wouldn't be able to have wasabi mayonnaise with his fish and chips or seared kangaroo fillet served with green peppercorns and borscht. So perhaps it was a valid story after all.

However, he'd already frittered away most of the morning and if he did ring these restaurants, any chef worth their salt would be working up a sweat; searing, frying, grilling, baking and swearing their way to feeding the Friday lunchtime hordes. He didn't feel like waiting on the end of the line for some stressed-out chef to imply he was a fucking moron, and to ring back later when the lunch service was over.

He did have a review to write, for Splash, a new venture for a former Olympic swimmer who, gossip had it, had invested all his earnings in the restaurant, but Adam was waiting for a detail of the menu to be emailed through. The food had been mediocre, the champagne very good. Still, in the interests of objectivity, there had been a spice that had made the pork belly different from all the other pork bellies he'd been eating. Only he couldn't remember what.

Instead of working, he calculated the likely payout if he were offered a redundancy for about the 50th time, sobered himself by looking up the remaining amount on his mortgage, then committed himself to at least a further decade of employment by going on the internet and buying a case of wine. Then he phoned Kate.

'Hello. I just rang to wish you luck.'

'Thanks, I'm going to need it. Miles Harpur just rang and said that Charlotte's angling for the contract too.'

'What Mrs Carrot-up-her-arse?'

'Don't be mean!'

'I'm not. Just biased.'

'How's your day?'

Adam checked if any of the office's efficiency pests were in earshot, before answering, 'Boring as batshit. Are you still on for 1?'

'Should be fine. Anyway, got to run. See you at Dosh.'

'Good luck!'

The Morning Glory occupied two floors of a skyscraper in the CBD with a bird's eye view over the city and the harbour all the way to the heads. You could spend a whole day there and do nothing but watch the boats. The paper used to be in an old labyrinthine building at the scummy end of town where the working conditions had been a source of constant gripes. A sweatbox in summer and freezing in winter, it was as byzantine as many a journalist's head. The new building, which stayed at a constant 22°, felt sterile and isolated. It was as if the paper was being written from a cloud about the world that lay below. Underneath it was an accountancy firm and the floors above were occupied by a bank. Some people liked it this way. They were the aloof sages of the AB demographic. But some, as can happen if you spend too much time at the pub, were nostalgic for the old days, where the printing and the writing were done on the same premises; where you could go and see the black ink being pressed onto the pages instead of it disappearing from the computer and reappearing on doorsteps in the morning. Others, such as the dwindling caste of sub-editors, who had spent so much of their lives fixing up other people's mistakes they had started to look at society as an extended grammatical flaw, would find something to grumble about no matter where you put them. They were in the process of being outsourced to New Zealand, where the Scottish heritage placed a value on the pernickety, and the wages were considerably cheaper.

Sydney by contrast was all about enthusiasm, about getting enough money so you could afford to unleash your id. Which was what the display advertising in the lifestyle sections of *The Glory*, after the loss of all the classified ads to the internet, the so-called rivers of gold, was all about.

The world had changed. And no-one had really anticipated how fast. What was the point of meeting a source in a pub when you could use email? What was the point of ink, when you owned an iPad? What was the point of investigative journalism when you could start a rumour then let it go viral on TikTok? What was the point of being a journalist when you could be a manager on three times the money with share options and an office that had a harbour view?

Still feeling work-shy, Adam went past several cubicles where people were furiously typing or talking to people on the phone, to the cubicle where his friend Bob Constance sat staring into space.

'Want a coffee?' Bob was a cartoonist and a buddy from the days when Adam had been a single man and the line between the office and the pub had been blurry. His working day consisted of chasing his subconscious in pursuit of a joke, then an hour or so of frenzied drawing to get it on paper before it was beer o'clock.

'Sorry mate,' said Bob, who was scribbling on a piece of paper. 'On the verge of something.'

With no-one to help him procrastinate, Adam decided he might as well do some work or he'd end up under the weekly quota of published words stipulated in his Key Performance Indicators for the second time in a row, which would mean words from Ingrid, and preference in the next round of redundancies, which was something he couldn't afford.

Ingrid's determination to master the jargon of management was evidence of her ambition. She was thirty and thought Adam, who was in his mid-forties, a has-been. Unbeknown to Adam, she had put him forward for a redundancy in the last round of cuts management had foisted upon the paper in a desperate attempt to show they were doing something other than pulling spectacular salaries from of a severely listing ship. It hadn't been approved and Ingrid had resorted instead to a brand of passive aggressive micromanaging she hoped would irritate him into quitting. They sat three melamine cubicles from each other but communicated almost entirely via the paper's internal message system. Ingrid, it seemed, had detected his procrastination.

I: How's the toilet expose coming along?
A: Good
I: ETA?
A: Soon
I: I need 2000 more words from you by the end of the week if you're to make your targets this month
A: I'll see what I can do
I: Brill.

Adam used to think that life as a journalist would be intrepid and that in the course of his career, he'd come to an understanding of the mysterious processes that ran the world. In the main it had turned out not to be true. Working on a newspaper, you learned how little of what actually happens gets into the news. Of course, a man tying a shoelace is hardly newsworthy and such actions constitute the vast majority of events. But even with important things, half the time, when you think you've discovered the truth about something, you can't use it. So much of the truly interesting stuff was off the record, or prone to attracting the negative attention of the lawyers. Often you could dig up the story but not enough of the facts to run it. Adam had once been a gun reporter at the paper. He'd been hard where now he was soft. He'd watched murder victims being zipped into body bags. He'd chased ambulances and interviewed grieving loved ones. He'd covered civil wars and famines. But his favourite round was politics because he couldn't help but despise the venality and mediocrity of the people running the state.

It was three years now since he had crossed from a newspaper section concerned with uncovering the outrages of the rich and powerful to one dedicated to the glorification of the good life. Funky terracotta pots, heated towel racks, white balsamic vinegar and Persian carpets, the hip restaurants and secret venues of the city's cognoscenti, the chocolate martini and its enemies, he had written about them all.

Adam was paid well and the work was fairly easy. Kate had been happy since his work complemented the business she was building. Having a husband who was a prominent food critic gave her a slight competitive edge in providing PR and event management. Couples talked.

With the help of an inheritance from Kate's grandfather, who had run a printing business, they had bought a small house on the hill between Bondi Junction and the beach a few years before the property market had gone truly nuts. And if it wasn't for the mortgage (Kate had three siblings) Adam could have sat on his back deck with a beer, the sea breeze and the detective novel he'd been writing and forgotten about work entirely.

But he also had the responsibility to maintain an enviable lifestyle. Instead of adrenaline, intensity, and delusions of importance, Adam's job now consisted of oysters naturale with a nice crisp Riesling, and the decision of whether to have the beef, the fish or the duck. He could look around at his fellow harbour city hedonists and feel like he truly belonged. Yet despite the easy-street satisfaction he got from making a living out of eating, something was eating away at him.

His phone reminded him it was almost time to leave for Dosh, a city restaurant that thrived on the corporate credit card and the digestion of heavyweight deals. As an antidote to the gritty purposelessness he was feeling, the wine list beckoned. He wrote his review of Splash with a blank for the missing spice, so could he file it later that day and look like he was being productive when he was getting drunk, a combination of dissipation and efficiency that the overpaid time and motion consultants moving through the office would not have understood.

Adam trawled through his email inbox. It was heavy with spam and scams. If everything he was sent was true, he could pick up his millions of dollars from the Nigerians, take his newly enhanced penis and spend the rest of his life shagging all the beautiful young Russian women who seemed desperate to warm his bed. Given that he was overweight and middle-aged, there were slimming pills and Viagra readily available, at Canadian prices, to help him fulfil this destiny. Other unopened emails included several press releases from various flacks, an invitation to the launch of a new boutique wine label and several restaurant menus, but not the one he wanted. In the past, the snail mail invitations contained product samples. Now, they invited you with an email, and you only got the show bag if you bothered to turn up. Is it just me, he thought, or is the whole world suddenly going to shit? He ordered an Uber to take him to Dosh, then returned to his unopened emails.

He scrolled, reading, trashing, thinking of replying, then one grabbed his attention. 'Fuck that MasterChef shit Osborne, here's a real story to get your teeth into.' He opened it. 'Twice cooked lamb and the eastern resurrection,' it said. Beneath it was a hyperlink: 'Follow the shit trail'. He liked a riddle. The link took him to what seemed to be a travel site. Probably some smart-alec social media savvy advertising wunderkind and their viral marketing campaign. On the home page were four pictures: one of the Egyptian pyramids; another of an icebreaker in Antarctica; a third of a picture of the Ganges in India. The final one was of the Sahara Desert. Easy, thought Adam, clicking on the Ganges, as famous for its pollution as its holiness. That page disappeared and another replaced it. Again, there were four more pictures. A jar of rice, a sugar cane field, a coconut palm and an olive.

'Pick the odd one out,' was the instruction. This was a bit trickier, even for a food journalist. Still, it didn't take Adam that long. Rice made sake, sugar cane made rum, and coconuts made arrack, or failing that malibu. Olives were the only crop not used to make booze.

He clicked on the kalamata and was rewarded with four more pictures: a pineapple, a bloc of chocolate, a vanilla bean and a mango.

His mouse weighed up a decision. But before he could make it, he received a text on his phone. His car was approaching. Time to go to lunch.

3

According to Patti Smart, *The Morning Glory's* gossip columnist, Dosh was a mecca for the city's movers and shakers, politicians, business moguls and finance types. A haven for some of the Lucky Country's most successful mediocrities. To the rear of the restaurant, in the all-important raised seating area, hidden from the entrance by an elaborate screen while offering elevation over the other diners, an important parliamentary pensioner, who had once been a communist, was lunching with a casino lobbyist, who also was an ex-MP. Next to them, Jock 'Schnitzel' Ogilvie, an Australian Rugby great from an era when the adjective could still be used, whose nickname derived from a fondness for tenderising his opposition in the ruck, was holding court. On retiring from rugby, he'd been silver-plattered into stockbroking. The 'boys' gathered around him were mainly superannuation fund managers. They liked to hear rugby stories while they splurged on shares, food and booze using other people's money. Rugby was the topic that prevented such conversations from becoming either interesting or dangerous. It channelled the animal instinct without turning it into war. Schnitzel obliged, gave them a whiff of the inside story, and picked up hefty commissions and some untraceable opportunities for insider trading as a result.

On the other side of the room was Candy Peak, a famous Sydney bikini model. She was married to a young internet baron, Connor Pile. According to Smart, the marriage of this power couple, both of whom had prospered from the versatility of silicon, was on the rocks. As if to confirm this, Candy was lunching not with her husband, but a younger man whose total tan, steroid physique and aggressive blue-eyed vacuousness smacked of the edgy hedonism of the eastern suburbs and its legions of personal trainers. Candy toyed with a salad while her hunk unwittingly teased her with the exaggerated chewing of a fillet steak; his large Adam's Apple sliding up and down with each mouthful as if he was giving himself deep throat. Sources close to the couple had remarked (off the record) that Connor had told Candy that her arse had started to sag. His best friend, Jonas Storman, with whom Connor was in conflict over a business loan, had told a gossip columnist while snorting lines in a nightclub bathroom that Connor's sudden nastiness towards his wife was a pre-emptive strike to conceal the frequent presence of a 21-year-old dancer on his motor yacht and the absence of an adequate pre-nuptial agreement at a time when shares in the company he'd founded were on the skids.

Candy had responded to the threat by going on a diet and fitness binge. She was thirty-three years old, still beautiful, if in a manufactured way, but sadly she no longer seemed to believe it. The light which had parted queues outside the best nightclubs only several years ago had gone from her eyes.

The other patrons were an earnest and arrogant bunch. Some were puffed up political bully boys who felt like they owned the city and the deals that allowed it to run as if they were the rightful heirs of John Macarthur and his entrepreneurial colonial marines. Others were quieter, greyer, men and the odd determined woman who worked seventy hours a week or more. They drank sparkling water when they lunched and were constantly checking their phones, which was a kind of umbilical cord to the offices where they spent their greatest moments. They got paid a lot of money and compensated themselves in their brief moments of leisure with the competitive consumption of property, overseas travel and boats. Fund managers, partners in accountancy firms, corporate lawyers and senior public servants, they embodied a cautious kind of greed that maintained faith in its own civility.

Fools, thought Houston, Minister for Development, sitting at his favourite table perusing the menu, eyeing the world with smug amusement while Justine was in the bathroom powdering her nose.

THE GUTS

He was one of the old school. He loved the cash and the gash. He didn't mind being crass. It gave him the edge over those grey-minded private school old boys who were prone to pull back when it came to risking the veneers of their respectability. An awkward silence at the golf club was more than some men and their wives could bear.

Houston had no delusions concerning the ethics of his industry. Although he offered the necessary lip service to the Sporty Party that had supplied him with his networks and his position in the parliament, his power and influence were dedicated to the accretion of assets to himself. His biggest edge was arguably his encyclopaedic knowledge of the goss. Before he became the Minister for Development, he'd been a long-serving Parliamentary Whip, where it was his business to know what the public wasn't meant to know and to work out how to keep it under wraps, or to cajole people into toeing the party line with the threat of revealing their indiscretions. He'd fallen into the role by luck, the result of a trade-off between the party's factions. He had begun with little idea of the job's true potential but had quickly gotten hooked. He was a collector by nature. Visitors to his house in the suburb of Woolwich, a peninsula wedged between the Parramatta and Lane Cove Rivers in the northern suburbs of Sydney, a domain mainly ceded to Daphne, his three wise monkey wife, and his two adult children, might be invited to peruse his collection of antique mirrors, or to visit the room full of knight's armour, a fascination begun in a Spanish castle while on a parliamentary research trip early in his career. When his appointment as Whip opened up privileged channels of information, he'd started collecting gossip and information with the same passion and used it to facilitate his other passion, which was the collection of real estate, largely funded from the gratuities he received from businessmen for the facilitation of politically tricky projects. There were farms, town houses, and apartments, though for the sake of the parliament's pecuniary register, they were mostly owned by shelf companies headquartered in the Cayman Islands. He owned a beach house, but was unaustralian in that swimming in the ocean didn't appeal to him. He preferred to breed pigs at the farm he had acquired near Mudgee on the dustier side of the Great Divide, while he waited for it to be mined for coal.

Of course, property wasn't the be-all and end-all. Part of what he had acquired with all this knowledge was insurance. No one was going to dump a bucket of shit on his head if they were more worried about the shit he had on them. Society, said Margaret Thatcher, is an illusion. An illusion, reckoned Houston, to be mined. For him, Australia wasn't something to be defended, it was an opportunity to be taken. His idea of history was simple. The Poms came and booted out the Aboriginals. The settlers booted out the Poms. Immigrants came from everywhere to fill the empty land. Eventually the place would probably be taken over by the Chinese, or some other Asian country in desperate need of rocks and *lebensraum*. So what? Life was all about making hay while the sun shone. It didn't matter what had happened before his time, or after he was gone.

In Houston's head was a dense map of compromising situations and under the table deals. For gamblers with bankruptcy, therefore expulsion from the parliament breathing down their necks, Houston had arranged discreet loans, whose repayment terms most would have considered irregular. Others not quite so vulnerable could be bribed. Sons-in-law were given high-paying gigs as consultants. Daughters who were at a loss after the completion of their arts degrees were appointed as media advisors. Fellow travellers who had proven their loyalty were parachuted into senior positions on all sorts of quasi-autonomous government organisations to make sure the autonomy never got out of control. The longer the Sporty Party stayed in power, the more it resembled an extended family. And due to boom-time conditions and the even greater mediocrity of the opposition, the Sporty Party had broken the patterns of the electoral cycle and remained in power for almost twenty years.

For Houston this business was all perfectly natural. Mayors received kickbacks from developers then became Members of Parliament as men already owned. People whispered things about companies at restaurants like Dosh before they were publicly known, before their shares on the stock market began to move. An MP might know for instance, the winner or loser of a government tender. It was all bankable information. Houston the politician had arrived in the great era of floats and privatisations. He had settled into the great Australian property boom. People were making money everywhere, and stacks of it, for doing not very much. As long as you were in the know. Life's a rort, and it's only a rort if you're not in it.

When Houston saw Adam Osborne enter the restaurant, his eyes lit up. It was five years since he'd last noticed him and it looked like he'd gone to seed. A fairly good-looking if poorly advised bloke in his youth, Osborne had since grown extra chins. His cheeks were florid from the restaurant stairs, and he had the beginnings of a drinker's nose. Houston's intuitions of the gaps between public confidence and private insecurity were well honed. To him it seemed that Adam's eyes had the false bonhomie of someone determined to maintain the veneer of worldly success, while they gazed inward on a self already defeated.

Osborne was sweating. A heart attack waiting to happen, thought Houston, who'd already survived his first. For two minutes, he actually had been dead. But there was no question of any spiritual awakening. Houston had returned from the underworld with his materialism enhanced. As Kerry Packer, whose maverick company Houston had enjoyed whenever the tycoon wasn't calling him a cunt had said, 'when I got to the light at the end of the tunnel, there was nothing fucking there.' Houston's experience had been slightly different. As the ambulance screamed through traffic on its way to Royal North Shore Hospital, he had seen a harbour-side mansion with a tennis court, deep mooring and a jetty. He celebrated his resurrection by buying himself a boat. For Houston, whose father had been a drunk, mother a martyr, harbourside Sydney and its undeniable beauty was the afterlife too.

It was not uncommon for a fat man to think himself comparatively thin and to super-impose his gut onto someone else where it can grow freely towards grotesquery. Where Houston had seen Adam's middle-age spread and read failure: Adam saw Houston's wilful piggy eyes set deep into greedy jowls and thought he resembled an ugly baby. He wasn't the first person of a certain age and cultural memory to call the state's Minister for Development, 'Boss Hog.'

People widely assume that fat people are lazier and stupider than thin people. Crap! Fat carried the right way can be an asset. It can impart an aura of power and prosperity, like statues of the Buddha's bountiful belly in cultures where there isn't always enough rice to go around. There was only so much you could do with looks. Unlike poor old Candy Peak, whose glory days were as truncated as any sportsman's, Houston liked to think he'd grown out of his looks, that looks were only ever a beginning. A fat man's confidence could surprise a thin man's expectation of superiority and put him off his guard. And it was in those moments when competitive advantage began to be established. Real advantage came from fucking with people's heads. Of course, fat and ugly was easier if you were a man, thought Houston, as an image of his new electoral assistant, Justine, briefly occupied his mind. The thought was a vestige of the fairness that had dressed his ambition in the early days, something he had also long ago outgrown. As Houston had expanded, he had learned how to throw his weight around.

When Adam appeared to have noticed him, Houston returned with an enigmatic smile. Houston enjoyed it when people were afraid of him, even if vanity left him prone to over-estimating his impact on other people's thoughts. Adam returned Houston's smile with a nod and a raised hand half wave, half stop sign. In response to the minister's beckoning wave, Adam pulled his phone from his pocket and pretended to answer it. He pointed to his table where a waiter, apprised by the maître d' of his status as a food critic, had already pulled out his chair.

The tablecloth was a rich purple, the white napkins thick and stiff. The floor was carpeted, the walls upholstered – to muffle the secrets. To the owners of Dosh, Adam Osborne was more important than the Minister for Development, a thought Adam happily swallowed with the day's first sip of beer.

THE GUTS

Adam inspected the menu. Soon after an attractive fleshy woman in her late thirties or early forties joined him. Her hair was black and curly, her lips dark red. She had a slight double chin and smart eyes. From his table Houston watched her breasts shudder as she laughed. Osborne's mistress, he assumed, his thoughts again dwelling on his electoral assistant, who seemed to be taking some time in the bathroom. Nobody lunched at Dosh with their wife.

'Why did that creep want to talk to you?' asked Kate, who had witnessed the exchange between her husband and Houston on her way in. Adam was wondering too. He'd only ever met Houston twice, and not to share a drink.

'Buggered if I know.'

'Buggered if you don't.' She raised her foot beneath the table and wedged it between him and his seat.

'Not with a shoe as sharp as that.' They didn't mind a dirty joke.

She brushed her hand over his, then said, 'I think I got the tender.'

'Aren't you clever?'

'I'm not completely sure yet, but Victoria rang me after the presentation and said how impressed they'd been. She told me, unofficially mind you, that it was pretty much in the bag.'

'Shall I order some champagne?'

'Not for me, I'm afraid. Maybe tonight. I've got so much work to do.' Kate returned to her menu, still looking pleased. 'The fish looks good. What are you going to have?'

'I'm thinking the duck. With a glass of the Tasmanian Pinot.'

~

The object of Houston's daydreaming was Justine Delph. Her looks were accompanied by a degree in politics and psychology, some deeply buried secrets and a low-boredom threshold that sometimes led her to flirt with danger. For several years after university, she had worked in the aid world, dealing with the consequences of civil wars, trying to help paper over wounds that would probably never heal. The initial intoxication of purpose that came from saving a starving family with a bag of flour, or a sick child through the provision of simple medicines had been incredible. But gradually those she couldn't save had a cumulative effect. She grew cynical about how aid was an industry where too much of the monetised kindness of first-world citizens was invested in brand new Toyota Landcruisers and confabs in five-star hotels. She grew sick of being a perennial outsider, weighed down by the constant reminders of the outrageous privilege of being a middle-class Australian, which she had hoped to disavow. And when one of the doctors she worked with had warned her she was burning out, she took her compassion fatigue and returned to Sydney, which was her home, only to find she didn't belong there anymore either. Sure, she loved it, the harbour, the beaches, the banksias and Moreton Bay figs; the jasmine crawling up the sides of inner-city terrace houses in spring, the mix of people, the cheap Asian food, the lack of murderous intent. But it bored her. Her old friends, who once might have talked philosophy or music or the next big thing, were getting married and talking of real estate, coffee and restaurants. It was all anyone seemed to be passionate about. They all remained technically left wing, they signed petitions on Facebook: for the refugees; against new roads; for animal rights; and marriage equality, but that was about it. Most of them were struggling to get ahead.

Babies would be next, and Justine wasn't ready for that either. Freedom was too important. And while she liked men and they liked her, she couldn't imagine spending decades waking up next to the same one. She wasn't quite thirty and she wasn't quite ready to settle down. Especially not with someone whose idea of achievement was a mortgage on an over-priced nest.

A series of dull contract jobs editing government reports upon her return hadn't helped her restlessness either. Why did work have to be so boring? Why was so much of the time you spent at work devoted to pointless bullshit? Not even a year and the itch was back. She felt decadent every time she ate in a restaurant. She bought her clothes at op-shops and felt like a fraud every time she bought a new pair of shoes. Wondered what kind of slave labour had produced them. She was a bubble dweller. There was civil war in the Congo, a famine in Sudan. Women being kicked out of a decent life by the Taliban in Afghanistan. Slaughter, starvation, oppression. Innocent people died to suit the self-aggrandisement of their leaders. Leaders were almost inevitably a disappointment. She had started sending emails to her contacts in the aid world. But she'd been there, done that, and she didn't really want to go back.

But she was going to until a chance meeting in a bar changed everything. In a life that wasn't short of debatable choices, this was possibly one of her worst. And now she was in the bathroom and she didn't want to leave. The white-tiled walls were cool against her skin and the artificial pine forest of the air freshener appealed to her. The place felt so sterile she had no qualms about chopping up a line of coke on the toilet seat and snorting it through a twenty-dollar bill. The coke was good. Her friend Sarah was sleeping with a Brazilian. He was pure bullshit, but it was pure Bolivian. She felt the tingles starting in her spine as the acrid powder hitched a ride on the mucus sliding down the back of her throat. Her mouth began to go numb. Soon she would be feeling invincible, a little bit stroppy perhaps, but loose. She shouldn't be doing it. Coke was a dodgy fucking yuppie drug. It was such a Sydney thing. But it enabled her to slip into her alter ego and strut out of the ladies, her brittle mood concealed by drug-fuelled sass. Justine looked in the mirror and wondered why she had gotten into this. Another addition to the list of unnecessarily dodgy situations she had gotten herself into. She liked keeping lists – she had a notebook especially for them. Favourite poems. Books she intended to read. Boys she had enjoyed and the countries they had come from. The word for butterfly in different languages. But *Derr Justine* was one of her longest. Hitchhiking through Turkey with a maniac, getting caught out by a blizzard in Nepal. Talking down the militia in Darfur. Staying behind with a sick child when the last of the Land Cruisers pulled out. Seducing a Masai tribesman – Kirui was his name – she wasn't meant to seduce but he was just too beautiful to resist. Sky diving. Motorcycle riding. You were supposed to grow out of these things. She needed thrills, though, to feel alive and her list kept getting longer.

Still, this was different. It wasn't too late to bail. She could walk back to the table, spill some soup in his lap and quit. It would be a pleasing way to end their short acquaintance. But her personal code of honour demanded that once she begin something, no matter how dangerous or hare-brained, she was bound to see it through. It was part of the ongoing battle she conducted with her deceased mother, whose rich imagination had been dedicated to reasons for saying no, and who had found an afterlife as a kind of intimate talk show provocateur in her daughter's head. Other than the occasional man, Justine hadn't defaulted on a challenge yet. It was unfair that the dirty job had gone to the girl. It was a rich seam of unfairness that had begun with her first period, she reckoned. All that sugar and spice and everything nice had been a cover-up. The boys playing this game only had to fiddle with their computers like they incessantly fiddled with their cocks. These anarchistic boy geeks with coding skills but no social skills had become the 21st century's Che Guevaras, working with zeros and ones instead of guns. But she had been cast to play the role of honey trap, like some Soviet era swallow. It was unfair, but so much of life was, unfairness, she reckoned, was an insufficient reason to quit.

The coke kicked in and her mind began to fly on the hot air of sloganeering. 'We must destroy in order to create.' Causes were more interesting than men. Justine checked her face in the mirror for signs of spillage and retouched her lipstick. Her mind was white, ready for anything. Now, back to the table. Fight power with powder.

Houston watched Justine keenly as she returned to him from the bathroom, flicking her blond mane behind her as she walked. Her breasts jiggled against the fabric of her blouse, which had its top two buttons undone to reveal a hint of the firm fat that lay within. He imagined her bum cheeks grinding the G-string he supposed was wedged between her and her tight black pants, then envisioned himself triumphantly unclad, kneeling behind her naked bottom as its

THE GUTS

spanked surfaces waggled an invitation. The heads she turned as she passed added to the lustre of his self-satisfaction. She was beautiful. More than just beautiful. She was sex itself. Young men, married men, men who'd long ago confined their thoughts of balls, sticks and holes to the golf course couldn't help but feel the resurrection of an ache. She was, thought Houston, the best electoral assistant a minister could ever hope to have.

Justine sat down, sniffling just a little and gave him what he thought was a horny stare. He brushed his leg back and forth against hers under the table. She kicked him in the shins, lightly, then apologised as if the contact had been an accident. Houston was not deterred. The waiter came. Houston ordered a bottle of Riesling, a dozen each of the oysters and two of the slow-cooked lamb. Justine did not protest. He removed his right loafer and was about to send out his foot in search of another kick, when his mobile began to ring. It was the tone he had chosen for the Premier – the theme to the Mickey Mouse Club. He fumbled for it in his trouser pocket. 'Roger, drop whatever you're doing. I need to see you now.' Winston Pond wasn't happy. Neither was Houston. If only he hadn't answered. His afternoon had been ruined before he'd even had the chance to eat his lunch.

'Who's the floozy?' asked Kate, who didn't much like the post-feminist insouciance of millennials.

'Dunno,' said Adam. His immersion in the menu had gifted him immunity from the animal magnetism of Justine's strut across the floor. Which was just as well.

The menu consisted of classics seasoned with power. Gambles of taste were confined to the entrees: grilled prawns wrapped in bacon with a caperberry sauce; an eggplant mousse studded with salmon roe; pork belly served with a truffled egg custard; and quail eggs dusted in dukkah on a bed of crispy seaweed. The oysters were unadorned. The mains were lamb rump cooked to order with a port wine jus and parsnip mash; milk fed veal in a lemon sauce with baby peas and a Jerusalem artichoke puree flecked with speck; hiramasa kingfish poached in Chinese masterstock with shiitake mushrooms and soba noodles; duck with cumquat sauce served with cavallo nero and wild rice. The special was rib-eye steak on the bone. Dessert included a refreshing trio of lemon, lime and lychee sorbets; butterscotch pudding with praline and Madagascan vanilla ice cream; and a candied pineapple and donut stack served with a coconut sauce, which was inventively named Hawaii Five O.

At about two-thirty, Adam said a heavy goodbye to Kate outside Dosh and walked back to the office. The email with the pork belly herb had arrived. It was *shiso*, a Japanese leaf herb whose taste in some ways resembled basil. He hadn't noticed it at the time, but with the *shiso* had been a hint of *umeboshi*, an intensely sour and salty pickled Japanese plum. He finished that review then drafted a review for Dosh while the meal was still fresh in his head. It took him about an hour. He went downstairs for coffee, then returned with a couple more hours to kill until he could go home without eyebrows being raised. The email riddle he'd been looking at before lunch was still on his computer. A question of vanilla, pineapple, mango and chocolate. His mouse hovered over the four pictures momentarily then clicked on the mango. His subconscious had done the hard work for him. It was the only food that hadn't originated in South America. Four more pictures came up. Paul Keating, John Howard, Peter Costello and Joseph Lyons. This one was a bit trickier, but not for Bob Constance, who was suddenly over Adam's shoulder and pointing at Peter Costello.

'All were ambitious Treasurers but he's the only one who didn't have the guts to fight for the top job. And thank fucking God for that!'

'Thanks mate.'

Adam clicked on Costello, but the server seemed to be frozen.

'I need to pick your brains about something,' said Bob, which in earshot of Ingrid was code for 'my work is done, have you got time for a beer?'

'Sure,' said Adam. He rolled out from his workstation and swivelled around to face Bob. He picked up his phone and keys and followed the cartoonist to the lift. There was a small pub down the road where the Friday after-work drinkers were beginning to accumulate. A game of cricket was on the television.

'Why the treasurers?' asked Bob, when Adam returned from the bar with their beers.

'Not sure.' He explained the email to Bob.

'Mmm. Weird. Do you mind if I pinch the idea for a cartoon?'

'Sure, just let me work out what it is first.'

When Adam returned to work an hour later, the computers were still frozen. Anyone on deadline was cursing and swearing, but since he wasn't, Adam decided to give himself an early mark.

Unable to message Ingrid, he went to her cubicle.

'If you need me, I'll be on my mobile. It's going to be easier to work from home.'

'I just spoke to Rod in IT. It should be fixed in about ten minutes.'

'I might go anyway. I've got some toilets to check out.'

'Just make sure you file by tomorrow. Sunday's the end of the month.'

'Sure.'

He went home, got changed, walked down the hill and swam off some of the day's excess with a lap of Bondi Beach.

4

What a prick-tease the Premier was! Houston bid Justine goodbye, walked out of the restaurant and into the ministerial car.

Next week he would take her somewhere special. Next week his wife would be in the Southern Highlands for a flower show. There would be time for him to spoil her then. He'd earned it, he thought. In gratitude for a deal he'd sealed for Virtue Constructions, Harry Virtue had given him free access to one of his Stevedore project's harbourside penthouses. The perfect place for sugar daddy assignations. As his driver negotiated the clog of buses, taxis and delivery vans, Houston filled in the Tuesday night blank in his diary with his fantasy pen. Dinner at one of the swank little eateries in the vicinity, then champagne on the balcony of his Harry Virtue penthouse, gazing out at the uninterrupted harbour vista and feeling like a million dollars. Then he'd count some of them trying not to come too quickly as he explored her hot young body. It had been a while. And now he was frustrated. Ever the optimist, he'd taken a Viagra in the hope of some post-prandial action. Sitting in traffic with a chemically induced hard-on, enroute to one of Sydney's unsexiest men, was not how he'd planned to spend the rest of his day. He could have kicked the Premier in the balls.

The car dropped him off at Chifley Tower. While taking the elevator up to the Premier's office, Houston tried to calm himself down. In the mirror he practiced his best deferential grin. The Premier was prone to getting his knickers in a knot over not much. Not that Houston would tell him. Well, not in those words. The Honourable Winston Pond, or Mr Premier as he preferred to be called, feared strong opinions and rewarded sycophants. His ego exceeded his abilities. He looked good on television and had an excellent radio voice, but as the Premier he was about as effective as a eunuch in a stud farm. Which was precisely why he was there.

In the five years of his Premiership, the electoral breeze had shifted. The Sporty Party would have lost the election of eighteen months ago, except for the late implosion of the Opposition Leader, Anthony Jones, after his wife publicly left him three weeks out from polling day. And in leaving him, she had revealed how many investment properties they had owned, several of them empty, and several other of them tastelessly renovated by a major Sporty Party donor for free. Still, the government's majority in the lower house had been reduced to four, and that majority had since been eaten away at by a series of scandals of sufficient magnitude that the members involved had been forced to resign. Janice Oates, MP for Blanche, had employed her husband as an advisor. The press had then discovered his links to a racist organisation and its virulent campaign against Muslims. In the resulting by-election – the electorate had a significant population of Lebanese – Oates's replacement had lost. The Member for Snedden, George Bayer, who had been assisting the Minister for Health had terminated his political career little more than a month after for failing to declare that the company he had awarded the contract to supply hospitals across the state with bandages, was owned by his wife's cousin. The Sporty Party had lost that by-election too. Now Joe Rosti had gone, the government was down to a majority of two, with a by-election to come. Judging from the polls they were going to lose that too. There were two more years of their term to serve. But if anything else happened the government would be at the mercy of the independents, or even the greens, for its hold on power. To win an election and waste two years of government, thought Houston, was like winning the toss at the SCG, choosing to bat, and getting skittled for under a hundred.

People got in and out of the elevator as it climbed through the floors, but no one talked. Houston hogged the rear right-hand corner with his vastness and allowed his irritation to crackle in preparation for meeting the Premier. He pushed his way past a number of apparatchiks to exit the elevator and made his way up the corridor.

THE GUTS

It was hot for November and the air-conditioning was in the process of being dismantled and checked because someone had found white powder in the filters. Houston felt beads of sweat trickle down his back as he walked past some expensive Australian artworks, his suit coat needed to conceal the persistence of his monument to American pharmaceutical genius. He passed a large open-plan office filled with mostly young men and women staring deeply into their computer screens, many with opened take-away containers beside them. With the air-conditioning out of commission, the place had the smell of an Asian food market. It was the afternoon office lull, and the policy gurus of the future were busy looking busy while their brains yearned for the under-touristed land of the siesta. One woman looked at him. She was vaguely familiar. Her eyes dived quickly when he met them.

In the next office, Pond's private secretary and Houston's unofficial enemy sat primly glowering behind her desk. Susan Hardcastle was the widowed daughter of a former scion of the Sporty Party, Lionel Potts – the greatest Postmaster General they'd ever had. Her husband, Chris, was a former Australian Trade Commissioner who had dropped dead mysteriously while on business in Dubai. Since then, Hardcastle had made herself Winston Pond's unofficial extra limb. Her age was indeterminate, but it didn't really matter, she'd been born middle-aged. Anyone with sufficient imagination to picture her as a girl was engaged in more fruitful activities than politics, while her colleagues in the Premier's office could only dream of her retirement. There were plans to buy her a one-way ticket to Wales in lieu of the golden watch. Her mouse brown bob, green eyes, freckled skin and pursed mouth housed a savagery of moral judgement that had accumulated over a lifetime of disappointment and had the uncanny ability to put powerful men in touch with their shame. With the women she was merely unfriendly.

Houston was sure that she despised him and was letting him know it, silently. The father was one of the old school, he'd dragged himself up by the bootstraps after leaving school at the age of 14. The husband had been more to Houston's taste. A pragmatist, Houston supposed

Chris could only have married this Susan for reasons of dynastic preferment. He was rumoured to have died on the job while working away from home.

'He's expecting you,' she said, though from the tone of her voice she might as well have added 'you disgusting doggy doo.' He felt her eyes linger where his suit jacket couldn't quite fully conceal the bulge in his trousers. Her mouth remained a sour purse, but was there the hint of a smirk? Houston consoled himself with visions of her lonely apartment life, surrounded by selfish cats and, because the world was leaving her behind, the voice of Alan Jones quietly shrieking from a clock radio in the kitchen. She had turned to pensioner radio before her time.

He went through the door and into the Premier's office. Pond was standing behind his desk, gazing into a window that merged a panoramic view down the harbour towards Manly with his own reflection. He was trying to pat a stray hair into place on the top of his head. Hearing footsteps, he turned to face his Minister. Although in his fifties the Premier still had the look of a belligerent baby. His face was a chubby moon that had maintained the pink cheeks of childhood. It was topped with a thinning shock of blond hair. His eyes were an indeterminate blue-green, simultaneously imperious and weak. Like many successful men, Pond had started out as a Mummy's boy. His father, a salesman, had rarely been home.

The generic handsomeness of the young Pond had been bankable, but now in middle age, it had faded. Little of character had emerged to take its place.

'Houston, we have a problem.'
'What's happened?'
'Parker's gone.'
'What do you mean gone?'
'Not here anymore.'
'Not here in parliament?'
'Not anywhere to be found.'
'How do you know?'

THE GUTS

'Take a look at this.'

He handed Houston a printout of an email and returned to stroking his hair.

From: Alexander Parker
To: wpond@premier.nsw.gov.au
Subject: Done the Harold Holt

Dear Winston, this is to let you know I've flown the coop. I once thought the process of growing old would make me more tolerant, but I have found myself becoming increasingly radicalised. There doesn't seem to me to be any point in being part of a government for whom good governance has become a secondary concern at best. I would like to say that I am sorry for the effect this will have on your career and your chances of remaining premier but cannot honestly do so.

This government – and I am ashamed to say I have been a part of it – is a disgrace. For the last five years, the state has been in crisis, but we have done nothing except pay consultants to write expensive reports. Unscrupulous developers who contribute heavily to our campaign funding have constructed all sorts of follies, and even then we have neglected to provide the necessary infrastructure so people can get to and from them. This party has a great history of legislating ideas that have made this country a decent place with opportunities for all, but now it seems intent on eroding it. We tell ourselves that we are the best people to handle the pressures of the market but in the end all we do is perpetuate ourselves with the money we take from pokies, property, and mining. The party for the people is now a party for itself.

I have recently been made privy to a raft of secret information concerning key members of our government, which has left me with an almost paralysing self-disgust. At first, I thought I might simply resign from the party and sit my term out on the crossbenches, but since the recent resignations have eroded our majority, that would mean constant pressure to join the opposition in forming a new government. And, to be honest, I don't like them any better than I like us.

You are not a bad person, but your success is a sad reflection on the society that has permitted it. For the people's sake and the Sporty Party's sake it's time for the dirty laundry of our political culture to be aired. I wish you luck in avoiding the fall-out that's to come since you are more of a consequence than a cause. But if you think the challenge of another by-election is all that awaits you, think again. I hope you will be shocked by some of the things you will soon discover. If not, then things are even worse than I have imagined. Don't try to track me down. You will not be able to change my mind.

Yours sincerely,
Alexander Parker MP

'What a cheeky cunt!' said Houston. But it wasn't just cheek. And that was worrying. Parker's letter was tinged with the sort of infuriating purity Houston associated with revolutionaries and university undergraduates. The intention of clearing the decks and starting again. Hadn't he heard of Kampuchea? Or the Caliphate. These were deadly dreams. If only the world's idealists could settle for sensible fantasies, he thought, mistresses who dressed up as schoolgirls, waterfront homes with motor cruisers, even a bit of mindless football hooliganism, then the world would be a much better place. But the debonair Mr Parker, always a bit of an enigma, his pleasantness just that bit too calculated to be trusted, but until now quietly compliant to factional and party lines, was suddenly sounding very much like a fanatic. A Unabomber in a Zegna suit.

Pond returned to his window. The room was too full of rapidly adjusting perspectives for speech. Houston ran through his mental filing cabinet. Before Parker had entered politics, he'd been a suburban lawyer. He wasn't married. Houston made a mental note to check out why. He had a series of coded files in which he recorded his

THE GUTS

knowledge of government MPs, opposition MPs and the people they dealt with. He was pretty sure that until now, Parker had been off the radar. Probably because he hadn't rocked the boat. It was time to dig into the man and find out what made him tick.

'What's he talking about?' asked Pond.

'I dunno,' replied Houston. A small part of him saw beyond Pond's mediocrity and felt sorry for his patsy Premier. 'One thing's for sure. He's lost the bloody plot.'

It didn't seem the kind of self-destructive grandstanding that usually came with nervous breakdowns in the bear pit. Parker didn't sound like an unlikeable ego making a desperate cry for love. He had been self-contained, but not loathed. And if this antipathy towards his colleagues was what he'd been containing, he'd done a scarily good job of it. Parker had spruiked the line of party solidarity, fiscal rectitude and law and order with the best of them. The idea of airing the party's dirty laundry was alarming. From the days of Robert Askin, and probably before, it was tacitly understood, with the help of the state's defamation laws and the provisions of commercial in confidence, that most NSW politicians, whether dry-eyed Balmain boys, mellifluous Maroubrans or bully boy Christians from the Hills, should have the benefit of death before their selling out of the state for the sake of vested interests became public knowledge. It helped secure the continuity of government. Now a loose cannon from the backbench might be about to put all this at risk. He had to be stopped.

Houston began to do what he did best, scheme. The first thing was to pacify Pond.

'We need to find him before anyone else finds out.' said Pond.

'Have you tried his house?'

'Yes. There was no-one there.'

'What about his mobile?'

'Switched off. I've had Susan ringing all morning,' he said.

'Has anyone else been ringing him?' asked Houston.

'Yes. None of his phones are answering and no-one's seen him since he went on leave.'

'Where was he meant to have gone?'

'Bushwalking, I think.' The Premier shrugged his shoulders.

'See if you can find out more. A favourite place, that sort of thing.' Houston stopped to think where Parker might have gone. 'Have you replied to the email?'

'Yes, but nothing's come back.'

'What did you say?'

'I told him that he was being very childish, and that this wasn't a kindergarten, rather the biggest game in town … that if he valued his career, he'd be at tomorrow morning's party meeting.'

No fucking idea, thought Houston. Pond's vanity prevented him from understanding that Parker no longer gave a shit. Houston had a sudden flash that Parker might have a holiday house on the south coast. 'Did you try his beach house?' It was the sort of envious detail that Pond did pay attention to.

'It doesn't have a phone.'

'Don't worry. Get me the address and I'll get someone to check it out.'

'Good. But what's he talking about?'

'What do you mean?'

'About the dirty laundry.'

'How would I know, Winston? Have you told anyone about this yet?'

'No, only Susan.'

'Let's keep it that way. We don't want anyone getting wind of this. It would make a lovely little addition to the papers, wouldn't it? MISSING MP LAME DUCKS POND.'

'But what are we going to do?'

'Let me make a few phone calls, and I'll get back to you. And if anyone asks, just tell them you've given Parker leave to go off on a hiking holiday, which is why his phone is out of range,' he said.

'Alright,' Pond sighed grumpily. 'But don't take too long about it. If this doesn't get sorted out we're going to have problems with the Shortland Towers development bill. And that's just for starters.'

Maybe you aren't so stupid after all, thought Houston. 'Don't worry, Winston. I'll sort it out,' he said, before walking out of his office.

THE GUTS

'I was hoping you'd say that,' said the Premier, softly under his breath.

Personally, Houston would have been content to dump Pond in it. However, Pond's last remark had reminded him that if the independents got control of the house, they were also unlikely to let through his coastal development bill. And if that didn't get through, he might be in trouble with some of the powerful and colourful business identities to whom his career was beholden. The Big Macaws, as he referred to them, had invested in his ability to get it through. They had paid him in advance for services rendered and if the bill didn't get through then he might have to return the money. His financial situation would take a big hit, just as he was beginning to think it might be a good time to retire. If they wanted the money, there was no question of not returning it. He didn't want to become the second New South Wales politician, after John Newman, to be killed in the line of duty. He couldn't afford to indulge the temptation to sit back and watch the Premier dissolve in a panic. He and Pond were one arse cheek each on the same precarious stool.

Houston left Chifley Tower and took the ministerial car back to his office in Parliament. Some ministers preferred to spend their time in their departmental buildings, but Houston liked his office in the parliament with its front office for secretaries, visitors and small meetings, and its inner sanctum that opened out to a balcony with views over the Domain to the harbour. When parliament was sitting, he enjoyed the buzz; when it wasn't sitting, which was most of the time, he found the peace and quiet conducive to scheming.

As his feet stomped down the carpet to his office, he was happy there was no one around to make him wipe the fury from his face. He briefly fantasised that Justine had returned. The Viagra hadn't relented. The thought of bending her over the desk and giving her one, his gut resting on the top of her buttocks as he thrusted, was almost enough to make him come. He turned the key and swung open the heavy timber door. Empty. Before he could fix anything, he needed to have a wank. He passed through the outer office, went into his inner sanctum and turned on the computer. From the bathroom he took a handful of toilet paper. He logged in using the password of one of his staff. When the Internet browser opened, he typed in the url: www.cumquick.com. A homepage opened with a series of sex scenes to choose from. A banner read, *For Busy Men with Urgent Needs*. He hovered over a few of the scenes with his mouse before selecting 'Secretary spanked and fucked.' It began with a woman with her hair in a bun typing on a keyboard but didn't stay like that for long. Before long, her boss emerged and began to abuse her in a language Houston didn't understand. The secretary's apology clearly wasn't enough. The boss instructed her to bend over the typing chair. She complied. He raised the chair to an appropriate level and unzipped her skirt. It fell to the ground, revealing a bottom covered with only a G-string. The boss said something sharp and landed a blow on her behind with his open hand. The woman raised the top half of her torso, turned her head towards him and made an angry remark. The boss pushed her back down. Her breasts flattened against the seat of the chair. His hands caressed her bottom in a circle several times, then slapped. It became a pattern. Houston unzipped his trousers and began to stroke himself under the desk. As the rhythm of his masturbation accelerated, Houston wondered how Justine would react if he tried to spank her bum. The boss lowered his trousers and entered the secretary from behind. It was all very Fifty Shades as she cried out in that peculiar porno dialect in which fake is indistinguishable from real, pleasure indistinguishable from pain.

Two minutes and 56 seconds into the video, Houston came. The relief was immense. When his knees stopped trembling, he wiped himself clean with the toilet paper then went into his private bathroom to mop up. His body was relaxed and suffused with warmth. He allowed himself five minutes on the balcony to enjoy the post-coital glow. Then he pulled himself together.

The first person he needed to call was his chief advisor, Murray Lime. Murray was a former tabloid journalist who had mainly worked

THE GUTS

the crime beat. He was not at all averse to smudging the line between the legal and illegal and over the years had become Houston's bagman and fixer. Although Houston hadn't gone so far as to trust him, he had given Murray a minor stake in his off-the-books arrangements, thus ensuring there was enough mutual interest to keep the relationship tight.

'Who is it?' growled Murray when he answered the phone. His voice sounded out-of-breath, yet dreamy.

'Who do you think it is, you great bloody goose?'

'What do you want?'

'Some of the precious time I pay you for.'

'Can't it wait?' he snapped. Murray's stroppiness suggested to Houston that he wasn't spending the afternoon alone.

'No! It's urgent.'

'What is it, then?'

'Meet me at Reggio's with the V-team in half an hour.'

'Give me an hour, will you.'

'No.' Houston had no regrets about passing his sexual disappointment down the chain of command.

'Fuck you,' said Murray and hung up.

Five minutes later, he rang back sounding cheerful. There was giggling in the background. 'The V-team are going deep-sea fishing. They can't make it till Monday.'

'Arrange a meeting with them as soon as they get back.'

'What's up?' asked Murray.

'Can't say. Meet me at the Sword Bar at eight.'

'But ... OK.'

'See you then,' said Houston and hung up. He rang his wife, Daphne, and after some familiar lies he gave her the good news: he was going out to dinner and wouldn't be home till late.

5

Adam got home from his swim a bit after six. The house was empty. Kate, he remembered, had gone to the annual Advertising Industry Awards, a glitzy extravaganza of champagne, cocaine, bullshit and backslapping. Sometimes he wished he didn't think like this. That he could simply accept and enjoy such things. After all it was advertising that paid his salary, or it had until the rivers of gold of the classifieds had dried up. His instinct for rightness was a self-damaging chunk of grit that Kate didn't always share with him. It made her the happier person. She'd been able to leave journalism and start her own business, something Adam doubted he could ever do. People were attracted to her positivity, as he got increasingly grumpy at the world (and his place in it) for failing to living up to its promise.

Having lunched, Adam wasn't very hungry, so he made himself a toastie with leg ham, artichoke, provolone and onion jam, which he ate on the couch. He watched the TV news, then a British show on extreme eating he hoped Ingrid wasn't watching too.

At about 8.30pm, Kate rang to say she'd met some people who were potential clients, that she'd be later than she'd originally thought. He took a second glass of red to the study, turned on his computer and returned to the email attachment with the pictures. Out of perversity he clicked on the image of John Howard, even though Bob had already told him the answer was Peter Costello. An image of Ronald McDonald colonised his screen while a parrot screeched 'What a Clown, What a Clown, What a Clown,' to the melody of the football supporters' song 'Here we go, Here we go, Here we go.' He hit the escape button on his computer, which took him back to the four photos. This time, he clicked on Costello. A picture of Tony Abbot came up. With him were pictures of Bob Hawke, Harold Holt and Roger Houston. This time the selection was clear. Roger Houston was the only one not wearing his swimmers. Strange, Adam thought, that's twice in the one day. He clicked on the image of the Minister for Development and a voice screamed. 'Warning! Warning! Warning! This a bomb! This is a bomb! This is a bomb!' His screen went blank. 'Fuck!' he shouted, thinking he'd just put some terrible virus onto his machine. He jabbed at the on button, but nothing happened. He unplugged the power cord and reinserted it. He hit the *alt tab delete* keys in an attempt to bring Windows Task Manager up. Nothing. 'Fuck! Shit! Shit! Fuck! Fuck!' He'd planned on working from home in the morning too.

As he was about to give up the computer came to life again. There was a message for him on the screen. 'Hey Osborne! Remember how you got burnt? Read on for your chance at revenge!'

Adam remembered it well. Around five years ago he'd heard through connections in the union movement that the government was offloading a piece of harbour foreshore at Balmain in the city's trendy inner-west, which had been leased for decades to a stevedoring firm that had made the decision to relocate to Newcastle, an industrial city of a few hundred thousand people about two hours to the north. In the initial stages the land was promised as public space, but this promise became contentious. A number of stakeholders were involved: property developers who reckoned it a licence to make money, the locals and environmentalists who were demanding open parkland, and a gaggle of architects, artists and society aesthetes, who wanted the place turned into a kind of cultural precinct with live-in artist's studios, cafes, galleries and a movie set with the exteriors of the grey maritime wharves and warehouses preserved as a living monument to the harbour's industrial history.

At the time, both major political parties were running scared of a populist wave of sentiment against the preferential treatment being given to the urban elites. Minor parties were winning seats in parliament on the pretext of standing for the battlers. 'Welfare for the rich,' they railed at the news of a cultural precinct that the people had little interest in. 'East gets to feast while West gets the rest,' they cried, and they had a point.

The protests made the parkland option politically difficult. The sale price of the land could be used, for instance, to provide a new botanical gardens out west, which was where most of Sydney's population, though few of its most influential citizens, happened to live. There was a big chunk of land out near Penrith the locals wanted for a park. A new botanical gardens with a small children's zoo, plus some other amusements had been mooted. The focus groups were showing there were votes in it and the local MPs in the vicinity were busy making the idea their own. With an election coming up and the proposed park fringed by marginal seats, the number crunchers in head office had added their blessing too.

Tenders were called for from property developers to purchase and redevelop the harbour site. The government gave public assurances that environmental considerations would be met and that there would be some preservation of the maritime heritage and public space. Ten developers tendered for the project, including most of the state's big players: Eden Apartments, Virtue Erections and CCP Constructions, run by the son of a senior member of the Chinese government. The tender details were commercial-in-confidence, and none were made publicly available until it was announced that Virtue had won the contract. The smiling face of Roger Houston, the Minister for Development, was pictured in company with Avery Lodge, the acting Premier of New South Wales and the managing director of Virtue Constructions, Ken Virtue. The Premier talked about how *The Stevedore Apartments Complex* would boost the New South Wales economy by creating jobs. It was going to be 'a landmark development incorporating the best in contemporary design.' Houston had beamed at the press and quipped that 'he wouldn't mind living there himself.'

A few days later Adam got a phone call from someone inside the Department of Development saying that the deal wasn't smelling of roses. Apparently, Virtue had tendered less money for the property and hadn't been rated the best bid on either environmental or aesthetic grounds. They'd slid around some of the tender specifications that stipulated a height limit to buildings. Now they had the contract, they were going to add two ten-storey apartment towers, citing the economic realities of property development, when the original height limit had been six. They had also reneged on the amount of land being left for public use by including an area for the private mooring of leisure craft as part of the public space. They had, however, made a large contribution to the government's campaign funds. Close to a million dollars, and apparently that was only the official part of the iceberg. Adam's deepthroat in the department claimed that if you looked at the deal, you'd find that people close to Houston were part of the Virtue team that had put the tender together and sold it to the government. A classic Sydney story of mateship. Mates from school, mates from the legal world, political allies and a series of shadier, more elusive connections. Unionists on the take, bikies, drug dealers and thugs. The deal broker, Dick Mahone, was a former employee of Houston, who now worked for Virtue as a consultant. While the Premier trumpeted that jobs were being created, the best ones it seemed were going to the boys.

With his source verified by some subtle nosing about, Adam started to put a story together. The government had been getting thousands of dollars from Virtue ever since it got into office. It was no secret that most of Sydney's property developers made large donations to both major parties. Even after it had been made illegal, the money had kept flowing.

What was a bit unusual here was who owned some of the Stevedore Apartments and how much had been paid for them. An ex-football player had paid about a quarter of the market rate for one, as had Chloe Daniels, a *Home and Away* starlet. A celebrity chef and one of Sydney's leading real estate agents also appeared to have bought apartments at a discount. It wasn't that surprising. Premium developments like the Stevedore often sold apartments to celebrities at under market value in exchange for being able to use their ownership in subsequent marketing campaigns. Some people were prepared to part with hundreds of thousands of dollars to live next door to a star.

THE GUTS

Adam began looking into some of Virtue's other recent developments that had occurred on premium, formerly government-owned land. The most direct comparison was the Emerald Apartments, which had been built on the waterfront site of a former mental asylum in the city's exclusive eastern suburbs. The apartments had sold off like hotcakes off the plan, and the prices for them had remained solid ever since. Which was why it was curious that the owners of four of them were unknown. Some digging into the records showed that the first had been bought by the Virtue subsidiary responsible for the over-priced strata management of the complex. This was where the concierge, a long-time Virtue employee lived. But the other three remained an enigma. In a building that could have sold itself three or four times over according to *The Glory's* property editor, why were there some for which the sale record couldn't be found? To answer this question Adam had embarked on an unofficial stake-out, to see who was coming in and who was going out. He parked outside the building in a rented Corolla with a thermos of coffee, a pocket camera with an oversized zoom and good low-light capacity, and a Cliff Hardy talking book to keep him company. He tried to get photos, but it wasn't always easy. Most of the time it was just cars with dark tinted windows going down into the garage beneath the building. A B-grade actor in a mid-life crisis red convertible with a woman who wasn't his wife was about as interesting as it got.

It was frustrating and after a few nights he thought of giving up, but then he got lucky. In the window of the nearby convenience store was a notice: *Car space for Rent at the Emerald Apartments, short term, long term, OK. Phone 0408987123.* Adam rang and went to pick up his keys from a bald guy in his early forties with a bank of computers in his lounge room who seemed extremely stressed.

The price was 300 dollars a week. In other parts of the city you could get an apartment for that. Adam leased it for a month. Each day he drove from home to the Emerald apartments in his rented Corolla, then caught the bus to work. After work he took dinner at a café or restaurant, making sure he was in his observation post before nine.

The garage was lit which made the task of photography much easier. But if anyone took exception to being snapped there was nowhere to run. The inhabitants of the Emerald, however, were mostly too self-absorbed to pay much attention to the presence of an unknown car in their garage.

One night as he waited for arrivals, there was a knock on his window. A swarthy man dressed almost entirely in black apart from a chunky silver ring on the hairy distance between the first and second knuckle of his right-hand ring finger looked down at him through the window. Adam opened it.

'If you think you're going to get any photos of Lance, you can get fucked.' Lance was the driver of the red convertible BMW that sped up the garage ramp soon after. In the passenger seat was the fallen soap star whose paranoia was probably the final remnant of his fame. If anyone cared, the photos would already have featured in some trashy magazine.

'Nah mate,' said Adam. 'I'm a private investigator. Rich old man, hot young lover. You know the drill.'

'Just don't take any photos of Lance. Unless you get my permission first.'

'Scouts honour.' Adam wound up the window and the minder returned to the lift. Adam decided to upgrade his surveillance car. The Corolla stood out like a poor thumb. He returned the following night in a black Audi hatchback.

Every few days, cars drove in and disgorged people Adam was later able to identify as union officials, council aldermen, policemen, and builders. Sometimes they were with a woman, sometimes without. Sometimes the women came after – dressed to undress. Adam's suspicions were heightened by the staggered arrival three times in the space of a fortnight of three or four men, closely followed by three or four women. The numbers always seemed to match. They normally arrived between nine and ten o'clock and stayed until late.

Adam knew the numbers of the apartments that were officially unsold. Needing to confirm his story, he dressed one night in a pizza

THE GUTS

delivery kit and waited to see if anyone he recognised arrived. When two men, one who resembled a senior council planner, the other a former Rugby international, drove in and ascended the lift, he waited. Thirty minutes later two glamorous young women were dropped off in the car park, and Adam ordered two large Supremes from Dominos. He picked them up when they were ready, donned his delivery garb and drove back to the Emerald apartments. There were three apartments. The first was on the second floor, and didn't have a water view. He ignored that for an apartment on the fifth floor that did. Footsteps greeted him when he rang the doorbell. Before the door opened, he could tell that he was being checked out. The door opened to the length of the security chain locking it from the inside and the ex-footballer appeared in the gap, wrapped in a towel, led by a large and misshapen nose.

'Whaddaya want?'

'Pizza delivery,' said Adam. He could hear a girl in the background. Some rap was extolling the life from the living room and she was singing along.

'Who is it?' asked the other male.

'Pizza.'

'We didn't order any.'

'I'm hungry but,' the footy player shouted back.

'Me too,' said another female voice.

The door closed. There was a pause. Footsteps went and returned. The chain was removed. The door opened again.

'What kind?'

'Supreme.'

The footy player reached out and grabbed the pizzas. He gave Adam fifty bucks. 'Keep the change.' What kind of a weird dickhead stole someone else's home delivery, then tipped the delivery guy outrageously, thought Adam.

The following week a crew of four turned up, shortly followed by four girls in summer skirts and stilettos. One of the men was a senior unionist; another was Murray Lime, former journalist, now fix-it man for Roger Houston. The other was Virtue's man, Mahone. The fourth man Adam didn't know. He decided to try the pizza gambit again. They were in the fifth-storey apartment again. This time when he pressed the buzzer, a voice said, 'Sorry mate, not for us.'

A few more nights on stakeout revealed little more. He reckoned he had enough to run with though. After a week of further checking and delving the story was ready to break. FUCK PAD FAVOURS was the headline that came to him. Not that it would get through. THE VIRTUE OF SEX might though. Barring the war on terrorism coming to Australia, a Royal Wedding, or a celebrity divorce, Adam reckoned the best real estate in the paper, the front-page lead, was his.

That's when the phone calls started. Somebody had caught on. Hard ocker voices or Godfather impersonators asking him if he'd like to go for a ride in a cement mixer: 'just like the Luna Park Rotor except everything sticks to you.' Each call offered a different fabrication of his demise. 'You're gunna make a nice speed bump in the carpark, Osborne. I'll think of you each time I run over you in my Merc.' 'Gunna mince ya and turn ya into fish food.' 'Knock you out and bury you in concrete. Put ya in an air pocket, so you'll be sure to wake up. Give you time to appreciate your tomb. Then I'll be going round to introduce myself to your lovely wife.' 'I'm gunna do you a big favour and give you what everyone wants: 360-degree harbour views – chained to a fridge at the bottom of the harbour.'

Adam had heard this sort of talk before. It went with the territory of investigative journalism. It was mainly wannabee gangsters who had been second-rate football players, watched too many episodes of *Underbelly*, taken too many steroids and were now full of bullying hot air. People like the pizza thief at the Emerald Apartments. Unlike many countries, nothing truly bad had happened to an Australian journalist investigating corruption since Juanita Nielsen went missing in the 1970s. He put it out of his mind and concentrated on getting the story out. Once it was out, they'd be going into damage limitation. Killing the guy who broke the story was not an effective way to do this. But he had to break the story first.

THE GUTS

A few pieces in the jigsaw puzzle remained before he could take the story to the paper's editor, Jim Sway. That night he had returned home half-cut from a Friday night at the pub and stumbled up the stairs to find Kate, whom he'd recently married, wrapped in a doona, white as a sheet, trembling at the end of the bed.

'What's wrong?' At first, she just stared at him with terrified eyes, but after he rocked her gently in his arms for a minute or so, she recovered her powers of speech.

'I was reading, and I must have dozed off ... I was having an Umbrian dream. Something to do with truffles. There was a pine forest ... Then a sound woke me up. A stone hitting the window and pinging off. Then another. And another. At first, I thought there must have been a hailstorm or something, but I could see the moonlight through the blinds and there was no rain sounding on the roof. Then the phone rang. I thought it might be you. I thought you might have forgotten your keys or something and were making a nuisance of yourself. But when I answered there was this horrible laughing voice that said 'Curiosity killed the cat. Make sure you're not next.' I heard a cat yowling and got frightened. I was worried it might be Ginger, but I was too scared to go and check. Then they started throwing stones at the window again. The phone rang.

'Who is it?'

'Shut up and listen bitch.'

'What do you want?'

'Tell your husband he's a dead cunt.'

'Why don't you tell him yourself!'

Concerned as he was, Adam couldn't help smiling at this last remark. Kate's pluck was one of the things he loved about her.

The voice at the other end of the phone had hung up. Kate had tried Adam, but his mobile phone had run out of juice, as it tended to in the pub. She'd been sitting in bed with the doona wrapped round her listening for the smallest noise ever since. Adam called the police, but they were short-staffed. There was a five-car pile-up on the highway. Four people dead and three still stuck inside their cars. They recommended locking the doors and getting some sleep. Promised they'd come round in the morning. Adam persuaded Kate to take a sleeping pill. He joined her in bed with a cricket bat beside him, ready to swing.

Just after dawn, he got up and went downstairs, the bat still in his hands. When he swung open the backdoor, he saw to his horror that Kate's cat, Ginger Meggs, had been nailed to the outside of it. He was mewling pathetically, only half-conscious. Adam called the police again. They told him not to touch anything and they'd be down as soon as they could. But he couldn't leave Ginger there. He called the vet, who was there within five minutes.

'What kind of sicko does that to a cat?' She was a tall and angular woman with curly red hair, around the same age as him. Adam nodded his agreement. 'Can you hold him still for me?' Adam kept Ginger immobile while the vet injected him with an anaesthetic, and once it had taken effect, she prised him gently off the door, removing the nails with a pair of pliers while Adam held the animal up.

'He'll be OK. Doesn't seem to have lost too much blood.' She washed and bandaged the stigmata. 'He might be a bit sooky for a while. He's suffered a major trauma, lucky really to survive.' She pointed to his leg. 'If they'd put the nail in there, he'd be dead by now.' She finished the bandaging, rummaged in her bag and produced a bottle of medicine. 'Here's some painkiller. If he won't eat, squirt about ten millilitres via this syringe into his throat.' She handed Adam some pills in a white envelope too. 'When he starts eating, put two of these in his food to settle him down. If he doesn't start eating in the next day or two, bring him into me.' The vet patted Ginger who had begun to shiver and muttered 'Arseholes!'

Adam was relieved that Kate, who was still sleeping, had been spared the worst of it. He wasn't looking forward to telling her, however. Ginger had been suffering for most of the night.

The police came ten minutes after the vet had left. He showed them where Ginger had been nailed to the door. They checked out the house, asked a few questions, and said it was probably kids. There'd been a spate of animal torture incidents in the neighbourhood, junior psychos (the neglected sons of merchant bankers) tying firecrackers to the tails of dogs, stoning cats and taking potshots with air rifles at the local birdlife (mainly seagulls, pigeons, Indian mynahs and the occasional cockatoo). 'Some evil little prick and his mates ratcheting each other up. Come down to the station when you can and one of the detectives will take your statement.' Adam started to tell them about the phone calls, but they were at the end of a long shift, and too convinced by the easy pattern of their theory to listen properly. By that time, he was too tired and overwrought to argue, and simply said, 'I hope you kick the shit out of them when you find them,' at which they nodded sympathetically, then left.

Kate woke up at about ten still feeling groggy from the pills. When she heard about Ginger, she freaked. Thankfully Ginger emerged from his anaesthetic haze and demolished a bowl of milk before crawling into bed with Kate like a sick child. Adam could see the relief on her face but saw too the hatred for anyone who could do such a thing. She would have killed them without a second thought.

When her immediate concern for Ginger began to wear off the interrogation began. She sat in bed with the doona wrapped around her and Ginger in her lap.

'What are you working on?' He'd told her he was working on a story with serious political ramifications, but she hadn't pushed him at the time. She knew he liked to keep a story close to his chest until it was sure to break. It was part superstition, part caution that someone else might steal it. But now she needed to know.

'Why didn't you tell me before?'

'I didn't tell anyone.'

'If people are going to be torturing my cat, don't you think I've got a right to know?'

'I didn't think they would go this far.' he said.

'Maybe you should think about taking that redundancy.'

Adam sensed potential danger in his answer. He was on the verge of breaking the biggest story of his life. The adrenaline had kicked in and he couldn't turn back. Rather than start an argument he ducked the question. One of the more difficult things with being married, he'd found, was the potential impact of his choices on someone else's life. It was no wonder the marriages of so many good journalists failed. Chasing a story could be an obsessive and selfish pursuit. It might be in the public interest, but that was the justification not the thrill. In this case, marriage made him vulnerable. Before they were married, those calls would have gone to his mobile phone. But whoever had rung had known that the best way to get to him was through Kate.

Adam wondered if Kate really would put pressure on him to quit. He had three weeks left to decide whether to apply for redundancy or not. If he did, he'd leave with a six-figure sum. But what would he do? Some of his friends had prospered in their new careers, other hadn't. Now wasn't the time to find out. He took off his pyjamas, slid into a pair of jeans picked from the bedroom floor and found a shirt in the wardrobe to go with them.

'I'm going into work. Want me to drop you at Gina's?' Gina was Kate's sister, a university lecturer.

'I've got too much work to do. The Bristol do's next Friday and I've got to sort out the catering today.'

Kate had taken a redundancy and had used it to start Caviar Communications, an event-based, hospitality industry focused, public relations consultancy. 'I'd rather be busy than hanging around worrying anyway.'

'OK. I'll drop you to work on the way.'

He dropped Kate off at her Pyrmont office then drove into town. He parked the car expensively, grabbed a take-away coffee and rushed to work. He emailed the first instalment of his story to his editor before could talk himself out of covering it at all. Just before lunch a message appeared in his screen from *The Morning Glory's* editor, Jim Sway, 'Please see me ASAP.'

He went up a flight of stairs to the floor where the managerial echelons of the paper lived, a realm where there were offices instead of open-plan space divided into cubicles. Adam felt envy, an emotion that

THE GUTS

often sucked people up into the rarefied world of senior management. Downstairs, he longed for peace and quiet just so he could concentrate on his thoughts and do his work instead of having to tune out multiple conversations.

Jim Sway shared a secretary with a couple of other suits. Her name was Laura and she politely ushered Adam into her boss's office, after first checking via the telephone to see if it was OK. Sway's office had glimpses of the harbour, but mostly looked upon the building next door.

He came out from behind his executive desk and shook Adam's hand.

'How's it going, Adam?'

'Not too bad. You Jim?'

'Can't complain. Nobody will listen. Did you see Joycey's ton against the poms?'

'Saw a bit of it at the pub.'

'What'd you think? Reckon he's the new Gilchrist?'

'I dunno. We're looking pretty good for the World Cup though. The team's regenerating nicely.' While Adam was normally more than happy to talk about the cricket, he was too pent-up and couldn't help giving his boss a look that said get on with it.

There was an uneasy silence before Sway spoke again. 'Um ... umm ... ahh ... about that development story....'

'Yeah?'

'We're not going to run it.' Sway looked ashamed. His head was slightly bowed and his lips were compressed. His eyes wandered sideways from Adam to the window. Adam was flabbergasted. It was not what an investigative reporter should be hearing from his editor. Of all the stories he'd broken before, some controversial ones too, he'd had the support of the brass. Sometimes the lawyers had pulled things because of the potential for defamation. But this time he had the facts.

'Why?' he asked.

'I don't know, Adam. Honestly, I don't. I don't even know if I want to know. The order's come from on high, that's all I can tell you. I'm sorry mate.'

'How high?'

'I don't know.'

Sway was caught between a rock and a hard place. Maybe he knew who'd given the order, maybe he didn't. Adam didn't care. Someone had just scared the shit out of his wife and tried to crucify their cat. And his boss was telling him not to do is job.

'Why the fuck not? Do you know what happened to me last night?' Sway looked weary. Creased and compromised, it was the look of a man who no longer liked himself.

'Take a holiday, Adam. Take as long as you like. Go and write some features on the slow food movement of Tuscany or something, so you don't have to use your annual leave. I'll sort you out a gig on the next cricket tour to the Caribbean. I'll do what I can, but I'm sorry, it's out of my hands.' The phone rang on his desk and he excused himself to answer it. As he picked up the phone, he looked at Adam and drew a circle with his finger in the air.

Adam replied with the bird and walked out without another word. As he left, he heard Sway saying in a tight, tired voice, 'yes ... yes ... yes ... yes ... yes.'

Downstairs, his colleagues pretended not to notice his purple-faced fury. Word of the summons had got around. Until the call out of the blue from his development deepthroat, he'd been having a lean patch. Leads had vanished into thin air. He'd been scooped by the opposition. The day-to-day stuff was fine, but he hadn't been breaking the big stories. His instincts were out of synch with the news cycle. And he was at an age where many journalists get bored, and it started showing up in their work. He'd become happily married.

As he steamed past colleagues some assumed he'd exhausted his line of credit and had been sacrificed to appease the vulgar gods of the superannuation funds who owned most of the company. Their careers had unluckily coincided with the great newspaper decline. Their eyes were a shy mixture of compassion for a fallen comrade and relief that they didn't have to worry about not meeting their mortgage payments, or getting a job as a corporate comms manager, yet. They watched for security to arrive and escort him from the building with

THE GUTS

his belongings in a box. Then they'd wait for the phone call to down tools and join him in the pub.

At his desk, Adam took a few deep breaths. He checked his voice messages. There were three. The first was a request from the travel editor that he write a few features on tropical island resorts. A week in Tahiti, three days in Noumea. Another week at an exclusive resort on an isolated coral atoll 200 kilometres off the coast of Vanuatu. News travelled fast.

The second message told him to keep things under his hat if he didn't want his election night indiscretion in Canberra two years ago to get back to his wife. A half-paralytic snog against a fake Ionian column in a hotel function room that never got anywhere near the bedroom. It had meant nothing, except embarrassment in the press gallery the next day. But it didn't help his filthy mood one bit. Nor did smashing his mouse into the wall. The cubicles around him went quiet. Adam toyed with taking the rock star approach to crisis management and tossing his computer through the window. He didn't relish the thought of his monitor landing on some unsuspecting head eighteen floors below.

The final message was from John Dykes, his deep throat in the government and simply said, 'There are bikies outside my house. Drop it, or I'm fucked.'

There was no point in being at work if they weren't going to let him do his job. He left without saying a word, went home, got his swimmers, flippers and a towel and stomped down to Bondi Beach for a bodysurf. By the time he'd crossed Campbell Parade and made his way down the grassy slope to the promenade, the beautiful people surrounded him. It was like being in a movie. Or a coke commercial. It wasn't real and a part of him wanted to take a hammer to it all. The suburb had changed since he first lived there. When he was this angry, only the ocean could placate him.

It didn't let him down. The cold water shocked his thoughts out of him. Three-foot left-handers crumbled slowly onto the sand banks. He surfed for an hour, taking one wave then swimming back out with an almost self-destructive intensity through the churn of broken water to the next, and so exhausted himself in a struggle with the sea. Sitting in the autumn sun and staring out to sea, he realised he would have to give in. Some things were like trying to fight the sea. The battle might be enjoyable, it might even feel noble, but it couldn't be won. His moral stubbornness urged against this pragmatism. 'Giving up's for losers. You can't turn to jelly at the first sign of danger.' Life as an Australian investigative journalist was safe compared to most places. Then the voice of reason, or at least he imagined it as such, began to undermine his stubbornness. 'Sometimes, son, you have to cut your losses, so you can live to fight another day.' It sounded conspicuously like his father. 'If there's fish in the sea and beer in the fridge and your family's all healthy, the rest of it doesn't matter.' No one in his family had ever been seduced by the idea of importance. But he was different. His mother and father had lived in country towns. Were happy with their routines. They were repairers rather than purchasers. Sceptical of the new. They didn't have a point to prove. For Adam, growing up in a country town had given him the space to think. When he had arrived in Sydney as a young man it had fused with the desire to act, partly motivated from a fear of being invisible among so many people. It had given him enormous satisfaction to see his byline first appearing on *The Glory*. It was a satisfaction that hadn't diminished over the years. His parents had been very proud. And from their love, he took on the responsibility of standing up for the people like his parents whose lives were shaped by the powerful and ambitious people into whose company he had been launched. As the sun warmed his skin, the heroic urge stirred in a part of his ego that shared borders with self-righteousness. It is rare for motivation to be both powerful and pure. How fucking dare they? he thought. I'll show them.

Adam tried to imagine what might happen if he told Sway to get fucked. It mightn't mean the end of his job. The union could come through for him. He could always take the evidence to his mates at the ABC. But would it make a difference? Probably a slightly altered apartment complex on the same prime waterfront land at slightly higher prices because the developer had been forced to conform to tender specifications. There might be a few fall guys, a ministerial advisor, or a town planner perhaps, the sacrifice all carefully delegated. If the Opposition was sufficiently on its game, there was the chance for an inquiry, but given the state's Commission Against Corruption had been nobbled, it was unlikely any of the power behind the decision would change. Backhanders, bribes and blackmail, I'll scratch yours if you scratch mine; it was the way things were done. Many people had gone into politics with the intention of changing this. Hardly anyone had.

In some ways, corruption was the natural way of things. It was all about helping those who helped you. But natural wasn't always best. All sorts of appalling things occurred in nature. Democracy certainly wasn't natural. It was an imperfect check on natural urges, the urge to dominate and profit at the expense of others, the urge to rule the herd even if it meant destroying it. If Adam went through with the story, ignoring the high-level resistance, he might become a democratic hero, he might win a Walkley Award, but at what cost to the people around him? It was a lot to ask of Kate to put up with the threats so he could bathe in the limelight. Or his deepthroat? They were onto Dykes already by the sounds of it. Adam's interest in the public interest was partly self-interested too. He'd get the glory, but his source would be sorted out. At the very least, not wanting the publicity of sacking a whistleblower, they'd shift him into a departmental dead zone, wait until the whole tawdry business was forgotten and then either try to pin something on him and sack him, or send him to some branch office out the back of Bourke, or maybe offer him a not so voluntary redundancy. All very well, for a man in his sixties, perhaps, already dreaming of afternoon golf and caravan safaris, but this guy was in his thirties, with two young kids, a schoolteacher wife, and a Sydney mortgage to pay off. He was deepthroating because he believed in public service, because morals prevented him becoming a passive cog in something that was corrupt. But there were limits. There wasn't much public service you could give from the dole queue.

It was a dilemma thick with consequences and there was no clear way out of it. To buy time, Adam accepted the gig reviewing the Pacific

Island resorts. He didn't feel like being in the office, anyway. He reckoned Kate, once her commitments with the Bristol do were finished, would be happy to come with him too.

Three weeks later they departed from Sydney Airport. It was a perfect holiday. They wandered along reef-fringed beaches, ate fresh seafood, wound down on banana chairs with throwaway fiction. Removed from Sydney with its insistent treadmill of ambition and competitive display, and enjoying the company of Kate, he resolved to give the story the flick. They made love with the ocean lapping at the deck of their bungalow and talked of starting a family. They talked of giving Sydney the flick as people on holidays often do. Of moving to some coastal hamlet and living their only lives slow.

Back from the South Pacific, he filled his computer screen with words like balmy, sleepy and pristine. He also saw the paper was looking for a food reviewer on the intranet. He enjoyed food. He found it relaxing to go home at the end of the day and cook. He liked to experiment with new ingredients, and while he wasn't the fussy kind of amateur chef that peopled the ranks of MasterChef, or one of the younger breed of journalists whose ambitions were epicurean from the very beginning, he could put on a pretty good spread.

The editor of the lifestyle sections at the time, Jemma Spring, was a colleague of Adam from his cadetship days. A hard-drinking, quick-witted old school journo, she'd started out in the 80s when the lunches were legendary. In fact, she'd woken up more than once on Adam's couch to the aroma of eggs benedict, fresh coffee and a bloody mary being conjured in the kitchen. She didn't think much of the new breed, their scepticism as to the value of a bender was beyond her comprehension. She had faith in Adam's culinary judgement and was happy to give him a go. Meritocracy in harmony with nepotism.

The deal met no opposition from the brass, though it did put a couple of the younger, arguably more qualified journalists' noses out of joint. It was another reason why Ingrid, without knowing the full details, couldn't help looking at Adam with contempt. Her current boyfriend, Sean Spicer, whose signature dish was a truffled almond

THE GUTS

soup, and who had cultivated friendships with at least half a dozen celebrity chefs, had applied for Adam's job and would have landed it had not Adam been imposed from above. Ingrid still dwelled on the missed opportunity of being her boyfriend's boss.

Within two weeks of applying for the position, Adam was in another pod of melamine cubicles, chewing on a whole new world of information. He even got a promotion as a reward for playing the game. He never found out for sure the connection between the company's chairman Julian Circle and the spiking of his story. Although he had his suspicions, he tried not to care. He had moved into the land of the endless lunch.

6

Houston must have fallen asleep. After ringing Murray, he'd reclined on the office couch and the next thing he knew it was dark and he had a rare second erection for the day.

He rang Justine on her mobile. 'Can you come here? I've got something important for you to do.'

'Sorry. I'm busy. I'm with Penny from George Milhaus's office. It's her hen's night.'

'Come on, Justine. You're missing out. Get a look at this one. It's a monster,' tittered a woman in the background. A chorus of shrieking women filled his phone.

'Where are you?' he asked.

'On a Harbour Cruise.' He heard raucous applause again. 'With the Chippendales.' The Chippendales were a troupe of male strippers.

He hung up.

He thought of another wank but resisted the urge. It wasn't often he got it up twice in a day and it would be a shame to let both go to waste. Too old, ugly and famous for Tinder, he started flicking through the callgirl pages of *The Evening Standard*, tossing up between petite Asians, leggy Europeans and sultry Latin Americans. He was halfway to dialling the number of a busty 23-year-old Svetlana when he remembered he was meant to meet Murray. Sure enough there was a cranky message on his mobile phone.

'Where the fuck are you?' It was quarter to nine and Houston was already three-quarters of an hour late. At some point, he was going to have to pull Murray aside and remind him of the hierarchy in their relationship. He didn't really mind the swearing, but these things risked developing their own momentum, and if his other staff started imitating Murray's attitude, he'd end up having to do something nasty and gratuitous to maintain his reputation as a hard arse. Murray answered after a few rings. He was still in the pub.

'Sorry,' said Houston, 'I got tied up.'

'I didn't know you'd become an English Tory,' came the reply.

'Very funny! You still right to meet?'

'Yeah, except I've just bumped into Mark Malouf and a couple of girls from the Premier's Department, and it might be hard to get away.'

Houston did know what he meant. Murray and Malouf had been copyboys on *The Evening Standard* together and had a long-standing competitive friendship. Both were serious bachelor types, hard drinkers and womanisers. Although he could trust Murray not to divulge professional confidences – Murray had too much at stake – he didn't want Malouf getting curious about the predicament the government was in. He'd been doing some work for the Deputy Premier, Giselle Hagan, and Houston didn't want Giselle to know about Parker just yet. She was already being touted as the face of change. If she was the one to break the news of Parker's disappearance, it might be her chance to cause a leadership spill. And that would not be in Houston's interests. And if he hauled Murray away for a tete a tete when there was tail to be chased then Malouf would be curious.

'How about a game of golf tomorrow?' he said.

'Yeah ... Good idea. About three o'clock?' said Murray.

'What are you doing in the morning?' he asked.

'In the morning? Ahhhhh ...'

Houston pictured Murray the following morning, relaying the bad news to whichever feisty beauty who'd fallen for his weathered looks: 'I've gotta go. My stupid prick of a boss.' It didn't make sense to push Murray to the point where he got all sulky and resentful.

'OK, make it two at the Lane Cove Country Club,' he said. It was the kind of golf course where any serious golfer refused to play.

'And remember Murray! Loose lips sink ships.'

'Yeah righto, thanks Rog,' said Murray and hung up before Houston could say and don't catch any diseases.

THE GUTS

The night was free and Houston was at a loss for what to do. The last of the Viagra must have worn off while he was on the phone and he'd gone as limp as a cocker spaniel's ears. Houston didn't much like being by himself. It was one of the reasons he'd entered politics. Aside from the power and money, politics was full of people. The days were stacked full of meetings, the nights with official functions. Being alone for too long made him edgy. When there was no one around to exert his will over, he felt an emptiness that scared him.

He turned the television on hoping to catch the late news and flicked through the contacts on his phone. His greatest factional ally, Silvio Patrese, with whom he was going to have to talk about Parker if he couldn't clean things up soon, was out of the country on a trade delegation to Dubai. Steve Bruin, his other factional colleague was a family man. It was almost ten o'clock. In days gone by, the nightlife had been part of being a man of influence. A lot of important business got done in pubs and restaurants. Deals were sealed with visits to a strip club. Now everybody seemed to rush home to via the gym. Quality family time in front of the flat screen TV. Women's business if you asked him. Society had been emasculated. It had started with Women's Lib, the end of the illegal casinos and the introduction of Random Breath Testing and had been going downhill ever since. Even the corruption was getting cleaner. Why bother importing heroin when you could be an insider trader? A piece of information dropped, a couple of clicks of the mouse, and that was that. Millions. Far more reliable than the nags. If you got the right information.

He went through his contacts, thought about ringing a couple of the younger MPs, but they'd be wondering what he wanted, when all he wanted was a drink. He thought going home to his wife, but scotched that too, for similar reasons. It was lonely at the top. He went out onto the office balcony and stood there looking down at the harbour which was filled with the fairyland effects of the lights of a thousand boats and the neon rainbow reflecting from the buildings. He started to feel sad, an emperor isolated by his power from being part of the thing he ruled. Then he had an idea. It was time to commit a crime.

Getting into Parliament House without an invite was hard. After all, you couldn't have all the voters and would-be terrorists running willy-nilly about the place eating the subsidised turkey sandwiches and drinking the cheap beer. But once you were in, the security was rather lax. Back in his property industry days, Houston had learned the basics of picking a lock. It was a useful skill when trying to get rid of obstinate squatters, if not as entertaining as a bunch of goons in balaclavas with crowbars.

He tested his own door by sliding a credit card in against the tongue of the lock. When it slid back easily, he closed it again and took a walk down the corridor. If Parker had deadlocked his office, he wouldn't be able to get in. But fortunately, he hadn't. Within five minutes, allowing a short break for the security guard doing his rounds, Houston was inside the office of the Honourable Alexander Parker MP. He shut the door, locked it from the inside, turned on his flashlight and started to snoop around.

Parker's outer office was a disappointment. Spartan clean. Not a single piece of paper seemed to be out of place. Houston rifled through the filing cabinets, but all they contained were policy documents, press clippings, letters from constituents and the minutes of parliamentary debates he'd taken part in.

The inner office looked more promising. As his mother used to say, it looked like a brothel, although he was never quite certain how she knew. The brothels he frequented were usually tidy. Parker probably had a tidy secretary who was banished from the inner sanctum, Houston reckoned. He hoped it meant there were things Parker wanted to hide. His desk was covered with piles of paper, while books were stacked at odd places on the floor and on the couch. The curtains were drawn across the door to the balcony. Houston closed the door between the inner and outer office before turning on the light. On Parker's desk was the usual accounting detritus that came with adult life: electricity bills, strata levies; water rates; a receipt for clothing alterations. Parker's home address, Houston noted, was only a street away from the Stevedore Apartments, where he had enjoyed the largesse of Harry

THE GUTS

Virtue over the years. A bank statement showed Parker was in a healthy financial position despite having withdrawn $20,000 about seven weeks ago. The only thing on his Visa was a purchase worth a few hundred dollars at a hardware store, while there was another on American Express of just under a thousand at one of those outdoor clothing shops. It corroborated the official story of a hiking trip, but since he'd made that one up himself, Houston wasn't reassured.

To the left of his bills were more piles of correspondence. Letters from constituents. We need a pedestrian crossing near the old peoples' home. An invitation to be guest of honour at a local high school's Italian Cooking Day. He was a more scrupulous local member than himself, Houston noticed. There were thank you letters too – for awarding the prizes for a local fun run; and for his work in getting the council to provide space for a community garden.

It seemed to Houston that Parker wrote his own replies to constituent letters and was not averse to turning up to functions in his electorate. Houston left the banality of everyday electoral politics to his electoral assistant who wrote the letters and put them on his desk to be signed. Occasionally he would rock up to a local function, but he liked to give his constituents the impression he was far too busy running the state to go round kissing babies at the local school fete. Listening to a bunch of senior citizens in a nursing home singing cabaret songs from their dimly remembered youth was hard work in anyone's book. And as the baby boomers aged, political demographics ensured there was going to be more of it. Houston could sing 'Yellow Submarine' with the best of them. but being a minister mostly allowed him to escape this democratic torture. So did holding a safe seat. A media release to the local paper every now and then pointing out all the new projects going on around the joint usually gave his constituents enough of a sense that he was looking after his own. Besides, having your local member as a minister imparted some reflected glory to the suburbs he represented. As did stacking the local branch with people who owed him. Except for a few cranks, most of his local branch were deferential. His patronage could help them into a cushy sinecure that governments got to hand out and Houston made sure his mates were looked after. A well-paid seat on the board of the Urban Development Authority perhaps, or a job on the recreational fishing advisory panel. Or what about one on the government/racing industry liaison committee? All they had to do was sound smart and say yes.

More interesting was another pile of letters on Parker's desk that seemed personal. Mostly they were printouts of emails, since it had become rare to write an actual letter other than for official reasons. A friend thanked Parker for his support during the recent sickness of a child and promised to have him over for dinner. There was an email from a Spanish woman getting up him for not writing: 'have you forgotten the magic so soon,' it remonstrated, 'a Basque has long memories.' Another was from someone called Nadia offering sage advice. 'Ideas be damned,' it said. 'Our duty is to live'.

Parker was a dark horse indeed, thought Houston, with exotic tastes in women it seemed. At the bottom of the pile was the RSVP profile of a young Brazilian woman. An absolute stunner. The text attached claimed she was 28 years old and single, a philosophy student, fluent in Portuguese and English. 'True freedom starts with the uncluttering of the heart,' was her motto. Her smile was such that Houston almost wanted to believe such naive guff.

Men in their forties are apt to do odd things, and he began to wonder if Parker had had a mid-life crisis rush of blood to the head and run off into some foreign sunset with a third-world nymphet. But if he had, why was he sending apocalyptic emails to the Premier? Surely it was more than just a prank. And what about Parker's declared intention to forgo the parliamentary pension? If he was going to turn his life into *Blue Lagoon*, why not do it properly?

Unfortunately, there was nothing on the desk that directly indicated why he'd done a bunk. The computer on his desk was shut down and Houston needed a password to open it. He tried the desk drawers, but they were locked. He thought of jemmying them open but was saved by the lack of a suitable implement. By the time he spotted a steel letter opener on the couch he'd realised it was a stupid idea. An

THE GUTS

office break-in would only fuel suspicions concerning Parker's disappearance. Houston didn't want the police getting involved in his predicament. He turned his attention to the books and papers that were scattered about the floor. As with many MP's offices, Parker's walls were lined with eminence generating volumes of torts and contracts, case histories and legislation. For all the shambolic legislation that got passed through the bearpit, Houston wondered whether MPs bought the covers by the metre. Not that he cared. The career move from lawyer to politician was often motivated by the same combination of arrogance, mediocrity and unwillingness to accept responsibility that inspired managers to become consultants.

In his former career in property the law was wasted time, regulations, stretchable red tape, and the reason why he had to pay bribes to local councils. It was his irritation at paying these bribes that had inspired him to run for council himself. Along with several failed developments that had left him in debt and in need of a salary. Most of his old mates were driving Maseratis by now, and although Houston could probably afford one, he wasn't fool enough to flash that cash.

Stacked behind the curtain going to the balcony were some books and magazines. Houston recognised none of them. Other than the newspaper and his bank balances, he wasn't really into reading. Several of the books were about butterflies. At least you can look at the pictures he thought. He picked a few from the shelf and sampled them. What a childish hobby, he thought. When he opened Bernard D'Abrera's *Butterflies of South America* some loose sheets of paper fell onto the floor. He retrieved them and unfolded them. About four pages in all, they were headed, 'Notes on Creative Destruction.' Houston felt a small unpleasant tingle in his spine. Something odd was going on in Parker's head and it wasn't just his interest in butterflies. He flicked through the rest of the book. Even odder was that when he reached the page that contained a colour plate of the Blue Morpho butterfly, there was a printout of the file Houston had kept on Parker, like he did for every MP, and all manner of other people too. His mind began to race. He remembered that he'd checked on Parker several months ago because of a proposal a publican mate had to extend his pub in Parker's electorate. But how in the fuck had he gotten his hands on that?

There wasn't very much there. Parker was a cleanskin. It contained so little he hadn't even bothered to encode it. A couple of taxpayer funded overseas trips of debatable value. Most of them to South America. So what! Parliamentary research was difficult to define. There were women here and there, again most of them South American but they were all over twenty and Parker wasn't married. To be honest, he hadn't ever bothered about Parker.

The worry, though, was that if Parker had his own file, then what else did he have? Houston chastised himself. He must have been carrying Parker's file loose in a folder to read while parliament was sitting. It had probably slipped out of the folder, and been picked up by someone, who seeing it was all about Parker, had returned it to his office. Hopefully no one knew it was his.

But what if that wasn't what had happened? What if someone had hacked his entire system? All the serious stuff was in code and there was enough gobbledydook in there, he reckoned, to keep them guessing for months. Or was there? The thought of his dirty laundry being aired chilled Houston like an Antarctic breeze ambushing a Melbourne summer. Losing government, if unavoidable, he could cope with, but there were other things he would do anything to keep out of the public gaze. Anything! The rest of the search yielded little of interest. There were two pen drives sitting on Parker's desk. Houston returned with them to his office and poured himself a scotch. He slotted them into his computer. The first seemed like a download of a holiday. A boat on a vast muddy river surrounded by tropical rainforest. There was a girl on the boat, a coffee-coloured girl next door, maybe ten years younger than Parker. Shots of animals competed with amateur arty close-ups of the sun and wind making patterns on the water. Nothing that offered any opportunities for his incrimination. The second pen drive crashed Houston's computer.

Parker had crossed the line, Houston decided. From its hiding place inside a hollowed-out volume of legislation, Houston retrieved a pen drive and several sheets of paper and returned to Parker's office. Ideally, he would have downloaded the contents of the pen drive onto Parker's computer. But there was little point trying to crack his password. Now his contact in Parliament's IT unit had resigned, he no longer knew where to begin. He was concerned too that any log in attempt would be recorded, risky given that Parker had already disappeared. Instead, he taped the pen drive to the bottom of the tray that contained Parker's personal letters. The evidence would suggest that Parker had abandoned parliament because he felt his interest in child pornography was about to be uncovered. It wouldn't matter what the renegade MP said after that.

7

At around ten-thirty, the M.V. Sunshine disgorged a boatload of drunk women. Some marched onto the busses that awaited them. Others made a grab for the few vacant taxis driving past. Justine and her party milled around the wharf, stabbing at their phones and discussing the next stage of their night. Penny from Richard Milhaus's office was a popular girl and the girls from Parliament House, relieved of the self-possession that had gotten most of them employed, were keen to kick on.

'You're coming out dancing with us, Justine,' slurred Blaise Newton, several years older than Justine, a first-class honours graduate in social economics, who was planning to stand for parliament at the election after the next. 'I'm going to find you a real Chippendale.'

'As long as he's not a Darlinghurst,' shouted Sonia Kaur, the legally qualified daughter of sugar cane farmers from Woolgoolga, who was prone to airing the truism that all the best-looking men in Sydney were gay.

'Better than a Cronulla,' said Selma Malouf, the younger cousin of Murray's friend Mark. She had grown up above her parents' corner store in the shire and was keen not to be treated in the remainder of her life to the same aggressive reserve.

'Cro Magnon,' more like it, said Justine.

'Yeah. Steroids, tatts and knuckle scraping,' said Sonia, who found it bizarre that someone might still tell her to go home when her great-grandparents had migrated from India more than a century ago.

'Of course, Penny prefers them right hot,' said Blaise. She ruffled the hair of the bride to be, whose cheeks were red from the copious amounts of champagne she had been forced to drink, but also from the embarrassment of having not long ago removed a Chippendale's G-string with her teeth. This was not, however, what Blaise was referring to. Penny had taken the unusual step of falling in love with a man on the other side of the political fence, a staffer for a National MP, a decent man by all accounts, just with some reprehensible ideas.

'Yes, she's going to marry a Singleton,' said Selma, referring to the location of the electoral office where Penny's fiancé worked when he wasn't in parliament, as much as the romantic status of the early period Bridget Jones.

They were on a roll. 'The biggest misogynists are all in St Kilda,' said Lucy Jewell, who had fled romantic disaster in the Paris of the Antipodes and found a job with the Member for Brighton Le Sands. 'The name says it all. They bump you off then get canonised.'

'Bruce the Chippendale was packing a canon don't you reckon,' laughed Blaise.

'Does anyone want to sleep with my boss,' laughed Justine, who had checked her phone to find a string of missed calls from him. The response was a shrieking chorus of 'yuck.'

Houston's sleaziness was well known to the younger set, he was a handyman in the manner of Harvey Weinstein. A dinosaur, but he had power and that was something these young women were interested in. If you were strong, Houston had the potential to open doors, which could help an ambitious young political staffer graduate to the ranks of electable politician. Most of her colleagues had pegged Justine as very ambitious. They understood if they didn't agree. Why else would you work for a fat old perve.

'Why can't they just invent a suburb called *ask me questions, make me laugh, kiss me softly, fuck me with feeling, make me come, make me come, make me breakfast?*' asked Lucy into a slight awkwardness.

The girls dissolved into laughter and Sonia provoked more by saying 'As long as it's near the beach.'

'Let's go dancing,' said Blaise, who grabbed Penny and tried to coax her champagne addled legs into a salsa.

'It's been a big week. I'm going home,' said Justine.

THE GUTS

'Julian will be disappointed,' said Sonia. But none of their protestations could change her mind. From Walsh Bay, she walked up the steep stairs of the convict-built cliff face and into the Rocks, which was full of revellers celebrating the end of the working week. A couple of men catcalled her outside the Observer Hotel. She ignored them and kept walking. It was eleven o'clock. Everyone had had time to get drunk. Soon they would all go home. For the moment the veneer of civilisation articulated by all the big buildings and clustered neon lighting, the gadgets, the smart suits and fashionable dresses had given way to releasing animal urges. Every Friday night, a tide of booze washed all the clever thinking the city generated in pursuit of a dollar away. There was singing, there was shouting, there was flirting and fighting and fucking. The party animals took over. This end of the week bacchanalia both excited her and repelled Justine. Her lunchtime lines of coke had been topped up a couple of times since and the cruise boat's cheap champagne – she had only drunk a couple – had smoothed her edginess. The choreographed raunch of the Chippendales, their toned and depilated bodies simultaneously sexy and cartoonish, had – against her better instincts – made her horny.

She walked to Circular Quay and caught the train to Sydenham Station. From Sydenham she walked to a terrace house in Unwin's Bridge Rd. As she knocked on the door, a curfew breaking jet, flying out of Sydney Airport, rattled the air overhead. She waited until the noise subsided, then knocked on the door again. The curtain of the front room window moved. Footsteps. The door opened.

'Paul,' she said.

'Did you get it?'

He was rude. Justine followed him down a dimly lit hall with cracked walls and peeling custard coloured paint to the living room, which was dominated by a table with four laptops on it. The main light was off and the room was lit by their blueish glow. Justine pulled out a chair from the table and sat down. Paul sat down in front of a screen and turned to meet her eyes. A game of wills. She waited, knowing she was going to win. His face creased with annoyance.

'Did you?'

'No, I couldn't. I didn't even get to have lunch.'

'Fuck!' he said. 'We need that password.' He stamped his foot on a loose floorboard, it rattled the whole house. It was one thing about anarchism Justine didn't quite get. Paul's legitimate business making apps for mobile phones earned him good money. Surely things would work better if he didn't live under the flight path in such a dump. Then again, she was twenty-eight years old, and more than half of her friends still lived with their parents.

'What happened?' he asked.

'The Premier called, and he had to go.'

'We've had a breakthrough. He plugged one of the spyware USBs into his computer this afternoon, but the bloody thing is encrypted and we need his password. We're depending on you more than ever.'

'I know. But the opportunity's got to be right. If I push his buttons at the wrong time, it'll fuck the whole thing up.' Paul gave her another frustrated look. It was as much an acknowledgement from him that she was right as Justine was going to get. The house rattled again as a plane broke the curfew. They waited until its noise faded. Having a conversation here was like watching a TV show studded with too many ads. 'What have you been up to?'

The screens of the computers cast a blueish glow. Lines were self-generating across them.

'Well since I'm being prevented from sabotaging a corrupt government, I'm trying to hack into the CSIRO to suss out the commercial-in-confidence provisions of their genetically modified crops.'

'Any luck?'

'Not yet.'

Justine put her hand on Paul's knee and stared into his eyes. 'Do you feel like getting lucky?'

He looked at her, the mind behind the eyes computing. 'Nah. Luck's for amateurs.'

'So, you've turned professional, have you?'

THE GUTS

Paul rolled his eyes. He could recognise jokes but he didn't really enjoy them.

'Reckon I'll go and find someone else to scratch my itch then,' she said. She took her hand off his knee. 'Hope you get lucky with the veggies.' Her experiences in aid work in Africa had left her ambivalent about genetically modified foods. The idea that some rich multinational might hold the patent for certain kinds of crops was wrong, but with the world's population expanding exponentially it seemed to her that the current ways of growing food were not going to be enough. It had taken until 1850 to put one billion people on the planet at the same time. Now there were almost eight. A plague. Sometimes nature was overrated.

She stood up and walked into the hallway. 'I'll speak to you tomorrow.' It wasn't like they were a couple. But they had hooked up. Paul's coolness annoyed her, but she was more annoyed with herself for wanting him.

He followed her up the hall and when she reached for the handle of the front door, he put his arms around her belly and slid them up to cup her breasts. He kissed the back of her neck and pulled her towards him.

'I was only teasing,' he whispered. He had a bullying streak. She couldn't decide if it was emotional clumsiness, the result of living too much in the black and white land of binary code, or a somewhat unanarchistic controlling streak.

She turned around and kissed him back. Her hands spanned across his thin smooth back. She rubbed herself against the front of his jeans until he began to harden.

'Only teasing.' She opened the door and strode off into the night.

By the time she got home thirty minutes later, she regretted it. Her apartment was empty. Lonely. Despite his oddities, Paul was one of the smartest boys she had ever met. If he was interested in making money, he could earn a motza as a white hat hacker for some large corporation. Their project was crazy, exciting, frightening. In some ways the hardest thing she'd ever done, and that included talking a drug-addled child soldier from shooting up a tent hospital in Central Africa. They weren't going to save the world, but it was just possible they might make a difference. But it was going to take guts.

And he wasn't bad in bed either, a bit quick perhaps, but willing. Why then did their chemistry always seem to sabotage itself? The world had enough unnecessary battles. Justine lay on the couch and imagined him making love to her – how she had showed him – with his tongue. She carried the thought to her bed and masturbated with Lana del Ray filling her headphones until the coke faltered to the point where she could sleep.

8

Adam stared at the computer screen with its offer of revenge. After a minute or so, the question appeared. 'Yes,' or 'No.' As his mouse hovered, he thought of Kate's reaction. He thought of the fable of Pandora's box. He thought of the future stretching out before him, of the long run into a retirement that, assuming newspapers survived, was more than twenty years away. It was easier, perhaps, to live with the consequences of doing something than of not doing it. Or was it?

Perhaps he should wait. Talk it over with Kate. But the thing about his marriage was that he already had a pretty good idea of what she would say. He clicked yes. And when nothing happened, he clicked yes three times again. Files started downloading to his machine. Adam refilled his wine. A few minutes later the download was complete. He opened then unzipped the files. Eureka! The first file he opened was a chart showing the chain of ownership of several shelf companies registered in Vanuatu, Nauru and the Cayman Islands. On one side were a series of entities that were effective, albeit off the books, subsidiaries of big development companies such as Virtue Erections and CCP Constructions. A second page showed the names of a chain of other companies, with origins in Australia, but no assets other than the ownership of other companies based in similar money laundering and tax havens. At the bottom of this list, someone had typed ROGER HOUSTON????????? A third page was a list of transfers between the companies on the first and second pages for sums in the hundreds and thousands of dollars.

It was the sort of background he could have used when he was trying to break the Stevedore story before.

A final file contained a copy of the email Alexander Parker had written to the Premier. Assuming it hadn't already been released to the public, that was a scoop in itself. Was it Parker himself who was supplying the information? Parker was one of those politicians he had never even thought about before, middle of the road, a bit of a goody-goody champion for science and the environment. He emailed back to the address. 'Who are you, and how can you prove it?'

When Kate came home effervescent after the Advertising Awards and Adam slipped his potential rejuvenation as a serious journalist into her account of the evening, there was a brief exchange of static electricity before she declared she was exhausted and needed to go to bed. He sat there watching TV, compulsively checking his phone to see if his mysterious source had replied, regretting what he'd said to Kate. Timing was everything. He should have waited. At least until he knew what he was doing. Until they could have a sober conversation. But he also knew that if he had waited, like last time, he might never have got round to telling her until it was too late.

The next morning, they slept in. After a night of gritty sleep, a hungover edge infiltrated Kate's voice. Danger. They chewed on their pile of the Saturday papers in silence. It was Adam, whose interests lay in change, who broke it.

'I can't work out what I'm going to with this stuff I've been sent.'

Kate was in the kitchen making an omelette. An egg flew through the arch that opened the kitchen to the dining room and hit the wall about a foot from Adam's head.

'Who do you think you are? Mikhail bloody Blomquist? Don't tell me you're doing anything with this other than handing it on to the news desk? Surely, you're not going to put us through all that again.'

'That was last time,' he said.

'Last time, people were ringing us up and threatening to kill you. Then someone came round and nailed Ginger to the door. Then your gutless bloody brown-nosing boss pulled you off the story anyway, because the fat cat CEO of the fucking company you work for, who by the way is now Chairman of the Board, and his greedy fat cat mates had their fingers in the pie. What do you think's going to happen this time? What's changed? This is Sydney. You know how it is. Life's a rort and it's only a rort if you're not in it. Give it up! You are not an investigative reporter anymore. We're having a life here and I'm kind of fond of it. If you're having a mid-life crisis, just remember there's a good chance you've got half of it still to go.'

Maybe he was having a mid-life crisis thought Adam. His career ladder had run out of rungs. It often happened to journalists, more so now the internet meant you were lucky to have a job at all. Despite being flattered by the city's restaurateurs in the hope of a good review, despite being feted by his friends for whom haute cuisine dining was an opportunity for competitive consumption, the gap between his worldly self and inner self felt like it was growing so fast that at some point they would stop talking to each other at all. Moreover, he was worried that Kate increasingly preferred his practical professional self to the truer one who inhabited an inner life composed of doubt, ideas and unfulfilled dreams.

'Jesus Christ!' he said. 'You've been reading too many detective novels. Things don't work like that in real life.'

'What? People don't get their pets nailed to their back doors?'

'Look, if I've got another 40 years in me, I want to be able to live with myself. This story has the power to change things, Kate. Don't you understand?'

'God help me,' she said. 'Why does my husband have to be the one who dresses his selfishness up as public duty?'

'Because I'm sick of this life where all I seem to do is point people to restaurants and bottles of booze, when I couldn't give a fuck if they all ate fish fingers and drank fruity lexia from a five-litre cask. Maybe, just maybe, I want a chance to leave my mark on this world before I get old and tired and my thinking fills with ailments and the bad manners of the young.'

Kate wasn't buying it. 'I've spent three months planning our trip to Italy. I've booked the villa and everything. And now you're telling me you want to put it on hold because you want to get yourself killed. Tell me how that's not being selfish!'

'I haven't said anything about not going to Italy.'

'Not yet you haven't. But I can see it coming though. You'll get obsessed. You'll be working twelve hours a day, you won't want to go.'

'Everyone goes to Italy. A year in Perugia. A month in Tuscany. Three midnights in Sicily. Two days in some filthy hotel in Rome. Just so we can come back and tell our friends how good the olive oil was and how the owners of the villa found us *simpatico*.'

'I'm not just anyone and I'm going to Italy,' she said. 'If you're intent on meddling in dangerous worlds, don't expect me to hang around and get killed as well. And while you're being so precious about your career, what about some thought for mine? How much work am I going to get if my husband's running around pissing off the wrong people. We're a good team at the moment. Why fuck it up? Why is your work more important than mine?'

Adam didn't answer.

'I've busted a gut to get this far. And now business is picking up. I've just put on two staff. I'm getting a reputation in the industry. And last year, for the first time in our relationship, I earned more money than you.'

Adam bristled. He didn't mind her earning more money than him, just didn't like it that she was using it to make him feel inadequate. 'Congraaatulations! So it's come down to money now, has it?'

'No. But money's related to my ability being acknowledged by the world.'

'What I'm talking about is not taking something from society, but giving something back, about ridding this city of the corruption that makes it behave so stupidly. Surely that's more important than money we don't really need.'

'Don't be so bloody naïve! There are over four million people living here. You get rid of one scumbag and another rises to take their place. It's the nature of things. Power abhors a vacuum. It fills the spaces opened by the greed and flaws in human character. People might seek power to cover their inadequacies. They might think that power will provide them with a defence. But in the end, power is always stronger than them. It never changes. And once they have it, they will rationalise anything to hold onto it. Like a pair of concrete boots for my idiot husband. And if you think I'm obsessed with the money, it's because in the long run I want the freedom to escape from all this. Get enough money and you don't have to answer to anyone. Where we live money's the only universal mark of respect. It shows that I can make it as a woman in this world.'

'You should listen to yourself,' he said. *Money's a mark of respect.* What about the respect that comes from fighting for a better society? All the difficult kinds of respect that require character and sacrifice instead of lifestyles and assets. That's where you can find real respect.'

Kate rolled her eyes. 'So, I should abandon my dreams and throw my lot blindly behind a husband who says he's fighting for a better society but is really just feeding his hunger for recognition.

'That's the kind of attitude that made Hitler possible. You mightn't be able to stop it, but at least by opposing it, exposing it, power is checked. That's what democracy's all about.'

'Well thanks for the Politics 101. But I've got a real world to be getting on with.'

Kate picked up her bag from the couch and snapped back over her shoulder as she left the room, 'And remember we've got a boring dinner to be at by eight.'

Adam was left on the couch to figure stuff out for himself. He replayed the argument in his head. Did Kate really mean what she said, or was it just that she was tired and hungover? His timing had been off but he hadn't imagined she'd react that badly. Or, to be honest, that he would reciprocate. There was no immediate solution, so he turned on the television instead and waited for his email to be answered. The first cricket test of the Ashes was on at the Gabba. It was the second day. In years gone by this would have been soothing. But with the retirement of all the greats, Adam found himself instead watching something that too easily fed into his middle-aged despair. Australia had won the toss and bowled out the Poms on a grassy pitch for 212. The ball was swinging, it was just after lunch and the home team were 5-69. Adam watched a rear-guard action from Smith and the tail. He finished the papers. He got out his laptop and sat with one eye on it, the other on the cricket, and tried to work out how to prove the suggested connection between the money trail and Houston in the documents he'd been sent.

When the tea break came, he hit the beach. After swimming a lap, he walked back, dodging the clusters of beautiful boys and girls who looked like they didn't have a care in the world. Back home he got a beer from the fridge. The first sip flushed the lingering salt taste from his mouth. It was the best thing he was going to taste all day. They were going to the Hendersons for dinner. The cricket was still on the TV. He let his mind drift until it was stumps. Time to get ready. He put on chinos and a Ben Sherman shirt Kate had given him for Christmas. Kate returned. She got dressed. She looked beautiful in her burnt orange dress. They didn't talk but managed, like so many couples did, to get into the same car and drive in silence across the city to see their friends without the argument flaring up again.

Bridie Henderson had just turned 47, and tonight was a low-key celebration. The Hendersons lived in Petersham, a suburb in the city's inner west about half an hour's drive from Bondi. With the help of a small inheritance, they'd bought a large old terrace cheap in 1996 from an Italian family, who'd been living in it since they migrated from Calabria in the fifties. The house had originally been built by a nineteenth century squatter as his city residence and had suffered in the suburb's subsequent reversion to the working class, but with Bridie's careful renovations and the gentrification of the inner-west almost fulfilled, it was now worth more than two million dollars. Just minutes *à pied* from Leichhardt's fabulous café and restaurant scene, their opulent estate had four big bedrooms, a large formal dining room, lounge, and a country style eat-in kitchen (complete with Miele

THE GUTS

appliances) that opened out via a family room and cedar doors onto the garden. The yard was large, there was even a patch grass left after they put a pool in. At the back of the garden, the original stables built by the squatter had been converted. Downstairs was the garage while the upstairs was now the office for Bridie's home-run PR consultancy, which operated in friendly competition with Kate's. In the main house, one of the upstairs bedrooms had been turned into a nursery in expectation of the baby that had never arrived. Increasingly, Adam and Kate found their social world shrinking to a core of couples who didn't have kids. After many exhausting cycles of IVF, the Hendersons were considering the options of surrogate pregnancy and adoption. Kate and Adam had decided that if a child wasn't going to come naturally, then it wasn't meant to be.

Bill Henderson was a tall thin man with tight dark curly hair and a beakish face, whose intense blue eyes contrasted with his long-bodied languor. Like many solicitors he found his work long and dull but had managed to adapt. He compensated for the long days spent inspecting the minutiae of commercial deals by collecting art. Paintings adorned the many walls of their house, mostly by up-and-coming Australian artists who were the focus of Bill's aesthetic investments. He was very proud of the fact that he'd just been appointed to the board of a contemporary art museum. He was very proud in general, if you asked Adam. It was the women who were friends. The men tolerated each other because it made their marriages easier, and because, beyond the workplace, they couldn't be bothered organising a social life for themselves.

Bridie opened the door and welcomed the Osbornes with an air kiss each. 'It's so great to see you both.' Adam put on his best bonhomie, complimented Bridie on the new Afghan rug she was pointing out to them in the hallway and followed the two women, who'd quickly moved from talk of carpets to carpaccio, into the living room where Bill was holding court while James and Nicola Driscoll, Martin and Jasmine Venery, and Jenny Cross, the first in their immediate social circle to get divorced, were passing round an iPad with photos from the Henderson's recent sojourn in Venice.

'Everybody thinks the Venetians are arrogant,' pontificated Bill. 'But it depends on where you stay. Although it wasn't far to San Marco Square, our apartment was in an area where the real Venetians live and, after we'd been there for a few weeks, they started to treat us much differently ...' Everyone nodded in agreement. They belonged to the Eurocentric rump of Australian society. They were fans of multiculturalism, but it was part of the public but not the private face of their lives. Their close friends were almost exclusively Anglo-Celtic and mostly made at uni. They made up for the accidental apartheid of their lives with travel. They had backpacked in the age of Lonely Planet Guides and were *travellers* not *tourists*. Authenticity was important. Their overseas trips functioned like their food as a form of competitive consumption, a process amplified by the explosion of social media. 'Of course, it helped that I was with the gallery,' continued Bill. 'We got to know some fantastic people. Surprisingly, there's still a bohemian element and some cutting-edge stuff going on there.'

'I suppose the Biennale has got something to do with it,' said Nicola, who knew how to stroke an ego, working as a producer in the film industry.

'Not really,' said Bill. 'They're not that keen on the Biennale. Not the people I spoke to anyway. It's just another form of tourism to them.' The dirty word lingered.

'Look who's here everybody, our very own pair of tucker scribes,' Bridie interrupted, to her husband's quickly suppressed chagrin. Bridie was blond and slender, though her face, thought Adam, seemed drawn from the effort of bringing her twenties body into her forties, a puritanical urge for thinness that clashed unhappily with her dedication to gourmandism. She was wearing a loose white mildly diaphanous dress that made him think of Ancient Rome. 'I've been fretting about what to feed them all day.'

Adam shrugged with an 'aw shucks' modesty, while Kate simply lied: 'I'm sure as usual it will be delicious.'

The other guests all turned and said hello, except for Martin, a fine arts academic who didn't like pictures anymore. He raised a cursory hand and gave Adam a knowing look Adam reckoned meant nothing at all. Bill shook Adam's hand, kissed Kate rather too close to the lips for Adam's liking, then reverted to his spruiking of the Italian way. He'd been in Italy to source an exhibition on the Future of Futurism, which he was planning to set up in 'his' gallery. After that, he and Bridie had taken a villa with some friends somewhere in the Veneto, where they'd, as was usual on their holidays, eaten well, drunk too much, and convinced themselves that this was real living: the simple things done well on the other side of the world.

Kate sat on a lounge next to Jenny. All the lounge chairs were taken so Adam sat on a chair borrowed from the dining room. Bill's pomposity, which was competitive but not malicious, enervated him. His mood wasn't helped by the sly pointed looks Kate kept giving him from the couch where he imagined she was making marital complaints, although the size of the room and the assuredness of Bill's voice prevented him from overhearing. He imagined he was home with a toasted sandwich and a book.

The feeling intensified when Bridie came out from the kitchen and ushered them into the dining room. If *Gourmet Traveller* was the platonic form of Bridie's dishes, her kitchen was a sharp reminder of the imperfection of the world. Despite all the Miele appliances, Le Creuset pots and Essential Ingredients, nothing Bridie cooked ever came out quite right. But social decorum meant she had never been told the truth about her cooking, and while she secretly suspected it, and was terrified of the suspicion, Bridie had to endure, along with her cowardly guests, while she struggled ever harder to make the grade.

Adam had argued about it with Kate before. 'You're her friend. You're a professional. She'll listen to you. All you have to do is suggest that she should stick to the simple things. Bill's always crapping on about authenticity after all. I dunno, get some fancy sausages and put them on the barbie, salad and crusty bread, rock melon and prosciutto for entree, fresh fruit and cheese for dessert. Now that's a meal.'

'I can't say that,' Kate had said. 'She'd be mortified.'

'But isn't that the kind of thing they eat in Italy?'

The night's entrée consisted of overcooked Jewfish on a bird's nest of sweet potato chips that had gone soggy with the too early application of an oily aubergine coulis. When pressed for his opinion by Bill (who unusually had refrained from expressing his) and with all the other guests keen to see how Adam negotiated the social dilemma, he found it hard to keep a straight face. His argument with Kate and Bill's Venetian monologues had brewed a cruelty in him that clamoured for release.

He managed to smother it in time. 'Greece via Fiji, very Club Med. Jewfish are great at this time of year.'

There was silence. It hadn't come out quite right. Club Med was a package tour place. It was a bit like saying Nescafe. At the far end of the table, Martin applied a napkin to a smirk. Adam passed the baton to Kate. 'What do you think, darling?'

'A fascinating combination,' she gushed. The balance between critical integrity and the expectations of friendship was something she handled far better than he did.

Bridie looked pleased. 'I made it up myself.'

This, in fact, was a lie. There'd been something remarkably similar in the back of *Fine Times*, *The Glory's* Saturday magazine only a few months ago. Bridie had swapped the hiramasa kingfish for jewfish, swapped the miso paste with coulis, confused it with some Vietnamese mint and changed the lemon garnish for lime.

The evening continued in a vein of subdued one-upmanship before getting around to the compulsory discussion of Sydney's real estate. Jenny was currently looking for a house somewhere in the inner west and was complaining that with the divorce settlement split down the middle, all she could afford was a two-bedroom apartment in a seventies red brick building in Marrickville. For the rest of them it was hard not to feel smug when the matter of real estate was raised. They'd all been sensible and bought when they were young in suburbs close to the city that had since skyrocketed in price. Their friends who hadn't bought before the property boom of the early noughties were finding the going tough. Martin, for instance, who didn't earn a lot of money as an academic (Jasmine some years younger than him, and not from their

THE GUTS

original circle of friends, was still trying to finish her Ph.D.) had bought a weatherboard cottage with water glimpses in Rozelle. With property prices having almost doubled in five years and salaries having stayed much the same, an academic couldn't even buy a house in Rozelle anymore unless they'd inherited money. While Adam and Kate and their friends were all in favour of Bohemianism, and in a way still considered themselves a part of it, Sydney's bohemian days were gone.

Martin's good luck with property didn't mean he was happy, however. If he were happy, Adam suspected he wouldn't know what to do with himself. Other than writing impenetrable articles and complaining about the unfortunate lot of the intellectual in the materialist wasteland of Australian society, and organising sabbaticals in New York, Martin was occupied chairing a resident's group that was at constant war with the spectre of property development in his suburb. It was the one thing that drew him from the cool theatre of his enigma. The state government's current plan to sell off part of a mental asylum near his house so townhouses could be built was the latest in a number of local issues that had provoked his righteous fury.

'I can't believe it. Even the bloody local member isn't protesting about it. I mean what's the point in democracy if your MP doesn't represent your interests. At least with the Greens, you know where you stand. There's no way I'll be voting for the Sporty Party next time.'

Everybody nodded in agreement, except for Adam, whose suppression of his urge to be cruel about Bridie's cooking had turned him into a contrarian. 'I read the report, Martin. It's not that bad. They're still going to be keeping 60% of it for public parkland. Don't you think you're being a bit selfish? What about all those people in the western suburbs with no infrastructure at all?'

The table gave him puzzled looks.

'But why only sixty per cent?' Martin countered. 'Have you seen what they are going to be building?'

Here he had to concede that Martin had a point. The problem with so much of the property development in Sydney was that it was allowed to be cheap and nasty. The architects, except for the occasional landmark building, were briefed to focus on costs and there was industry resistance to innovation and quality control. Furthermore, the local councils, the Land and Environment Court and the Department of Development under Roger Houston were rigged in ascending order in favour of the developer. If a council refused building permission, it went to the Land and Environment Court and even if the refusal was vindicated there, which was not often, since the framing of the law made this difficult for judges to do, Houston could still force a rezoning, for example, on the grounds of a project's importance to the state. In the process, money that would have been better spent on things like acoustic insulation or keeping development on a human scale ended up being wasted on sweetheart deals, lawyers, political donations and bribes.

'I know it's not that pretty, Martin, but I've seen worse. Go to any major city in the world, especially in Asia, and tell me that apartments are about aesthetics. People live inside them. That's the most important part. The outside shouldn't matter so much.'

'Yeah, and I suppose you're a fan of the Bauhaus movement and the tower blocks of the sixties.'

'Not really. But there's a long way between a bunch of slightly tacky townhouses and a tower block. Why don't you look at the benefits? The improvement of the urban infrastructure that comes with a higher population density, for instance. Better public transport. (Martin was one of those people who had never learnt to drive.) More buses, more frequently. A greater variety of shops. The provision of low-cost housing to the young.'

Martin wasn't impressed. 'And my favourite walking track gone, the park full of people and hundreds of cars driving down my street every day. And, as for funky shops, you know what they'll be, don't you? A new convenience store, almost identical to the one two hundred metres down the road, a soulless café on the ground floor of a building I find repulsive. Another crappy boutique. Fantastic!'

'It doesn't always have to be like that,' said Adam, unwilling to cede that Martin was probably right.

THE GUTS

'So, when are you going to give up your Bondi semi with its backyard and come and live in one of the concrete boxes that Ken Virtue will make millions out of by ruining my favourite park?' asked Martin.

'Leave him alone, Martin,' butted in Bill. 'I don't understand you. You whinge about the lack of world-class museums, the state of the universities, the lack of cultural depth, but you still want to live on a quarter-acre block with a Hills Hoist out the back. Look at any great city in the world and you'll find that the majority of people live in apartments, and the apartment, my friend, is the way of this city's future.'

'So, when are you moving then, Bill?' asked Martin.

'As soon as The HMAS Apartments down at Garden Island are finished.'

'Another Ken Virtue special,' said Martin disdainfully. 'So, Bill, do members of the Urban Consolidation Institute get a discount?' Bill looked uneasy. 'It was on their website,' added Martin.

'What's the Urban Consolidation Institute?' asked Adam, whose embarrassment at not knowing was outweighed by his curiosity.

'It's a group of civic leaders who believe in the cultural and economic benefits of the densely populated metropolis,' said Bill whose interest in the art world had introduced him to some wealthy and influential people. 'We commission research, produce educational material and hold public events to encourage an awareness of the benefits of urban consolidation.'

'Come on. Stop kidding yourself. It's a front for the property developers,' snorted Martin. He emptied his glass and looked for more wine to put in it. Jasmine mouthed no, but Adam, who was starting to enjoy the argument, pretended not to see this and refilled Martin's glass. 'They've learned a lot since the *good old days* of Juanita Nielsen.'

Bill rolled his eyes, a self-assured man of the world expressing bemusement at the naivety of his guest. This annoyed Martin even further. Despite his professorial pursuit of obfuscation, he was sensitive to attacks about the unworldliness of life in the ivory tower. Adam experienced a fleeting urge to tell them of the information he had received but didn't.

The escalating clash of male ego was headed off by the arrival of the main course and the argument stopped to taste the food. It was a fusion disaster. Bridie had concocted a home-made curried pumpkin ravioli with a leek and pancetta cream sauce. It forced Adam to drink his wine much faster than he wanted to. Again, he was obliged to pass judgement on the creation.

'Delicious.' Not good enough. He tried to pass the burden of commentary onto Kate. She looked at her watch and smiled. He knew what he had to do. It was part of a game they sometimes played called 'thirty second grab,' the rules being that no matter what the situation, the responsibility to offer commentary couldn't be shirked. She wasn't going to be the only one to sacrifice her integrity for the sake of friendship by telling a barefaced lie. It was a dirty call.

'It's an intriguing combination of traditions,' sputtered Adam, resorting to another scull of his wine. 'The smokiness and heat of the curry really dig into the sauce, while the cream binds the combination beautifully.' He glanced at his watch. Fifteen seconds to go. He bit into a ravioli pillow to help chew the time, exaggerating the tasting of it. 'The best baby Italian soft-skinned samosas I've ever eaten.'

It was a winner. Everyone nodded in relieved agreement, while Adam hung onto his bonhomie and smiled ingratiatingly at his hostess, who demurred before breaking into a smile.

Unbeknown to her, Kate's self-satisfied smile celebrated a pyrrhic victory. If he didn't chase the Houston story, Adam decided, he would end up hating himself for the caricature he'd become. The patriotic urge to lop tall poppies was blossoming. He only had to survive dessert before he could start regaining pride in his life. It wouldn't be easy, he thought, but once Kate saw how central it was to his being, she mightn't like it, but at least she'd understand.

9

If Justine had known how close to the Gut she was going to have to get, she might have bailed. There were plenty of other battles to be fought. Plenty of other places to be. She'd met Peter years ago working a boring job as a university enrolments clerk, which she'd taken to pay the rent after finishing her honours while she worked out whether or not she was going start a Ph.D. As they processed the next intake of commerce students, Peter had talked to her about his interest in anarchism. It had seemed like a philosophy that might suit her. She had tried a few already, had a list in her journal called Abandoned Isms: Buddhism; Marxism; Eco-Feminism; Pointillism; Fabianism; Structuralism; Optimism. She read some stuff on the net, and started another list called Anarchist Authors: Bakunin; Jean Jacques Rousseau; Kropotkin; De Bord; Bookchin; Goldman; Saornil; De Cleyre. She and Peter went out one night, got drunk and slept together. They did it again. Got to know each other. He liked to throw paint at things: the large glass windows of the yuppie restaurants taking over the inner city; the bonnets of BMWs. He was studying to be a teacher. Sometimes when he didn't have paint he pissed on things. One morning he turned up to work with a black eye. He'd been caught by the Young Liberals painting *Fuck off rich cunts* on the sandstone of Sydney University. They hadn't called the police. He wore it as a badge of honour. Justine was less convinced. 'If only it made a difference,' she told him. 'Models will be wearing it on T-shirts next.'

Two months later, she left the country for a new career as an AID worker. She hadn't kept in contact with Peter, but her interest in anarchism had survived. In the developing world power was cruder, more overt than in Australia. Those holding it were almost always a disgrace. It was heartbreaking to watch children die because of the warring egos of strong but foolish men. Australia was protected from the stupidity of its leaders by prosperity, but in Africa it was stark. Even if anarchism wasn't the most natural or practical way of organising a society, it seemed right. Putting neither money nor ideas above people. She had started another list: Places Where I've Seen People Do Terrible Things: Darfur, Congo, Ossetia, Pakistan. The temptation had been to blame colonialism, but her experience told her this was not the case. She lost her optimism, but her desire for justice seethed.

Four years later, back in Sydney for several months and already restless, she'd run into Peter in a bar. He had the beginnings of a beer belly under his faded blue T-shirt and his hair had started to thin. Justine was out with her journalist friend, Sarah. He was drinking with a friend too.

'Justine, meet Paul,' said Peter. 'He's dangerous.'

Paul nodded 'Hi!' About medium height, he was thin with a pale complexion highlighted by the stubble on his face. He wore old jeans, daggy sneakers and a T-shirt that spruiked a fun run from 20 years ago. His eyes didn't like making contact.

'And this is Sarah. So how come you're so dangerous, Paul?'

Paul made an irritated face. 'Peter's just talking crap.'

'Isn't that what you're meant to do in a bar?' said Justine, who was more than a few cocktails into the night.

'He's a hacker,' said Peter.

'Or maybe just a hack,' said Sarah, who was a suburban newspaper journalist and prone to self-deprecation.

Paul looked at the three of them as if he didn't care.

Justine was intrigued. 'But the internet's so boring,' she said. 'It had so much potential. But now it's just a place where people buy things, stalk each other or look for help with wanking.'

'You're right,' said Paul. 'On the whole, it has been very disappointing.'

'But what about WikiLeaks?' said Peter.

'Just another glory puss,' snapped Justine, 'feeding off the risks taken by others. He was shagging Swedish girls while his sources were

THE GUTS

locked up in jail. That American soldier. Bradley, Chelsea … what's their name. He's the real hero.'

'I wonder what Lisbeth Salander might have done with him if he'd tried to seduce her?' asked Sarah. Salander was the hacking genius and furious heroine of Swedish author Stieg Larsen's *Millenium Trilogy*.

'She would have kicked him in the balls,' said Justine.

'You know she's based on a real person,' said Paul.

They all looked at him incredulously. 'You're shitting me,' said Sarah.

'Why would I?'

'Who?' asked Justine.

'She's a hacker. Her online name is *Fleur Dumal*.'

'Who said so?' asked Justine. Lisbeth Salander was too good to be real. She thought about Mikhail Blomqvist, the other star of the trilogy. He was too. A fantasy of how men would like to be treated in their middle-age. Women seemed to fall for his out-of-shape, workaholic charm like flies. Justine reckoned he was just another Blandinavian, an Ikea hero available in blond veneer or walnut. If Lisbeth Salander was real, she wouldn't have fallen for Blomqvist in a pink fit. 'Come on! Tell us!'

'That's for me to know and you to find out,' said Paul.

He was cocksure, reckoned Justine, clearly very clever, yet with an awkwardness that implied vulnerability. She wasn't sure if she wanted to kiss him or slap him.

It was Peter, however, who put the word on Justine at the end of the night, to which she said no. She didn't believe in reliving things. Just as she didn't want to return to Africa, she didn't want to return to Peter. Still, she gave him her new details and they talked about catching up for a drink again soon.

It wasn't Peter, however, who texted her three weeks later while she was editing a booklet on Road Safety for NSW Transport. The message read 'Lisbeth?Gd2meetU. Date OK? Botany View 9.30. Friday night.'

'Who the fuck ru?' she replied.

'Last of the Gospels, done by the Romans.' Although the beneficiary of an Anglican education, Justine had never paid much attention in divinity class. Wikipedia it was. Half an hour later after following a chain of links down a rabbit hole that that had ended in off-topic in Gnosticism, she replied, 'A date with a gay apostle? Why not?' before returning to the intricacies of orange traffic lights.

The Botany View Hotel was one of the last unrenovated pubs in the gentrified bohemian suburb of Newtown. A country and western band was playing in the front bar when Justine walked in. Uninterested in the lovelorn truck driver being sung about by a skinny guy for whom the Texan phrase, 'Big hat, no cattle,' might as well have been invented, Justine moved out the back. Forty-five minutes later, Paul sat down on the barstool next to her.

'Another beer?' She nodded. He was late. She was tempted to walk out while he was at the bar. He returned with a beer and a schooner of Coke. Justine raised her eyebrows.

'I don't really drink. I got drunk on rum and coke when I was fourteen. Had to get my stomach pumped. Haven't liked it since.' It made sense. Justine had done a lot of vomiting. The food you ate in the aid world wasn't always the best. Meal worms were sometimes a delicacy. The essential thing about vomiting, she'd found, was to get her hair out of the way first.

'What do you do for kicks then?'

'Mainly hacking.'

'Hacking what?'

'All sorts of stuff.'

'Like what?'

'That's what I'm here to talk about.'

'I thought we were having a romantic date,' said Justine, giving herself an inner high-five when she saw a flash of awkwardness cross his face.

'Ummm.' Paul looked at Justine and blushed. 'Not exactly. I've got a proposition to make.'

'So have I. How about we go back to your place and fuck?' She skolled her beer, stood up from her bar stool and started walking to the front of the pub. She stood outside on the street for a minute or

THE GUTS

two, long enough to feel the thrill of uncertainty. Would he come or not? She wasn't normally that blunt. Her restlessness and his rudeness had reacted in her head.

When he came out the door, she breezily threaded her arm through his and in this way they walked unspeaking to the end of King Street, then down the Princes Highway before they turned off at May Street and followed it as it became Unwin's Bridge Road.

'What a dump!' Justine turned Paul around to face her in the hall and playfully kissed him on the lips. He didn't resist. She kissed him again. He was stiff at first, like some sub-cultural Ken doll, but eventually his hormones overwhelmed his passivity and he became stiff in the way she preferred. He guided her into the bedroom off the hall, then pushed her onto the bed. Justine drew him down on top of her, undid his buttons and buckles while he kissed her face and neck. She took a condom from her pocket and opened the packet with her teeth. She rolled on top of him, jerked down his pants, rolled the condom over his already erect penis, bunched up her skirt, tweaked her undies to the side and came down on him. A cowgirl, one hand whirling an imaginary Stetson the other balancing on the skinny pommel of his chest.

'So, what's your proposition?' she asked Paul. They were in bed surrounded by traffic, trains and planes as the glow of physical intimacy faded. Paul sat with his back resting against the wall behind his bed and his knees drawn up to his chest. Justine lay beside him on her belly, her upper body raised on her forearms like a lioness.

'We need a honey trap.'

'Why me?'

Paul gave her a thin smile. 'I reckon you've got what it takes.'

'But who do I have to trap?'

'I can't tell you that. Unless of course you decide to do it.'

'Don't tell me I've just slept with the messenger.'

'It wasn't my idea.'

'No, I don't suppose it was.' She rolled onto her side and reached between his legs. 'Don't you think there's something sad about a shrunken penis?'

Paul took her hand away and got out of bed. 'Sorry but I've got work to do. I'm trying to hack into something in the US and I need to do it during their business hours.'

'But what about the honey trap?'

'Will you do it?'

'That depends.'

'Someone will call you; I suppose.'

Justine got out of the bed and adjusted her clothes. They stood on either side of the mattress. Paul scratched his balls.

'A shrunken penis is a sensible thing,' he said. 'It gives the sperm and its organs of delivery protection.' He picked up a pair of underpants from the floor with his toes and put them on.

'I think I like you better when you're not being sensible,' she said.

A week later, Paul hadn't rung. Justine began to wonder whether she had merely seasoned a male geek fantasy with her mischievousness. It was possible, she thought, that her brazenness had scared him off. Still, the more time she spent editing poorly constructed paragraphs about speeding and seatbelts, the more she wondered what being a honey trap might be like. She even rang Peter and arranged to have a drink with him. But he and Paul hadn't spoken since the night they'd all met up. His face dropped when she said she could only stay for a couple. He was a decent guy. She didn't have the heart to tell him she'd slept with Paul.

Then one morning a phone call. A deep and charming male voice informing her a vacancy in the office of the Minister for Development, Roger Houston, had come up and wondered if she'd apply for the job.

'Why would I want to work for that scumbag?'

'To make the world a better place, of course.'

'But why would he give the job to me?'

'Because you've got the kind of skillset he admires.'

Justine had seen the Minister for Development on TV. Fat, smug, ugly. A cane toad. 'But he's repulsive.'

The voice at the other end of the phone had laughed. The rich and slightly evil laugh of a ringmaster. 'I'll call back when we can find you someone better looking. Let me know by the end of the week.' She memorised the number and deleted the call.

That afternoon she appeared at Paul's uninvited.

'I didn't think it would be as bad as that,' he said, when they were lying in bed and she told him her news.

'I should have gone to acting school. How much honey do you think the trap will need?

'I don't know. You don't have to do it.' Paul's face seemed conflicted.

'Do you think I'll have to go all the way?' She felt like she was a teenager again.

She turned on her side not wanting to give her feelings away. Paul put his arms around her and spooned her

'I don't know. Not if I can help it,' he said. Justine relaxed into him and they drifted off to sleep despite the aircraft overhead.

Two days later Justine presented her work on road safety at a meeting with the project manager, Marion Flint, who proceeded to rip it apart.

'I'm so sorry,' said Lyn, the woman who had employed her.

'Why?' asked Justine. 'I've worked on it for a month. Why wait until now to decide how she wants the whole thing done?'

'It's not your fault. I'm afraid you're collateral damage. She's really trying to get at me.'

'Great. And why does she hate you?'

'Because she has no personal life, so she over-invests in her work. And she hates the fact that I leave on the dot of four every day to go and get my kids. And because ...' Lyn checked to see if anyone was in earshot, 'she's a fucking bully who is only just smart enough to do her job. And she's paranoid that I'm trying to take it from her, which would probably be a good thing for everyone.'

Lyn's explanation made things clearer, but it didn't make them any easier. Justine was going to have to write the whole thing again in the format outlined by the stupid bitch. Talk about bullshit jobs! The instructions were already waiting for her in her inbox when she got back to her desk rendering all her work to date futile. It had been hard enough to write the damn thing the first time, the material was so incredibly dull: to pull it apart and reorganise it all would be harder still, especially since she couldn't see how the new format would make the booklet any better.

By halfway through the following day, she'd had enough. When she told Lyn she was quitting, Lyn was suddenly less understanding than she had been the day before.

'You know you're dumping me in it, leaving like this.'

'I'm sorry but I can't just hang around being your collateral damage.'

'What's it matter? You're still getting paid. I'd offer to pay you more but I can't because of Marion.'

'It's not you, or the money, it's just that I can't bear to waste my time like that.'

Lyn looked at her with judgmental envy – the size of her mortgage, the fact of two young children meant she didn't have a choice – then gave up. 'Ok then, I suppose you better email me everything you've done then and make sure you hand in your pass to security on the way out. Otherwise, they'll start worrying about terrorist infiltration.'

Justine nodded. That afternoon she rang the mellifluous voice. 'I'll do it.' An email arrived in the morning offering an interview time for the following Tuesday. On the Saturday night she caught up with Paul. His eyes were bleary when he opened the door. He invited her in. They went to the lounge room, where four computers were running lines of code.

'I'm searching for a password. It's been a long day.'

Justine put her hand on his shoulder. 'I took the job.'

'I heard. I'm going to be pulling an all-nighter, but if you want to have sex, we can do it now.'

Justine bristled. She had wanted more acknowledgement. It wasn't how she expected to be treated. 'OK.' She went down on her knees and blew him. His knees quivered when he came. She gave him a couple of minutes to recover. He checked the screens. Hit a few keys and checked them again. 'Now it's your turn buddy.'

THE GUTS

'What do you mean?'

'I'll show you.'

Justine took him by the hand and led Paul to the bedroom. She removed her clothes and stood on the edge of the bed. She reached up to the top of Paul's head and pushed it down. When he got the idea, she lay back on the bed. He kissed her on the mouth. She pushed his head down. He sucked on her right breast until her nipple was hard and tingling. She pushed his head down further. 'Lick me!'

She felt his tongue on her. Its inexperience. 'Higher!' she demanded. It wasn't the 60s anymore, the revolutionaries were no longer the best lovers, if indeed they ever had been. Her hand was on the back of his head guiding him. 'Slower! Make it a surprise!'

At least Paul was a willing contestant. She was surprised how many men she'd encountered who were perfectly willing to accept fellatio but then baulked at cunnilingus. Before long Justine's instructions devolved to moans which grew louder until her whole body shuddered while Paul pinned her, hands on her thighs, to the bed. 'Enough!' She pushed his head away. He lay down beside her. She kissed him and tasted herself. Before long he returned to his work. Justine lay there a while longer, then got dressed. She found him in the lounge room, kissed him on the back of the neck and left without another word.

On the Tuesday morning, Justine chose a push-up bra then a subtly sheer blouse and piled all her blond and starry-eyed charm into a black suit. She curled her lashes and put on lipstick. She caught the train to Wynyard and walked up to Parliament House to meet the Minister.

'I try wherever possible to support young talent,' said Houston, willing his eyes away from her cleavage, 'and you seem like a very competent young woman indeed. No need, I think, to beat around the bush. I'm impressed by your efforts to improve the lives of people all over the globe. When can you start?'

And that was that. Electoral Assistant to the Dishonourable Roger Houston MP, Minister of the Crown. After a week off hiking in the Blue Mountains with a morning to purchase some corporate attire, the following Monday she was in his Parliament House office sorting out the correspondence from constituents, writing responses to their entreaties and complaints and leaving them in neat piles on his desk for him to read and sign. The office was divided in two, an outer room where Justine sat in the receptionist's position and an inner office where the Gut, her private nickname for him, had his desk. This in turn led onto a balcony with a beautiful view down through the Domain to the Harbour.

'I prefer it here,' he said, on her first morning on the job. They were drinking coffee on the small wrought-iron table he'd installed on the balcony of his office. He had made the coffees himself using an Italian espresso machine – a gift from a constituent – in the process of showing Justine how. 'When I work out of the ministry, every single little bureaucrat wants a piece of me. It's just meeting after meeting after meeting. Nothing ever gets done.' As for his other office, the one in his electorate, Houston avoided it at much as possible. He lived at Hunters Hill and the office was in the Western Suburbs, a forty-minute drive if the traffic was in a good mood.

The first weeks of her new job were spent at Parliament House. When the Gut was there, she played the dutiful secretary, much as she had for her father in his clinic when she was on school holidays, and he was still alive. Julian, the dreary heartthrob from the office next door, who sang in a band when he wasn't writing letters to his boss's constituents, told her that Houston had been spending even more time than usual in his Parliamentary Office since she'd joined his staff.

And it was true. She felt his fascination. As if she were a new and beguiling toy. At first, everything was above board. He was charming and polite in showing her the job, but it wasn't long before he began to test the boundaries. A brush of the hand in passing. His breath on her neck as they looked to her computer screen. 'Just checking to see how you're going.' His eyes on her bum whenever she left the room.

Three weeks later, the Gut arrived early for a breakfast meeting with a coal lobbyist before parliament sat. Justine was on hand to take the notes. When the meeting finished, he invited her into the inner sanctum. He rode his chair on its swivels from behind his desk and offered her the lounge.

'I'm very pleased with your progress,' he began.

'Thank you.'

'You've got the right instincts for the job. With the right advice, you could really go places, an intelligent young woman like you.'

'And what might that advice be, Roger?'

'Have lunch with me tomorrow, and I'll let you into a few secrets about how things really work.'

10

Adam's Sunday began with making Kate breakfast in bed.

'So, you've changed your mind and this deliciousness is a wordless apology?' Kate asked, as he came into the bedroom bearing a tray with a truffled omelette, toast and coffee for her to digest.

'No,' he replied. 'It's a butter-up job.'

'What? Italy's off but you're on for a tango in Paris? I'm sorry darling, but I think I'm getting a headache.'

'Would you like an aspirin?

'You know what I'd like ... I'd like you to stop acting like an idiot. I'd like you to give our marriage the priority I think it deserves.'

She sliced off a piece of the omelette and rolled it up before popping it into her mouth with her fingers.

'Please,' he pleaded. 'I can't tell you how much I need to do this. I'll make it up to you, I promise. We can go to Italy next year, can't we?'

'These shaved truffles aren't as nice as the ones we had before. In fact,'

'Please Kate. I'm serious. You don't understand. It's my last chance.'

'Then give me one good reason why your career's so special, why I should risk my career and possibly my life just so you can get your rocks off doing something that in the long run will hardly make a difference at all.'

'Kaaate!'

'Well, that's what you're asking me to do. You're asking me to jeopardise the health of my new business, postpone our trip to Italy, and risk being unable to sleep because I'm scared shitless of the slightest sound in the night. Can you let me know in advance if the dog's going to be burnt at the stake this time, or will they be coming for one of us instead.'

'Come on, Kate!'

'No! You come on! This is not a Boy's Own Adventure. And you're no longer a boy.'

'But this time it's going to be different. I promise.'

'If I had a dollar for every time I've heard that from Madam Osborne's crystal ball, I'd have been rich enough to leave this circus years ago.'

'Now you're being silly.'

'Adam, that's exactly my point. Why take a perfectly good life and waste it?'

'Good living isn't everything,' he countered. 'I need meaning. I don't feel like I've given anything to the world.'

'So living with me is meaningless?'

'No, of course not.'

'Merely something you take for granted, then?'

'No.'

'Well, it can't mean too much to you. You'd rather be a bloody hero propping up a new apartment building as part of the concrete foundations.'

'Don't be hysterical,' he said. 'You've always been the most meaningful thing in my life.'

'Then prove it!'

There was only one proof. And Adam couldn't give it. He'd crossed an invisible line. The consequences were the consequences. The conversation faltered.

Kate stayed in bed with the door closed while Adam sat at the kitchen table reading the papers.

An hour later Kate walked through the living room dressed in baggy Indian trousers with a suitcase trolleying behind her. 'What are you doing?' asked Adam.

'I'm going to yoga. Then I'm going to my sisters,' said Kate. 'I want you to remember, this is your choice. And I don't want you calling unless you're thinking of changing your mind.'

Kate closed the door gently behind her. Adam stared at the door, too gobsmacked to even say goodbye. In nearly ten years of marriage, this had never happened. Why did she have to be so bloody stubborn? So impossible to argue with? Why didn't she understand? Why did he feel like a toddler having a tantrum when he was on the verge of breaking the biggest story of his life?

By sunset his temper had ebbed. He opened a bottle of red wine and worked. There was a mass of stuff to get through. The timing of the story and its discrete components needed to be thought through. He had to get the most mileage out of it before the wheels of justice were set in motion with the likelihood of injunctions. The office politics needed consideration too. Food critics didn't usually try and bring a government down. Would they let him run with it, or would they try and get him to hand it over to one of the young guns who were currently doing the rounds? Of them, Jackie Barbour was a real gun. He was going to have to be careful if he wanted to keep the story for himself.

He sent another email to the sender of the coded pictures. *Did you get my email of yesterday? I need more information.* The reply came soon after. '*Run with Parker. We're working on the rest.*'

Running the Parker disappearance story made sense. It wouldn't alert Houston to the main story, but it would still be an excellent scoop. One that would give him enough points with management to continue. He wrote the story of Parker's defection, quoting at length from the email he'd been provided. He then rang Jim Sway to tell him what he had.

'Can you confirm it, mate?' asked Sway. He couldn't. His own confirmation came from the files detailing the activities of Houston. He didn't want to divulge these yet, especially given what had happened last time.

'Yes.'

'How?'

'Horse's mouth,' he lied.

'Ok, type it up and email it in. We'll run it.'

'Front page.'

'Yeah mate, front page. But you're going to have to hurry. We'll put it up on the internet tonight, too.'

'Great.'

'And we're going to need follow-ups tomorrow too. You know reactions from the government etcetera.'

Adam smiled at the thought of telling the annoying Ingrid she might have to do the toilet story herself. 'Sure. No problem.' He made some phone calls to get comment on the story, people he could trust not to break it. He wondered whether to include Parker's email to Pond but decided it would buy him time if he held off on that until the following day. Delaying it would also give the Sporty Party the chance to manufacture an excuse, only to be contradicted. And this would give the story legs, while Adam tried to work out how to tell the rest of it.

Afternoon became evening and evening night. Adam sat at his desk poring over the files, tapping notes into his laptop. If the information was right, it really was a chance to shoot the Minister in the nuts. Adam hadn't allowed himself to think it at the time, but Houston's smile at Dosh the other day had said: 'I fucked you up Osborne and you couldn't do a thing to stop me.'

Why should dickheads like Houston be above the rules, especially when it was their job to make them? For people like Houston goodness was tantamount to weakness. Power was all that counted. Even Adam sometimes wondered if the overlap between goodness and mediocrity was niceness. Adam Osborne, Mr Nice Guy, snickered a mean little voice in his head. The overlap between Nice Guy and power is duplicity, it said. But if he put Houston behind bars, he could silence that worm of doubt for good.

Dawn spilled into the apartment. Adam reached across the bed for his absent Kate. Unable to sleep, he decided to go for a walk. He loved Bondi early in the morning. The wannabees were all asleep after a hard night's showing off and, apart from a few fishermen, some fitness freaks, and the odd backpacker who hadn't made their way back to their bunk bed after a hard night on the lager, he felt like he had the ocean to himself. In the gentle light and still air, cool even on the cusp of summer, he listened to the waves pounding onto the sand banks and was infused with a natural awe that was hard to find in most major cities, knowing there was no land in the straight line between him and South America. A quick swim cleared his head of the wine. On the way home, he picked up a copy of *The Glory* and there he was, front page, for the first time in almost five years.

Where is Alexander Parker?

Adam Osborne

With Parliament due to resume on Tuesday, the government's slim hold over the balance of power could be at risk. Alexander Parker, one of its senior backbenchers, has gone missing. An unnamed source in the Sporty Party said he didn't show up for a meeting last Thursday and has not been seen since. A call to his home last night was answered by a woman claiming to be his cleaner. She said she had expected him on Thursday night, but he hadn't arrived.

Parker is something of a maverick in the Sporty Party. Despite his talent, his career has been curtailed by an unwillingness to toe the party line, threats to cross the floor, and an interest in the environment at the expense of the mining lobby. With the Government majority currently at one, if Parker has not returned by next Tuesday, when Parliament resumes sitting, the government will be forced to negotiate with the Greens and independents for the passage of legislation. With bills such as the controversial Development Industry Protection and Environmental Safeguards Act due to be voted on, the chances of success without Parker are slim.

According to Dr Anna Ng, lecturer in Government at the University of Sydney, if Parker doesn't turn up, 'the government faces at the very minimum serious frustration of its program, at worst an early election at a time when the polls aren't looking good.'

The Greens and two of the three Independents in parliament have described the proposed

Development Act as a disgrace. While the opposition is also supported by the development industry, they will find it hard to resist knocking back the unpopular bill, especially if it leads to an election they stand an excellent chance of winning. With Parker gone, a no-confidence motion in the government may well be on the cards. To avoid this, the government might have to sacrifice the support of some of its biggest campaign donors. Dr Ng said, 'the situation is delicately balanced. If Parker truly has defected, it may well change the way politics is conducted in this state.'

Adam ignored the temptation to go to work early and crow. He was still a bit worried that he'd been set-up. But of all the texts and emails that came through to his iPhone before he reached the office, none were about a government denial. He reached the office at about ten. As soon as he logged on to his computer, there was a message from Ingrid: *I need the Dosh review by lunch.*

He felt like writing back to her, *what's the fucking hurry?* But she was his boss, and he was feeling good. It took an hour to write what much of the time would have taken him half a day. It was a good idea anyway to clear the decks if, as he hoped, Sway was going to give him the go-ahead to pursue the Parker story, though the toilets might have to wait.

He sent Ingrid the story, who sent him back the message: *Middle Eastern sweets – ten best places to buy in Sydney and their individual specialities, 1000 words by Wednesday.*

The stupid thing was there'd been a similar feature only six months ago. Ingrid had seemingly forgotten. For a has-been, Adam had a good memory for what had been done and when.

Didn't we do that six months ago?
That was different. This is a tie-in to the visit of the Sultana.
Who's the Sultana?
Lesley Figgins. The Australian girl who became an airhostess, then married a middle-eastern prince. They're coming out next month on their first official visit.

THE GUTS

Very exciting.

It was hard to be ironic via *The Glory's* internal messaging system. But at least it pre-dated the invention of the emoticon, and Adam wasn't receiving his instructions with a smiley face.

He wasn't going to do it, but there was no need to tell Ingrid that just yet. He was off to the newsroom's morning conference instead.

'Nice scoop, Adam!' barked Sway.

'Hendo, can you follow it up with the pollies.'

'Yes,' she said.

Jackie's out already hunting down last sightings.

'Has anyone got a statement from the Premier, yet?' asked Adam

'Not yet. Why?'

'I'm sitting on more of the story.'

'What have you got?'

'An email.'

'What's it say?'

'I can't say that until someone gets a response out of the Premier.'

'No worries. But just so you know I've already had that bloody Ingrid complaining that the newsroom's stealing her precious resources.'

Adam raised an eyebrow as if to say, 'So What.' Sway caught the subtext. 'OK. You broke it. But you've got to keep up with your food work, so I don't get her whining into Jack Vine's ears.'

He was going to have to write the bloody baklava story. 'No worries, but as long as you don't mind me putting the real journalism first.'

'Yeah sure. Just don't tell Ingrid I said it.'

Adam rang Kate to tell her the good news before he remembered she'd be unimpressed. He then took a leaf from Sway's book and went down to the Monkey King in Chinatown with Bob.

'Hello mate, how are you?' came the familiar greeting as they entered the King. The owner of the place was an unpretentious millionaire, who'd gotten rich by dint of hard work and saw no reason to stop. He was almost always there in a short-sleeved polyester shirt greeting the punters at the door. Adam had been going there for years.

Before he got married it was one of his favourite places in the world. The decor was vintage laminex and there was a big round table at the front where all the solo diners were put – Chinese taxi drivers saving up to get themselves a wife, homesick students from Hong Kong, and a few stray gwailo such as himself. The food was good. Succulent BBQ pork and duck, a sweet corn and chicken soup to die for, prawn dumplings, choy sum steamed with oyster sauce. Best of all, it was open until 2am. In recent years, however, the King had gotten trendy, though the food remained just as good. Partly, it was Adam's fault. He'd written it up in the paper. Since then, the North Shore and Eastern Suburbs crowd had been descending on the place in droves. It wasn't unusual to have to queue for a table on a weeknight even. The prices had gone up too. Adam had half-complained about this one night.

'It's not the same as it used to be, boss.'

'What do you want me to do? Stop making money?' had come the incredulous reply.

The King was also a haunt of some of the city's more colourful powerbrokers. While the grey suits and platinum card set were lunching uptown at places like Dosh, the King, especially in the warren of semi-private rooms upstairs, was a hive for trade union leaders, backroom politicians, lobbyists, stand-over merchants and flacks.

Adam wasn't surprised to see Dick Mahone, a former colleague from *The Glory*, wiping some pork juice from his chin. Mahone had sidestepped from journalism into PR, but a certain affinity with the underworld discovered while covering the Wentworth Park Dogs, consolidated in a stint as a crime reporter had professionally shaped him. He'd developed an unusual network and his clients included some of the more colourful business identities around town. The developer, Ken Virtue, however, was his main employer.

Mahone was rumoured to have earned millions, but other than a flat somewhere in the Eastern Suburbs most of it had been lost at the races or in the casino. Like his boss, who could afford it, Mahone, who could not, was an inveterate gambler. It was common gossip that Mahone was not merely employed by Virtue but owned by him, even

THE GUTS

if he operated under the guise of an independent consultant. One rumour was that Virtue had rescued him from a nasty situation in the Philippines. Mahone resembled an underfed greyhound; tall, thin, edgy, prone to moods. Thin lips spilled over his mouth as if he had grown up in permanent anticipation of a smacking. The top of his head was bald, the sides closely cropped. A trim moustache sat like a caterpillar on his long upper lip. It was, Adam supposed, Movember, the month where some men grew moustaches to raise money for charity. Only Mahone didn't seem the charitable type. His eyes told the story. Black, aggressive, quick to anger. Hungry.

Mahone's luncheon companions were building industry figures, a town planner Adam had once interviewed for a story, a union boss, and some guy in a Nike tracksuit who looked like somebody's muscle. The final member of the table was Virtue. The unionist and Virtue, tall men in their fifties, looked like they still did exercise, but not the kind that put too many calluses on the hands. They both sported blue suits and smugness.

With a small triumph and a couple of beers under his belt, Adam was feeling a bit cocky. He'd ducked Virtue's mate, Houston, at lunch several days before, but now with some runs on the board, he felt like getting a reaction. With Bob talking to his wife on the phone and the BBQ Duck demolished, he found their table and gave Mahone a slap on the back.

'I've never thought of you as a peacemaker, Dick,' he said, nodding at Virtue and the unionist, who were enemies by historical convention only.

Mahone's look suggested that he had never thought of himself in that way either. 'Good to see you, Adam.' he said.

Adam turned his attention towards Ken Virtue. 'What are you guys going to do if the Development Bill doesn't go through?'

Mahone put himself between them. 'Don't be a cunt, Adam,' he said. 'If you want an interview, you've got to ask for one. And as far as I'm concerned you already know what we think of our lunch. Excellent as usual. Best BBQ Duck in the southern hemisphere. Otherwise, no comment.'

While Mahone had bristled, Virtue remained unruffled. Yet Adam's question had aroused his curiosity. 'Enough Dick! Why ... Adam, isn't it, would you think there's going to be trouble getting the Development Bill through?'

'Well, you know Alexander Parker's disappeared.'

'Yes, I read it in the paper. Urgent personal business I hear.'

Adam wondered if that was the line Pond was spreading. 'That's not what I'm hearing,' he said.

'What are you hearing?' asked Virtue.

Adam looked at him with calculation. 'Just a little birdy, but I'm afraid you'll have to wait for tomorrow's paper,' he said. 'Enjoy your lunch gentlemen.' He went back to his seat where Bob was still defending himself on the phone.

An hour and a half later, feeling sluggish from the daytime beer and MSG, Adam went back to the paper, wrote up the frame for the story that featured Parker's email and put it onto the system to be edited. He then caught a taxi home. Without Kate, the place felt empty. He cracked a beer and got some Indian home delivered. He channel-surfed between forensic detection on Netflix and an erotic Scandinavian thriller on SBS. At around ten, he switched to the late news on the ABC. The show's talking head, Simone Neil, was previewing the next day's papers, and on the front page of *The Morning Glory*, Adam saw the headline; *MP is for Missing Person* and the write-off, As the Pond government scurries to cover itself, is it becoming more likely that a lost MP will cause them to lose government?

A thrill ran down his spine. He was back in the main game.

11

On Monday morning, Houston hoovered up three pieces of toast and jam and muttered goodbye to his wife, Daphne, who still made the breakfast but had long ago ceased farewelling him from the driveway. His driver headed towards the city. As they negotiated the traffic, Houston demanded *Cats* on the stereo. He liked the melodrama of a good musical. Andrew Lloyd Webber was probably the only person living capable of making him cry. The traffic across the Harbour Bridge was good and by 7.30am he had arrived at the office. He'd arranged to meet Murray, who lived in Manly, in a café down at Circular Quay at 8.00am. On the way, he checked the headlines on his phone. The story about Parker having disappeared was not what he wanted to see. He preferred doing damage than controlling it.

The driver dropped him off at Parliament and Houston strolled down to the Quay past thousands of grimly focused office workers. He felt like the overseer of a great democratic chimera. A pyramid builder. This happy feeling assuaged his growing concerns until he saw Murray in bicycle lycra already poring over the news. Why did all these middle-aged men do it to themselves? What was wrong with a pair of shorts and a polo shirt? If he was the police minister, he'd arrest Murray for offensive behaviour.

'Morning. You look fucking terrible,' he said.

'Thanks. Have you seen the paper?'

'Yes. Some cunt's already onto it. It's starting to feed into the radio too.'

'What do you want me to do?'

'Dunno. Have you spoken to the V-team?'

'Yep.'

'Are they coming?'

'Yep. We're meeting them at the Toaster in 45 minutes.'

'Have they got any idea where he is?'

'Dunno. They don't like talking over the phone.'

'Right. Might as well have a coffee then,' said Houston.

He ordered a flat white for himself and a macchiato for Murray, who left for a few minutes and returned in the more aesthetic attire of a dark blue suit. One of Murray's old schoolmates was a deckhand on the ferries and let him leave his suit in their change rooms. He was full of odd friendships like that, a relic of the old Sydney and its mates. Houston read what *The Morning Glory* had to say about Parker. Not much. But the fact it had been reported meant Pond would be shitting his pants. He reached into his pocket and turned off his mobile phone. The Premier could wait until there were answers. Until Houston had some idea of how he was going to play it.

'Why do you think this story has been written by a fucking food critic?' asked Murray. Houston hadn't thought of the byline. But there it was, Adam Osborne. Strange. It was only a couple of days since he'd seen him at Dosh, now here he was again. He wasn't superstitious, but from his experience coincidences were rarely just that.

'What do you reckon?' he asked Murray.

'Dunno!'

'A fat load of fucking good you are, then. You're meant to be a media expert, mate.'

Murray rolled his eyes. 'Well, he did used to be a political journo. And,' he continued, with a nasty grin, 'if I remember rightly, he's fairly easy to scare.'

Houston laughed. 'It's probably nothing. Maybe they're a bit short-staffed after the latest round of redundancies. Rumour is they're about to merge with a TV station. There's an industry dinner this week. I'll ask Jack Vines then.'

The chat drifted off into some political gossip Murray had picked up from his night on the turps with Mark Malouf. Houston got the attention of the barista who was discussing his upcoming role in a play with a

THE GUTS

woman whose breasts were poorly restrained by her summer dress. 'Come on, mate. This isn't Bondi, you know. Some of us have work to do.'

They walked from the café to The Toaster, a triumph of expediency over aesthetics. Some years ago, there had been one ugly old-school skyscraper between Circular Quay, where the ferries dock, and Joern Utzon's beautiful if impractical Opera House. On the rest of the walk around, there was a high sandstone wall beyond which were the beginnings of the Botanical Gardens. The company that owned this building decided to change premises and sold the land to a developer, which decided it was going to utilise the land more efficiently. A plan was submitted with three squat buildings that swallowed all the land as far as the beginnings of the Opera House and cut off its visibility from Circular Quay.

If the people of Sydney care about anything, it's waterfront land, and if they aren't rich enough to own it, which the vast majority aren't, then at least they like to be able to walk along the bits of it that haven't fallen into private hands. There was an outcry, which in Houston's opinion was little more than the politics of envy. Too often the rich were often treated as second-class citizens, particularly by the press, when they were the people who kept the economy growing, making it possible, through the generation of employment, for the punters to pay their mortgages and buy the big screens that kept them relatively placid. By protesting against the Toaster, a bunch of selfish do-gooders wanted to deny a developer millions of dollars in profit, merely to preserve the capacity to gawk through an empty piece of sky. It was a joke and there was no way he'd have let the matter build up such a head of steam on his watch.

However, it had happened on the watch of the former Minister for Development, Hugh Bills, a former unionist and not the sharpest tool in the shed Houston thought, not least because he still subscribed to the anachronistic idea that workers and bosses had competing interests. In the battle for the Toaster, the developer made some serious mistakes. To begin with, the old office building had been destroyed before the permission to build the new one was in place. For several years, the development had languished, with the lawyers making a motza while the matter was kicked between the council, Macquarie Street and the Court. The developer was forced to sell the land to service more pressing financial concerns. In the interim, the public had enjoyed an uninterrupted vista from Circular Quay that opened the city out to the Opera House and the Botanical Gardens. They had never had it before and now they did, they wanted it to stay.

By the time the furore hit its peak, there were people marching with banners on a regular basis between the Opera House and Circular Quay. When the government approved the plans, it claimed its hands were tied by the contract the previous government had signed. If the public wanted the site, the state would be forced to buy it at the going commercial price. The government was unable to justify spending hundreds of millions of dollars to buy the site, since it would have to come out of the budgets for hospitals, police and schools.

People had chained themselves to bulldozers at the beginning, but the protest soon became exhausted. The buildings Houston and Murray were walking towards were pretty bloody ugly. Even Houston wasn't about to deny that. Their squat grey squareness had led to the 'Toaster' nickname after the domestic appliance. It was a good analogy. There were three buildings, all with a misplaced sense of grandeur.

But even if these buildings were an ugly crock of shit, Houston approved of their right to be there. It was important to remember how quickly the punters forgot. Disapproval of the development had been something in the order of 90 per cent, but as they strolled along on a nice November morning, there they were, punters aplenty in the cafes having breakfast. At nights and on weekends it was even more crowded. Humans will colonise anything usable, he thought. Some of the Toaster's most prominent critics were inside its art-house cinema watching second-rate European films, or eating and drinking to their good fortune at one of the swish and expensive eateries.

They walked to the second building, then took a lift to the fourth floor. When they exited the lift, they turned left. Murray knocked on the third door.

THE GUTS

'Who is it?' barked a gruff voice from inside.

'Billy and the Pig,' said Murray. Houston wondered for a moment who was who, then let it slide. There was the sound of a chain being released and the door opened. 'Who did you think it was, you big goose?'

'Fuck off Muzza! You never fucking know, do ya?' said the voice which had acquired a suspicious pair of eyes.

'I thought that's what the security cameras were for,' said Murray.

'I'm afraid they're having some technical problems today.'

'You're not as stupid as you look, are you?'

'Save the compliments, why don't ya?'

The door opened fully. Murray and Houston entered the apartment and followed their host into the lounge room. His accomplice was already there, enormous, even more so because of the compromise the developer had made on the height restrictions. Instead of losing a floor, the floors had been squashed together. This pair of thugs in Nike tracksuits looked like they belonged in a boxing gym. Houston wasn't sure how they'd got their mitts onto this place, nor was he going to ask. But it wasn't on the fifty grand a year retainer he gave them via Murray for their services.

'Roger,' said Murray, 'this is Benny,' indicating the one who had opened the door. Houston had always kept the V-team at one remove, leaving them for Murray to deal with. But this time he had a feeling, a bad feeling, and he wanted to impress the seriousness of the matter upon them with his presence. Benny was a smallish, stocky, fit looking man, with a receding hairline, designer stubble and eyes like steel ball bearings. Officially, he was a private detective who dealt with surveillance and industrial espionage. He was someone who broke the law with discretion. Murray, who had known Benny since Manly Primary School, was the closest thing Benny, a sociopath, had to a friend. He had stopped five kids from beating the shit out of young Benny when he was walking home from school one day. Benny, from a broken home where kindness wasn't the currency, had never forgotten. He'd repaid Murray with a loyalty that had lasted more than thirty years. If Benny had to do a job that was not in the interest of Murray's health, Murray was likely to get a warning.

Benny shook Houston's hand while keeping his eyes on Murray.

'Gentleman, this is Bruce.' Benny nodded towards his offsider who was pacing the floor while shouting into a mobile phone.

'I don't care what he says. Just fucking do it! ... What's your fucking problem?' Bruce threw the phone on the couch.

'Problem at home?' asked Houston

'None of your business.' came the reply. Bruce shook his fist. He was six-foot four and built like a brick shithouse. His massive, shaved head was in danger of scraping the ceiling. His face looked like the consequence of a chilli suppository. Benny gave him a look. Bruce pulled back from the threshold of violence into a menacing attitude.

'Let's get down to business,' said Houston.

'Why don't you go outside for a smoke, Bruce?' said Benny

Once he had, Benny began to talk. 'So far, it's not looking good. I've put the word out but nobody's seen him. His secretary, his lovers and his neighbours all claim to have no idea where he's gone. They either don't know or they don't want to say. I could up the aggro a bit and find out, but I'm not sure it's going to help.'

If Benny was going round threatening people on a fishing expedition, the media was going to find out. But Houston needed to find Parker, or at least work out where he'd gone before parliament resumed sitting the following week.

'Let me think about it,' he said.

'Don't take too long,' Benny replied. 'I've got to be on a building site by twelve. And I'm not going to be talking about this over the phone.' Houston went out to the balcony, ignoring the scowling Bruce, who went back inside, while Benny took a call.

Ideally, Houston wanted Parker to come back to parliament so the balance of power could be preserved and his new development legislation passed. For this to happen, Parker had to be convinced it was in his interests to return. But how? As far as he knew Parker wasn't bribeable. That was the thing about the Sporty Party, most of

THE GUTS

its members weren't. The power and influence, however, had concentrated in the hands of the few who were.

If Parker wasn't bribeable, the next best option was blackmail. Hence the USB drive that was now sitting in Parker's office. Houston had a talent for blackmail. He had once caused an obdurate judge to depart his bench via a car with a hose connected to its exhaust pipe. Holiday snaps. It intrigued him how often public virtue and private corruption co-existed in the one person: that someone who liked sleeping with teenage boys on overseas trips could be a stickler for the letter of the law; that people who campaigned on Christian values were the most likely to get caught with prostitutes; that wealthy women who devoted their lives to charity were in the habit of cruelly mistreating their domestics.

The only problem was that Parker was a political cleanskin. No bribes, no rorted travel allowances. No huge favours owing. He hadn't even stabbed that many people in the back to get to where he was. A certain absence of ambition had insulated him from the nastier kinds of power struggle at the same time as it had made him a popular local member. An attempt by Phil Dunleavy, an apparatchik from the right, to roll him in a pre-selection battle by stacking the local branches had proved a career-limiting failure. Dunleavy was someone Houston could have worked with. He was working in insurance now.

The only real fault line Houston could think of from his break-and-enter expedition into Parker's office was the member's fondness for third world beauties. But he was a single man, so he couldn't threaten to tell his wife. Houston supposed he could email the various women in Parker's life and introduce them to each other, but what was that going to achieve? No sign of prostitutes nor evidence of kinkiness. They weren't male and they weren't underage. Was it time, he wondered, for the world to discover that Parker was a paedophile?

But if he was going to try and blackmail Parker over the pornography he'd planted in his office, he had to find him first. He went inside. Benny got off the phone to a police contact. The news was not encouraging. He'd managed to track the email Parker had sent to Pond, but it had been sent from an internet café in Sydney, which gave them nothing except the possibility that Parker was still in the state.

Benny wasn't so sure. 'His mug's too well known not to be spotted. If he's serious he's either holed up somewhere in the bush, or he's skipped the country. Does it solve your problem if he's already done the bolt?'

'Not by a long shot.' Houston replied. 'Do you have anyone in immigration who can check whether he's used his passport in the past few days?'

Benny's mobile phone rang again. 'Yeah?... Yeah ... No bullshit? ... OK ... Keep a lookout, but whatever you do, don't let him find out or I'll have your balls for breakfast. We're coming now.' Benny pocketed his phone and turned to Bruce, 'Get your shit together sunshine. We're going for a drive in the country. I've got some good news,' he said. 'A source up in Dorrigo reckons he saw Parker driving down to a log cabin hidden in the forest. Do you want me to check it out?'

'Absolutely!'

'It will cost you. There's other work we'll have to cancel. Might put a few noses out of joint.'

'I don't give a fuck.'

'No worries, then. What do you want us to do if we find him?' asked Benny.

'Take it easy! There's no point coming on heavy if he knows jackshit about it. Try and suss him out. If he fesses up freely to who he is, give him this message.'

Houston handed Benny a letter from Pond, addressed to Parker, requesting him to cut short his holiday and return immediately for urgent pre-sitting consultation on crucial policy matters.

'What if he doesn't 'fess up?'

'If he tries to do a runner, bag him. Tie him to a chair and ring me for further instructions.'

'No worries.'

'And whatever you do, this is sensitive. Don't fuck it up!'

'No worries, boss,' said Benny with just a hint of contempt. 'C'mon Bruce, we've got work to do.'

THE GUTS

Bruce grunted back. A couple of minutes and they were ready to leave.

'Might be an idea to stay here for a while after we go, boss. Wouldn't want you to be seen mixing with unsavoury characters, would we now?' Houston detected class resentment. Another tawdry moment in the politics of envy, he thought. Wasn't the world easier for people when everyone knew their place? 'I'll let Muzza know when I get there.'

For some minutes Houston stood with Murray in the loungeroom enjoying the view. It did make you feel special. Murray poured himself a vodka from the drinks cabinet.

'I'm not paying you to get pissed in the morning,' said Houston, surprised.

'It's something I picked up from my Russian grandfather,' said Murray lamely.

'Oh, so your name was Limonruski before it was anglicised to Lime?'

'Gorky actually. It's just that my grandfather liked reading Graham Greene.'

'You'd better watch it,' said Houston. 'If it gets full-time, you'll have to give it up. And going to all those AA meetings telling the world how weak and pathetic you are is like being Catholic except the confessions aren't secret and you're deprived of the thing which brings you closest to God.'

'Apparently it's a good place to pick up chicks.' said Murray, ever the optimist. 'Once they give up the booze, if they don't go all Jesusy, they can get wild about sex.'

'Yeah, but it's not going to be like wham, bam, thank you mam, no strings attached. She's going to be looking for something life-sustaining.'

'But,' said Murray, with a Machiavellian glint, unwilling to concede the point, 'You've got the best excuse in the world.'

'What's that?'

'You're a recovering alcoholic. I'm sorry darling, I'm just too fucked-up now to get into a relationship.'

'But so is she. And before you know it, she's ringing your mobile phone three times an hour, because it makes her feel strong just to hear your voice. Then she starts knocking on your bloody door at three in the morning, saying I can't sleep without you.'

'Block the call, and always play away,' countered Murray.

'How long's she going to swallow that for though?'

'Long enough. Tell her your life is so fucked up, you had to move in with your parents who are Baptist preachers.'

Murray would pull it off, he was sure. Probably more than once. Some people knitted for a hobby; others did the gardening: Murray lied. It was one of the reasons why Houston had employed him. As the sun streamed in through the windows, Houston dreamed of Justine undressing in front of him in their own little waterfront love nest. It was going to be amazing. An elegant dinner, some expensive wine, a king-sized bed with soft Egyptian sheets. He imagined his hands stroking and squeezing her smooth skin, the smell of her, his nose buried deep in her neck, the taste of her, and her gasp of surprise at the moment he entered her, then the sound of all the million dollar yachts clinking on the harbour and the waves lapping the waterfront as they took the slow road to orgasm.

'Calling Houston, Calling Houston!' said Murray, breaking the reverie. 'It's Justine.'

He took the phone from Murray and only just managed to suppress the urge to say, 'How did you know I was thinking about you?'

'What's the problem?' he asked, a bit too gruffly.

'Pretty well everything. I've got Winston's secretary on the phone every five minutes asking where you are, but you've turned your phone off. There's a pissed off constituent waiting for you in the lobby, who says he has an appointment to see you. And the press are on high rotation seeking a comment on the future of your development legislation if Parker doesn't show up by the time parliament sits. I've got a mountain of work to do, but every time I make a start, the phone rings.'

'Never a dull moment, eh? Here's what we'll do. I'll ring the Premier now. Tell the muckrakers I've got no comment to make at this particular time, but that there might be a press conference later this afternoon. Then go down and apologise to the punter ... who is he?'

'Some guy called Nicholas Falk.'

'Small fry. Tell him I'm very sorry but urgent government business. Invite him to dinner in Parliament House next month and we can talk about his concerns then. Make a note of them and add him to the diary.'

'Thanks a million,' said Justine.

'That's what you're getting paid to do,' he said bossily. That was the problem with these millennials. They thought they only had to do the fun bits. But the lingering daydream of them in bed softened him. 'Then take yourself out to lunch.'

'To the Parliamentary Canteen?'

'Anywhere you like. On me.'

'Will I be seeing you this afternoon, boss?'

'It depends on how many mosquitos have been breeding in the Pond,' he replied, and hung up.

'What?' Murray was giving him a droll look. It took one to know one.

Next was Pond's secretary, 'Susan Hardcastle here. The Premier needs to talk now.

He dialled Winston's office. 'Hardcastle,' the voice at the other end said. 'Houston,' he replied. 'Get me the Premier!' He thought he heard her flinch. After some hesitation he was put through.

The Premier was in a dither. 'Roger, we need to meet. ASAP. The press are hounding me and I don't know what to say to them. And the executive's freaking out too. We need the legislation to get through if we're going to fund our campaign for the next election.'

'Say as little as possible,' said Houston, knowing that the journos would be picking up on Pond's emotional state.

'Do you know our current position on drought relief?' asked Pond.

'I can find out. Why?'

'Frank Graves, one of the rural members, rang to say he'd heard there was a leadership crisis and he wanted to declare his loyalty.'

'Bullshit! What did you do? You haven't been ringing people fishing for declarations of loyalty I hope.'

'Ummm.'

What a fucking idiot, he thought. 'That's exactly what you can't do. If you do that then people will think that where there's smoke, there's fire. Keep calm. For the moment the best thing you can do is nothing.'

'But what if they're ringing someone else?'

Sure enough there were at least four messages from MPs on Houston's phone. 'So, what if they are?' he said.

'You saw the paper, didn't you?' he said.

'Which one?' Houston asked.

'Roger, this is no time for mucking about!' Pond's voice was cracking about the edges.

'Yes, of course I saw it.'

'Well, what are we going to do about it?'

'We can't do anything until we find Parker.'

'I got another email,' he said.

'What did it say?'

'That this is just the beginning.'

'Is that all?'

'Yes. It's getting out of control.'

'Try not to panic,' Houston told him. 'It's going to be fine. I'll get back to you as soon as I hear something more.'

He didn't tell Pond about the sighting. To begin with he wasn't sure. Also, the more desperate Pond was, the more grateful he'd be, and Houston had a couple of schemes in the back of his mind that could do with his leader's support. The best time to ask for a favour was in the moment of immediate relief, before the gratitude wore off.

The talk of relief put an idea into his head. Murray had let himself out while he was talking to the Premier. Houston took note of the apartment number they were in then made a call. Fifteen minutes there was a buzz on the video intercom connected to the front door. He let the young woman and her massage table in. It was the last happy ending he would enjoy for some time.

12

Justine woke up uneasy. The dregs of an ugly dream. The bathroom was painfully light. The shower itchy. She ate a banana, drank a cup of Japanese tea, got dressed in a suit, sensible shoes and sunglasses, and hopped the train from Marrickville into town.

The underground air of Town Hall station felt like a giant armpit. More bad thoughts. Anticipations. Thursday night. A romantic dinner with the Gut. This time she had to go through with it. The banana revolted in her stomach. She turned up her headphones. Amy Winehouse. What kind of fuckery ...? Music for angry girls.

The stupidity of self-sacrifice flashed in her brain like an advertising banner. She pushed up the volume until the world became a video-clip and she an actor in it. Warning bells. Be careful, she told herself, else you'll be a basket case by the time your revolutionary deed is done.

At work the phones were on fire. The sour crab in the Premier's office every ten minutes. Every man and his dog in between.

'The Premier wants to talk to the minister now.'

Justine didn't think she was believed when she told the old bat that she didn't know where he was and agreed to give him the message (again).

The Press were also fishing for a sound byte from the Gut. When she finally got onto him, she was tempted to give him a piece of her mind then reminded herself that from her perspective the more chaotic the better.

Then she had to go down to the lobby and soothe Mr Nicholas Falk, CEO of Overlife Retirement Resorts. Clearly questing after influence, even if his suit coat did look crumpled after an hour of twiddling his thumbs in sight of the security guards in the lobby. Justine sensed he was expecting an apology and to be rushed off to meet The Gut. When she gave him the bad news, there was a short crisis of self-importance. For a moment she thought she was going to cop it. His face flushed, his voice got louder and higher.

'But he promised to meet me ...'

'I'm very sorry,' she lowered her eyes before looking back up to him. 'He's been called into a meeting with the Premier.'

Falk clearly needed a favour and that meant he couldn't afford to lose the plot, not even with the underling. His eyes, which had started to tunnel into Justine with the sordid machismo of a wife-beater, glowered on the cusp of incandescence before turning back in upon themselves, allowing his store-bought charm, a kind of crystallised insecurity, to return. The anger was still humming just under the surface and Justine was tempted to tickle it, just to see what would happen. But that wasn't what she was there for.

'Mr Falk, Mr Houston would again like to extend his sincere apologies. He has asked me to convey to you that he is looking upon your proposal with interest and wondered if you would have the time to dine with him in the parliamentary dining room next month and discuss the matter further. If that's amenable to you, please get your secretary [that always made them feel important] to contact me to arrange a suitable date.'

Falk brightened up with the promise of a ministerial dinner. The Gut was in the good books again, which meant that she was too.

'My secretary will be in touch. Please give Roger my very best regards.' His plummy private school voice concealed the shoddiness of the nursing home chain – the bed sores, slop and exploited staff – that funded it.

'Of course,' Justine nodded. If only he knew how little Roger cared.

After dealing with Falk, Justine went out to lunch. It was Sarah's birthday. Surely he didn't expect her to eat alone. Sarah chose the Opera Bar, down on the water. She left Parliament House and took the same walk her boss had taken only hours before. A hint of cool in the air made the sun on her skin feel good. She arrived on time at 12 and

THE GUTS

took a seat facing the harbour. Even on a shitty day, it was hard to argue with its beauty.

Sarah arrived in a fluster. 'Sorry, I'm late. I was on a story. The real estate guy wouldn't shut up. And there weren't any taxis. So, I had to get a lift with him and pay for it with a sympathetic ear. Took me ten minutes to get out of the car. You should have heard him. By the end of it I wanted to say, 'if it's that bad, you might as well top yourself.' You would have thought with the property boom and everything, he'd be laughing. Then after telling me all his problems, he asked me out on a date.' She rolled her eyes and sat down. She was wearing a black skirt, black calf-high boots, and a purple top cut low that revealed more than a hint of her considerable cleavage. Sarah was shorter than Justine. Her hair was dark brown. Her body curvaceous. Her father had migrated from Croatia. Her mother's family had originally come from Ireland. She drew male eyes wherever she walked. It was unsurprising the real estate agent had asked her out on a date. Sarah lacked confidence, but she didn't need confidence to attract attention from the opposite sex.

The two women had met in a political science tute at uni and gotten involved in student politics. They had run together as part of a feminist Trotskyite team for the student council, Hot to Trotsky. For a year or so, they had been flatmates in a dodgy Dulwich Hill terrace. Once they'd even had a threesome – Justine's first and only – with a Marxist Freedom fighter from Waterloo after a long day of listening to Billy Bragg and drinking Stones' Green Ginger Wine.

The experience hadn't prevented them from becoming best friends, connected to some degree by their sense of being outsiders. Sarah's dream was to be a star reporter on a metropolitan daily, but she lacked the right connections, and the confidence to overcome this. She was living out her dreams at a suburban newspaper writing about auctions, shops and local alderman without quite knowing how to make the leap to the next stage. She compensated for this with an exotic love life; her current Brazilian lover was just one in a long line of men (many of them more trouble than they were worth) and the urge to try new things. Tango, sailing, pole dancing, spoken word, sculpture, she always seemed to have a new hobby on the go.

They ordered fish and chips with Riesling. The waiter was a pretty snoot. Justine decided to keep the tip for Oxfam.

'Why are so many of the good-looking men gay?' said Sarah when he left them, his walk somewhere between a mince and a brood.

Sometimes their conversations sounded too much like *Sex in the City*, thought Justine. As if the gloss had become the model. The sky was so clear the day seemed almost cartoonish. Justine imagined herself in a bikini on the prow of one of the yachts tacking their way to the heads, leaving Sydney on an adventure, hearing only the wind on the sails, the gusts jangling the stays, the whoosh and thud of the hull ploughing through the waves.

Sarah looked at her with curious amusement, 'So things are going well with Paul?'

'He's a bit on the spectrum, but he's not dull.'

'You've always had a thing for space cadets.' It was true. Justine found her own self-containment easier to manage in relationships with people who were also self-contained. She didn't deal well with needy. 'How's work?'

'Better than writing safety guides three times over for the fucking RTA. By the way,' she whispered. 'Do you think you can get me another gram of coke?'

'Sure.' Sarah rummaged in her handbag. She pulled her hand out and slid her closed fist towards Justine across the table. Justine couldn't help but notice what looked like a big emerald ring on Sarah's finger.

'Are you getting married?'

'No, blitzed with charm. South American men are the bomb. They love the drama.'

'It's beautiful.'

'It's full-on.'

Sarah opened her hand so the palm of it was facing down then slid it back to reveal a small zip lock bag that contained white powder. Justine slid her hand across the table and covered it. She lifted her arm and deposited the coke in her bag.

'Thanks. How much do I owe you?'

'What it cost me. One fifty.'

'I'll sort you out with the bill.'

As she walked back to work, it struck Justine that scoring coke from Sarah had been a bit too easy. The rock in the ring a bit too big. But who was she to judge? Sydney was a flashy place. And even in her time in South America, she had never come across a place whose inhabitants were so fond of snorting white powder up their nostrils. It had become part of Sydney's cultural fabric in the way she associated hash with Amsterdam and pilling with Berlin. People in Melbourne tended to prefer smack.

The wine had made her sleepy. She wrote a draft Press Release about the reinvigoration of the southern fringes of the CBD as an education and entertainment precinct and left it on his desk to sign. She then bit the bullet and booked a table for two under Houston's name at a place called Fetish on Thursday night. Using the fiction of a doctor's appointment, which she texted to Houston, she left work, swam some laps of the Enmore pool and went home.

'Did you read the paper?' Paul asked when he rang her that night.

'Yes, Alexander Parker's gone.'

'What did your boss think of it?'

'I dunno. He seemed a bit stressed.'

'Good. We're getting closer.'

'He's taking me out to dinner on Thursday night. Hopefully I can get what you want then.'

'Cool. I'll drop the stuff round now.'

Twenty minutes later there was a knock at her apartment door.

Paul seemed more business-like than before. It was his first time at her place. It was an old flat and not a particularly nice one, bedroom, lounge room, bathroom, kitchen, low stucco ceiling and flying saucer light fixtures. They walked past her bedroom and into the lounge room. Justine went into the tiny kitchen to make tea while Paul sat on the couch and checked his phone.

'Nothing more to report. Parker hasn't been found, according to *The Morning Glory*. And he won't be.'

'How do you know?'

Paul's face wore the self-importance of a secret. 'I'm pretty sure he's no longer in the country. The ABC is predicting other MPs are going to go too. We're at the tipping point. Now's the time to find out what your boss knows and where his unofficial records are kept.'

'Thursday night. I promise. What's the stuff you've got for me?'

Paul reached into his messenger bag and pulled out two small vials with screw-on droppers for lids. 'This one's SD-117 – it's a truth serum the KGB used. Tasteless, odourless, painless. Fill the dropper once and squeeze it into his drink. It should start to take effect in about around 30 minutes. Give it to him as early as you can.'

'What about the other one?'

'That's Rohypnol, you know the barbiturate. Give that to him about twenty minutes after the first one, half a dropper this time. Don't give him too much especially if he's been drinking. He might die.'

'Worse things could happen.'

'True. But it won't look good for you when the toxicology report comes back from the pathologists.'

'So, you're talking about date rape in reverse?'

'What do you mean?'

'Well things are getting friendly after dinner. We go somewhere. I give him the drugs. He talks. Then he goes to sleep. I leave. He wakes up feeling groggy, thinking we must have had sex, but the intimacy has been of an entirely different nature.'

'Pretty much. You might have to wank him off, but.'

'Really?'

'That way there'll be evidence that something must have happened.'

'Is that really necessary?'

'You don't want to have to do it again.'

'Shit. I better buy a pair of gloves.'

Paul's phone rang. He answered it then went into her bedroom. Justine wasn't sure whether to follow him in or not. She stayed on the

THE GUTS

couch and finished her tea. She heard his voice, low and urgent, but couldn't decipher his words.

'Who was that?' she asked when he came back.

'Can't say.'

She was annoyed. 'I'm about to get naked with a nasty old fat man and you can't tell me who you're talking to on the phone while you're in my house?'

'I'm sorry. It works better that way. We only share information on a need-to-know basis.'

'So, who knows what I'm about to do?'

'Me, you and two others.'

'Who are they?'

'I can't say.'

'Then you can't stay.'

'I can't stay anyway.' Paul picked his bag off the couch and walked to the front door. 'Good luck. Ring me and let me know how it goes.'

Justine's anger kept her awake until after 2am. Here she was about to get into a dangerous situation and her lover wouldn't tell her crucial information. She realised she knew hardly anything about Paul. His enigma was an irritation. He didn't even seem jealous over what she was about to do. How possible was it to actually know anyone, she wondered. You could share the same bed and bodily fluids with someone for decades without ever getting to the bottom of them. People were a mystery. But what if he was sleeping with her as part of getting her to do the job? If that was the case, she didn't want to know.

She slept in. It was 8.30am when she woke up. After nine by the time she got on the train. Almost ten by the time she got to work. The Gut was already there.

'You're late,' he said.

'I'm sorry,' she said.

'What good is being sorry going to do?'

The phone rang. It was Pond. 'Yes Winston, I'll be there in half an hour.'

'I booked a table for Fetish on Thursday night.'

'Well good for you.' He really was in a sour mood. 'Today you're going to take a little trip. Mrs Smith's second cousin twice removed has died and she has to go to the funeral in some shitty little country town. Which means the electoral office is unmanned. She's leaving tomorrow. So I need you to go out there today and learn the ropes. And if you can manage to behave yourself out there, I will take you to Fetish on Thursday night. Well, what are you waiting for? Haven't you got a train to catch?' She walked to the door. 'And remember, keep your mouth shut out there. No need to stir up the constituents.'

Why suddenly was she the meat in everyone's sandwich, she thought as she waited at Museum station for a train to Blue Hills. Fuck them all!

13

It was great to see his byline on the frontpage again. When he got to work on Tuesday morning a few people even congratulated him. 'Nice scoop,' said one. 'Good get,' another. The phone on his desk blinked with messages. He turned on his computer and checked his emails. A spokesman for the Premier reiterated the official denial of Parker's disappearance. There also were some Elvis-style sightings of Parker: in a Caravan Park at Ulladulla; a Roadhouse out of Coober Pedy. A log cabin up in the Dorrigo forest, in Peru, and on a P & O cruise ship heading towards Tahiti with a concubine in tow. The bank wanted to know if he needed to increase his credit limit, there were two invitations to upcoming culinary events, and somebody wanted him to be a judge on a cooking show. But before he could do anything, there was Ingrid.

Where's the toilet story?

Up shit creek

What do you mean?

I haven't had time.

It's meant to be your top priority.

What against the biggest story in the state?

I need it by section deadline tomorrow. Otherwise, there's going to be a hole in the paper next week.

I might have to go away.

Six restaurants, six bathrooms. Surely someone of your drinking prowess can manage that.

A piece of piss.

Then do it.

Ingrid might have lacked imagination, but she did know how to protect her patch. Adam opened Word and started remembering the toilets in Dosh. 'An ideal place for Finance types to snort their coke ...' She could do with it what she liked.

Adam hoped one of his phone messages would be from Kate. No such luck. Maybe she hadn't read the paper yet. Maybe she had and was still angry. He didn't know. He felt calm and potent. On leave from his mid-life crisis. He took this newfound confidence and rang her.

'Hi,' she answered.

'Hi. How are you?'

'I've been better.'

'What's wrong?'

'You know what.'

'You saw the paper?'

'Yes.' The flatness of her tone disappointed him.

'It's a good story.'

'Adam ...' Kate hesitated, as if she were building up the courage to say something.

'Yes?'

'I had a dream. A terrible dream. Something bad is going to happen. I can tell.'

Adam sensed that she was crying. 'It's OK sweetheart. It's just a story. This is Australia. It's more dangerous being a food critic.'

'Unless of course you're a cat. Look, I've never had this feeling before. Not even then. Please, can't you just let it go?'

It was unusual for her to say something like this. Kate was the more rational one, it was Adam who tended to get paranoid and Kate who reasoned him out of it. And she wasn't making it up for the purpose of emotional blackmail. That he did know. 'What was the dream?'

'I don't want to think about it.'

'What happened?'

'I don't want to say.'

'What was it?'

She pulled back a big sob. 'I was trying to talk to you. But you were like a ghost. You just looked back at me, but it was like talking through glass. I couldn't hear a word you said. You were desperately saying

THE GUTS

things, I was listening as hard as I could, but I couldn't hear you. All I could hear was the wind. Then a dark shadow fell over us. And that's when I woke up. My heart was pounding. Promise me you'll give it up.'

Adam drew a deep breath, then another. The silence between them was potentially bottomless. 'I'm sorry. I'm not sure I can.'

'I can't support you in this.'

It felt like a knife to the ribs. He sucked at the phone for air. 'What do you mean?'

'You know what I mean.'

'No. I don't. Tell me.'

'I'm sorry. I've got to go. Be careful.' Kate hung up. She had given him an ultimatum. The story or her. He didn't want to choose.

Before he had time to dwell on it, another email came in. The sender was darkrose@hotmail.com, the same address, unbeknown to Adam, that Parker had used in his email to Winston Pond.

Good news travels fast. Looking forward to coming instalments. Here's something you can throw at them too. AP

If Parker had left the country, thought Adam, he must be reading the news on the net. Adam wondered whether he'd be able to trace Parker's location through the computer he was using. They'd caught terrorists that way. Then again, he wasn't the CIA. Still, he wanted to be sure of his sources or he'd end up with egg all over his face. It was possible his correspondent was an imposter. Anyone could open an email account and pretend to be someone else. But his gut was saying otherwise.

Attached to Parker's email was a press release.

PARKER'S PISSED OFF?

In response to reports of his disappearance, the missing MP for Nile, the Honorable Alexander Parker has announced he has abandoned the Pond government and that his seat is up for grabs. Mr Parker said, 'The current regime has led to the government of this state according to a buffet logic. Parliament should not be treated as a ticket to riches and currently it is. I want nothing further to do with a government composed of the self-serving and those who are wilfully blind to evidence of their colleagues' corruption. It's a dangerous blend of the incompetent and the criminal, and the people of New South Wales should be given the chance to know this. While I am far from sure that the opposition if given the opportunity will do any better, for the sake of clarity and democracy, the only real option is to do what I can to help bring this government down.'

In a written statement exclusive to The Morning Glory, Mr Parker apologised to the people of New South Wales for any inconvenience caused. He also said that the government should tackle the balance of power crisis resulting from his departure by declaring fresh elections. Mr Parker advised he would not be standing for his seat and recommended that his constituents vote for an independent candidate when elections are held until the Sporty Party is reorganised to once again represent the true interests of its members and the electorate. He finally added that he has submitted his resignation one day short of the period that would have qualified him for parliamentary superannuation. 'It would be a disgrace,' he said 'to take such a course of action and then continue to suck on the teats of the taxpayer. I would like to thank the people of New South Wales for their support over the course of my political life.'

A touch of glory mongering, thought Adam. Politicians were notorious for their difficulty in separating the public interest from their own. With Kate's warning fresh in his mind, Adam wondered for the first time whether he was running the story, or whether the story was running him. Journalists who swallowed and regurgitated the words that staffers and spin doctors wrote for their politician bosses weren't that uncommon. Legend had it one old soak in the Parliamentary press gallery had pinched so much from politicians' press releases that when he retired a ministerial media advisor had sent him an invoice for freelance work at fifty cents per word. Most of the time, the flacks encouraged it. Plagiarism by lazy or over-stretched journalists

THE GUTS

was one of the most effective ways to get their bosses' messages across. They took pride in writing pithy sentences that lodged in the brains of tired hacks and were regurgitated, slants intact, in the paper. Politicians often went a step further by keeping pet journalists, to whom they released select information ahead of the rest. The fat egos of some political journalists were unearned given that their scoops came only on the condition they parroted the positions of their source. Adam really hoped that Parker wasn't playing him like that. He had already taken the bait. He knew he wasn't going to pull back and wait until he had solid proofs of Parker's whereabouts. Until he had spoken to Parker himself. If he did that then someone else would get the story. It was risky, but his gut told him to keep going.

He formatted Parker's press release as a report and filed it, then it was time to pump out his toilet piece so he could keep Ingrid off his back. In quick succession, he rang Pufferfish, a newly opened, slightly funky, second tier Sydney's restaurant. The tables were being laid for lunch. The restaurant was taking bookings. After identifying himself as Adam Osborne from *The Morning Glory*, he asked the critical question: 'What are your toilets like?'

'What do you mean, what are they like?'

'Describe them to me.'

'Running out of ideas are you?'

'Not my idea.'

'OK. Hang on.' After a short pause, the voice returned, with reverb. 'The floor tiles are kind of like a wavy navy blue. The basins are white.'

'What about the urinals?'

"fraid I'm not built to use them. But I've heard they're water saving ones'

'Fair enough.'

'What about the soap?'

'Verbena.'

'Any extras.'

'Towels stacked on a wooden plate for hands and faces. An electric dryer on the wall. A bowl of mints next to the basin.'

'Anything else?'

'Water music in the ladies to prevent any embarrassment. I think that idea came from Japan.'

'Air freshener?' There was a pause on the phone while Adam's source took a conspicuous sniff.

'Well, it isn't Glen 20. Smells a bit like sandalwood. Upmarket hippy.'

'Thanks for that.'

'Anything else you need to know.'

'Nah, that's great thanks.'

'Well don't write anything nasty, or I'll be in trouble.'

'No worries. Thanks again.'

The four subsequent calls to Flake, Castro, Commander Grill and Babyface, which he was due to review, were much the same. Within the hour he had typed up a series of tables: Air, Water, Towels, Scent, Soundtracks. The water music had intrigued him. Most of them just piped the music through from the main dining room. Babyface, the first Sydney restaurant to cater to the soft food movement, primarily wealthy senior citizens who could no longer masticate properly, had cups filled with Polident for the washing of dentures next to the basins. All their toilet cubicles had been especially widened to allow for wheelchairs and Zimmer frames. Commode chairs were available on request. The toilet music inclined towards early Beatles and Frank Sinatra. Pink Floyd, apparently, was good for constipation. Commander Grill, which like Dosh was a conservative restaurant catering to the finance elite, was notable in that they cleaned their toilets during the lunch and dinner service too. 'It's a problem with men who sit down all day then eat too much meat,' said the waitress at the end of the phone, who sounded like she was bored with her job. The one good thing, Adam imagined, about serving the clientele at Commander was big swinging dicks showing off to each other with the size of their tips.

It took another half an hour to write up the article then another 45 minutes to write a review that would usually have taken him all morning.

The service was crisp, the seafood fresh, the wine list disappointingly over-burdened with sauvignon blanc. The flathead roulades

THE GUTS

were truly inspirational. The Murray Cod on a kumera stack, solid but unspectacular. The dining room was loud, but the energy was good. He didn't even have to hunt for new superlatives. The words his fingers conjured from the keyboard were sticking to the screen like a Chiko Roll on a milk bar bain-marie.

By lunchtime he had polished off a week's work. But he had to feed it slowly into the system in case Ingrid noticed and upped his KPIs. The work made him hungry. He messaged Bob to see if he was interested in lunch. Bob was hungover and in need of miso therapy, so they went to a little Japanese place in a Chinatown foodhall that served an excellent ramen. The sun was shining, the city was full of energy. He would have been feeling on top of the world if only he wasn't worried about Kate. A naughty voice insinuated that perhaps it was time to move on. Surely there would be someone who would appreciate the public service he was performing. But the allure of becoming a bachelor again was immediately countered by the presence of Bob who had. He was recovering from an accidental bender the night before. His skin was spew pale except for the splotches of red around his nose, where capillaries had burst. The sun's heat had irritated the tiny spiders embedded under his skin. His wife had moved to the Gold Coast.

Lunch was a deep miso broth, fresh beanshoots, shallots, two chunky slabs of pork and a tangle of glutinous noodles. The condiments included raw garlic, strips of nori and powdered chilli. Bob slurped at his miso ramen like a Japanese salaryman with a train to catch. It was hard to get anything out of him.

'Have you ever noticed the connection between hangovers and lateral thinking?' he finally asked when his soup had been reduced to a tiny puddle at the bottom of his bowl.

'Yeah?'

'I got the cryptic out in under five.'

'Not bad,' said Adam, who had tried on the way into work and only landed four clues. 'But if I were you, I might be substituting lateral thinking for more horizontal thinking. A bit more dreaming, a bit less waking nightmare. You look like shit.'

'Thanks Mum.' Bob stared into the wall. 'I see you're back to being a hot shot. So, while we're on the subject of meaningful advice, there's one thing that's got me puzzled. Why do you think Parker's doing what he's doing? What do you think's in it for him? And why has he dragged you into it? How can you be sure it's not all just some gigantic practical joke?'

Bob's question amplified the doubts Adam had been having that morning. Perhaps the stuff he'd been feeding Adam was just a smokescreen for something completely different. Something Parker hadn't let Adam in on. And if the stuff Parker had fed him wasn't true, there'd be more egg on Adam's face than there was in a Beluga sturgeon.

Adam responded with a worried look. 'What do you reckon?'

Bob shrugged his shoulders, 'Fucked if I know. Just be careful.'

When Adam returned from lunch, his phone was beeping on his desk. There was an urgent message from Sway to meet him in the boardroom. Adam had never been to the boardroom before. He didn't have to be a genius to realise it wasn't going to be about his ambivalent review of Dosh. His palms sweated as he went up two floors in the lift. Suddenly he was busting. Fortunately, there was a toilet next to the lift. Somebody was straining and farting appallingly in the cubicle next to the urinal. There were things even human resources couldn't fix. While the lay-out of the newsroom was a modern warren of laminated, particle board workstations in a bland grey that aspired to neutrality and efficiency, the boardroom was an ersatz relic of a nineteenth century London club. The walls were mahogany-panelled and lined with the portraits of former editors and publishers. In the corners were two clusters of armchairs gathered around antique coffee tables, where three or four people could cluster and share secrets. The room was dominated though by an immense rectangular timber table, encircled by sixteen leather upholstered chairs. The concessions to modernity were the thirty-fifth floor vista over the harbour, and a projection screen on the opposite wall with Power Point display of a marketing strategy lingering from the meeting before.

THE GUTS

Sway met him at the door. 'Come in and sit down, Adam.' he said, a little unsteady on his feet as he ushered him in with his arm.

Closest to Adam and nodding hello was Chloe Saville, the paper's inhouse lawyer. She was tall, dark and button-mouthed with smart brown glinting eyes. Adam had met her soon after his move to food journalism, when a restaurant had tried to sue him over a review in which he'd complained about a cockroach in his soup. Adam had wrapped the cockroach, which must have drowned, in one of the restaurant's embossed napkins and put it in his jacket pocket. It had been the last cool day before summer and he had put the jacket away in his cupboard with its cargo preserved. Three months later, when the restaurateur had launched his defamation suit, Adam had been able to produce the roach. Confronted with the offending insect in one of his own distinctive napkins, the restaurateur had dropped the action. Chloe told Adam he'd probably saved the paper half a million bucks.

Her hobby was humanitarianism. When she wasn't sorting out the legal problems of the newspaper, she was an advocate for refugees and had appeared for many of them pro bono. She was one of the only people Adam had ever met who had moved from Sydney's eastern suburbs to the western suburbs out of choice. The daughter of an Afro-American musician who had come to Australia via Vietnam and a third generation Australian born Chinese mother, she found the west more culturally dynamic than the gentrified inner rings.

Sitting opposite Adam was Jack Vines, the CEO of the company that published *The Morning Glory*. Vines had once been a journalist, but after a relatively inauspicious career editing the property and personal finance sections of the paper, he'd gone off and done an MBA somewhere in America and returned to take up a management role. Rick Walsh, the fifth-generation proprietor of the family company that had started *The Morning Glory* in the heady days of the first Australian Gold Rush, had decided that there was more money in gambling than news. Disabused of the idea of *noblesse oblige* by his friends in the eastern suburbs party set, Walsh had sold out to an American private equity firm, Cayman Crocodiles, who were mainly interested in manipulating *The Glory's* debt for tax concessions then floating the company at a profit, rather than actually running it. The company had been floated and the Americans had made a tidy almost tax-free profit. Within two years, *The Glory*, now owned by several superannuation funds and overseen by a board with corporate but no media experience, had lost more than half its value. Journalists had been retrenched, executive renumeration had increased. Jack Vines's timing had been impeccable. Unlike the board, he did have media experience and his newly imbibed mastery of the mumbo jumbo of management consultancy meant that when the paper publicly listed on the stock exchange and became prone to the influence of bean counters, investment analysts and superannuation fund managers, his star had risen. He could downsize, rationalize, monetize, operationalize and incentivize with the best of them, and had successfully brown-nosed the new company Chairman, Sir Julian Circle, one of the best-connected men in Australian business, by dressing him up as his mentor. 'If it wasn't for Sir Julian's generosity with his business smarts, I'd still be chasing ambulances,' he had once remarked to an unimpressed interviewer. Having escaped the fate of being a journalist, Vines had come to believe they were an over-unionised bunch of malingerers who interfered with the mathematical elegance of economic efficiency, and who failed to get, despite being paid to be curious, the gist of how the world actually worked. In his three years as CEO, he had charmed the financiers, and grown the management team, while shepherding the paper towards the banality that comes from an over-reliance on the findings of market research. Most importantly he was looking for someone to buy a controlling interest in the company, so he could make a few more million on his bonus options and get out.

'Good to see you again, Adam,' he said. Adam didn't necessarily believe him, but nodded nonetheless. Vines was wearing a number two haircut, a ski tan and a blue Italian suit. Behind his metal-framed spectacles, his blue eyes were aggressive.

Next to Vine was the unmissable bulk of George Pepsis, director of corporate relations, whose job involved keeping the paper's investors

THE GUTS

and major advertisers happy, mainly through an elaborate circuit of lunches, dinners and sports spectating in corporate boxes. Adam had dealt with him a few times when covering events generated by the paper, such as *The Morning Glory*'s Big Fork awards. Adam had been surprised to find himself liking Pepsis. Behind the immensity and smiling eyes that simultaneously charmed and warned, was a good listener. But where the schmooze ended and integrity began was hard to read. 'Hi George,' said Adam.

'Good to see you,' His tone of voice and fidgety fingers put Adam on edge. The person sitting next to him, despite all the eating at the Monkey King, looked like a stick insect that had crawled inside an expensive navy suit.

'Adam, this is Dick Mahone,' said Vines. 'He's consulting.'

'We're acquainted,' said Adam. He nodded at Mahone, who nodded back. 'Consulting for who, Dick?'

'My client prefers to remain anonymous at this time,' said Mahone. His mouth curled into a sneer that turned his speech almost into a lisp.

Before Adam could drop the name Harry Virtue, George picked up the ball. 'This is some story, you've broken, Adam. And it looks like you've got it all to yourself. A bit of a leap from the restaurant gig, eh?'

'Yeah, it's quite refreshing,' he replied.

'I can imagine,' said George.

'But if we're going to follow this story, Adam, I need to know that your sources are one hundred per cent on the money.'

'I've got the documents to prove it,' he improvised, knowing that the documents he had were not quite enough to pin the story down.'

'We also need to know,' said Vines, 'where those documents came from.'

'A source is a source, Jack,' said Adam, casting a glance at Mahone.

'Dick is here at the company's invitation and has given us an undertaking of confidentiality,' said Vines. 'What is said in this room, stays in this room.'

'No can do.' Adam knew that at some stage he would probably divulge his source to Chloe. But for all he knew what was being said in this room was being recorded and listened to by a bunch of people in another room.

He wasn't going to get kicked off the story like he had last time. And if he did get kicked off the story, he'd call in the union and leak what had happened at this meeting to every journalist he knew. The room fell into a tense silence before George intervened. 'Dick represents the interests of some of our largest advertisers. He wants to know if any of these firms will be adversely affected by the material you are in possession of.'

'That's hard to say when he hasn't told me what companies he's representing.'

'If you read out a list of the companies that are implicated. I'll be able to work it out from there,' said Mahone.

Adam didn't know yet who exactly was implicated, and this was a gap in his knowledge he didn't want known. 'What about you read a list of the companies you work for, and I'll give you the nod if they are.'

'That's not how I want to do it,' scowled Mahone, looking to Vines for support. 'Your cavalier attitude underestimates the importance of what we are dealing with. Don't be a fool, Adam. This is important. Tell me who is mentioned.'

'No.' He wasn't going to mention Ken Virtue, or CCP Constructions, or anyone else. Mahone was playing poker. You show me yours and I'll show you mine. But what was shown first would alter what was shown second. 'Why don't you take a guess?'

'Why don't you go jump in the lake?' said Mahone.

'Look Dick, I'm not convinced of the necessity nor the benefit of divulging my information to you,' said Adam, rising as if to leave. 'We'll have to talk about this some other time. Gentlemen.'

'Another time my arse!' exploded Vines. Hardly Harvard Business School that, thought Adam. 'What's your fucking problem? Sit down now and tell Dick what he needs to know. Do you know how much revenue you're playing with here? Millions. Millions and bloody millions. Don't be a bolshie prick!'

'Worried about your share options, are you Jack?

THE GUTS

A spasm of rage passed through Vines like an electric shock. His face lost all its colour. He took a few deep breaths and his voice became calm. There were rumours he had heart troubles. The senior executive team-building sessions had traded in mini-marathons for yoga retreats. 'Look,' said Vines, adopting a contrived tone of world-weary patience, 'that's all very well and good in the ideal world, but you've got to understand the economic realities of the situation. If the paper doesn't sell advertising, there won't be any paper. The only way to cope with the loss of any of the accounts Dick is representing here would be to cut the newsroom budget by five per cent.

'But the primary purpose of a newspaper is to deliver news,' argued Adam. 'Advertising is just the means of making that possible. If one advertiser doesn't want to share the page with this kind of story, so what! Other advertisers and readers will be attracted to the paper's reputation for integrity. The only shareholders affected are your short-term speculators ... and,' he added, 'the kind of management whose bonuses only get activated if the stock hits a certain price by a set date. So, before I cough up information which has the capacity to make a difference to some PR flack, I want to know whose mouthpiece he is, whose knee he'll be sitting on, whose ear he'll be whispering my secrets into.'

'Don't be a bloody idiot,' said Vines. His face tomatoed. Yoga only went so far. 'You don't want to come in here with the biggest story of the year and walk out without a job, do you?'

'No, it's you who's acting the fool now,' said Adam. 'How are you going to explain yourself to the board when the union gets wind of that? They may be pretty useless but I've been a paid-up member of the MEAA for nearly twenty years now. SACKED FOR A SCOOP. Make a nice headline, wouldn't it. Bit hard to sell advertising when you haven't got a paper coming out, isn't it ... mate. Besides with a story like that, it shouldn't be too hard getting a job somewhere else ...'

'Harder than you might think. You don't know what you're messing with.' said Vines. A touch of fear clouded the aggressive clarity of his argument. But the outer manager won over the inner animal and his temper subsided. 'Don't be difficult, Adam. We all want to get along here. If you calm down and hand over what Dick needs now, you can edit the section of your choice. I'll even put Ingrid under you. We could come to an arrangement with Kate. I hear her business has been struggling.'

'Not true, Jack. She's earning more money than me.'

'Not for long,' said Mahone, which was a mistake on several counts, not least because it meant that Kate might be right.

'Thanks Dick. When I want to hear from an arsehole, I fart.'

The ambience of the boardroom was designed to mute such vulgarity, but it had seen bullies aplenty. Chloe moved her hand towards Adam's forearm to calm him, then countermanded the instinct. George looked like he was doing worry beads under the table. Mahone appealed to Vines with his eyes. Vines was struggling with the onset of another fit of rage. Adam didn't care. His boss had misread his ambitions completely.

It wasn't meant to be like this. Any decent newspaper publisher would respect you and protect you for uncovering such a story. Like the way Katherine Graham, owner of *The Washington Post* had gone in to bat for Bob Woodward when he uncovered Watergate. Vines should have been slapping Adam on the back and salivating over the prestige and extra circulation it would bring *The Morning Glory*, but instead he was worried about the shareholders and whether any of the paper's major advertisers would be implicated. A little red light oscillated in Adam's head. Vines. Mahone. Vines. Mahone. Vines. He hadn't punched anybody since school. But he regretted those moments when he had failed to fight back. Last time he'd crumbled when the heavies had come round and nailed the cat to his door. And he hadn't really liked himself since. This time had to be different. Sorry Kate! Sorry!

'If you don't want the bloody story, Jack, I'll take it somewhere else.'

'Listen here you stupid cunt ...' said Vines

Adam stood and shaped to smack his boss in the head.

Chloe was quickly between them. 'Now, now gentlemen. We don't want to do something we'll all regret, do we. You don't want this to end

THE GUTS

up in court.' The two men stood shaking their fists at each other, but the moment for violence had passed.

While all this was happening George and Mahone were urgently conferring at the end of the table. Mahone was highly agitated, and George was trying to calm him down.

Raised fists became scowls then death-ray stares. Insults were muttered and after some final posturing more ludicrous than threatening, they sat back down. Jack's face was purple and the muscles on his neck were fanned out like an angry lizard. Adam suspected that had there been a mirror in the room his would have looked the same. George and Mahone returned from the corner, and things started to resemble a proper meeting again.

'Jim,' said Vines, seeking weakness in order to re-assert his authority, 'can you pull the story?'

Sway's face drooped. He hesitated, wringing his hands. 'Probably, but I don't know, Jack, if it would be a good idea. You see we've already begun to run it. The subs have already read Adam's copy for tomorrow. You know what a rumour mill this place is. People are talking. If the story is pulled, they'll be asking questions, building theories. They'll be talking about you and the board. There's nothing they love more than the thought of management being screwed over a conflict of interest. There's a lot of talk about your salary going up for making journo numbers go down. Try as you might, they don't give a shit about the shareholders. What have the shareholders ever done for them? So you won't be able to seal it off with an appeal to company loyalty. You could try and force loyalty on them, but then the media's incestuous. They'll be telling their partners and friends who work for the radio, the TV and of course *The Inquirer*.' Vines bristled at the mention of the opposition. Sway's words were making an impact. For someone best known as a drunk, he was offering sound tactical advice. 'At least if we publish, we're in control of the situation ...'

'Jack that's not what we agreed upon,' interrupted Mahone. 'They're not going to like it.'

'Who's they?' asked Adam. 'Whose errand boy are you?'

Mahone sneered but said nothing. Outrageous! It took balls though to walk into a newspaper and tell the publisher and the editor they should go against all journalistic principles and pull the biggest story of the year. Either balls or desperation.

'You used to work for the Sporty Party didn't you, Dick?' asked Adam.

Mahone was surprised. 'What's that got to do with anything?'

The information seemed to pull Vines out of his thoughts. 'Did you really, Dick?' he said. 'Must have been while I was in the states. Who did you work for?'

Mahone shifted in his seat and looked uncomfortable. Everyone was interested now.

If Adam had accidentally given Vines a lifeline, Mahone's silence sealed it. 'Look I'm sorry Dick, I think Jim's right. I'm going to run the story.'

Mahone's anxiety turned bright red. 'This is NOT what we agreed upon.'

'I know. I'm sorry, but sometimes circumstances change. As soon as you've legalled it, Chloe, it's clear to run.'

'This is not the last you'll hear of this,' said Mahone. He stood up and stamped his way towards the door. 'I'm not sure you understand who you're dealing with.'

'If we knew that,' snapped Adam, 'then we wouldn't be dealing with you.'

Once Mahone had gone, Vines reverted to being a journalist. 'Go for it, Adam. You're a pain in the arse, but at least you've got the courage of your convictions. But tread carefully and make sure you stick to the truth. Jim, make sure this story gets to press before Sir Julian starts throwing his weight around. He's on a plane from London to Singapore and he'll find out about this later tonight. But if the story's fully blown by then, there's nothing he'll be able to do about it. Nothing like a bit of editorial independence is there? Sorry gentlemen, but I've got another meeting to go to. Can I leave this in your capable hands?'

Sway nodded. Adam thought of calling him a hypocritical fuckwit until he realised he had gotten what he wanted. Vines left. George

THE GUTS

Pepsis went with him, his thoughts not showing on his face. Chloe smiled at Adam and rolled her eyes. 'You know where I am if you need me,' then left too.

'I didn't expect it to end up like that,' said Sway, who wore a look of cynical bemusement.

'Me neither,' said Adam. 'I feel like I've just done a firewalk.'

'Well, I better go and get the front page changed again!'

Adam was left by himself in the boardroom. Baffled. A cruise ship passed under the Harbour Bridge. Through the double-glazed windows, he heard its deep horn. Ferries and leisure craft moved across its bows on their own missions. A tugboat sat at the stern of a ship, whose passengers were too small to discern on its decks. Soon they would all spill out into the city to buy boomerangs and didgeridoos. They would eat at a series of mediocre restaurants. They would stock up on their medicines and clothes. Some of them would go to the casino and gamble. Others would take the ferry to Manly Beach and walk the promenade along the row of Norfolk Island Pines. A few brave souls would take the plunge into the Tasman Sea. Other jaded souls would stay on the ship and whine. Three days later, they would glide out of the harbour with their bounty of souvenirs and photos and enough to discuss, hopefully, until the next port. Further up the Harbour at Garden Island an American Navy ship had berthed. It was late afternoon and Adam imagined the sailors asleep on their bunks, preparing for a hard night of eating, boozing, dancing and seducing the ready supply of women who were keen to shag a sailor. The vista from the boardroom window stopped at the Botanical Gardens, but Adam knew what he would see if he had been gifted with X-ray vision; more buildings like the one he was in, each with its hierarchical obsessions expressed in the limited space, each angling as much as possible towards the leisure mecca of the harbour, but at the same time bullshit busy busy busy with only intangible products to show for it.

As he sat there and enjoyed the solemnity the empty room and its heavy decor projected, he began to form an overview of what had happened at the meeting. Vines's backflip started to make sense. If the story did get out despite the fact that he'd tried to block it, it would make Vines look bad, firstly because it would look like he couldn't control his staff, but more importantly because a publisher who was known to block stories concerning high level corruption couldn't help but be tainted by that corruption even if he had nothing directly to do with it. Vines might be selfish but he wasn't stupid. If the cards fell wrongly this was the sort of thing that could stain him for life. Maybe the story would put a dent in advertising revenue. Maybe the share price would drop as a consequence. But maybe it wouldn't. Share prices were as much about perceptions as realities, and the cracking of a big story, even if it didn't bring direct financial gain, was nonetheless capable of lifting *The Morning Glory*'s stock. Besides, even if it didn't and the financial consequences in terms of withdrawn advertising revenue were severe, at least Vines would be able to take the moral high ground (and probably a golden parachute) with him when the axe fell on his head. At the very worse, there'd be a job waiting for him in the Media Studies Department of some university. But if it got out that he'd blocked the story, it would be bad for his career, since the sort of people likely to hire him because of his willingness for deep compromise would be unlikely to hire him if that willingness came with too much conspicuous baggage.

That the Chairman might not be in favour of the story came as no surprise to Adam. He could remember how the meeting with Jim Sway had ended three years ago. Julian Circle was one of the new breed of business celebrities. In addition to being Chairman of *The Morning Glory* Pty Ltd, he was the chairman of a smaller company based on the south coast of New South Wales which manufactured cement. He was also a board member of other companies including Slow Decline, a rapidly expanding private hospital and nursing home chain, as well as Virtue Erections and Chip Pty Ltd, the company which supplied *The Morning Glory* with its newssheet. Circle had also been appointed as an industry expert to a government committee whose brief was the reform of the building industry following the Royal Commission of 2002. It had recommended further deregulation of the industry, the

THE GUTS

restriction of appeals to the Land and Environment Court, and the right of the Minister to intervene directly in development applications when they were considered to be of state importance. As the Chairman of a newspaper company, Circle was a walking, talking, officially encouraged conflict of interest.

Chloe Saville came back into the room. 'Planning on taking the place over, are you?'

'Sorry.'

'I forgot my pen.' She picked it up from the boardroom table.

'You did well. I didn't think it would get this far.'

'Thanks.'

'Watch your back, though. Some of these people play for keeps.'

'Ok.'

'If you need any help let me know.'

'Thanks.'

Chloe left the room, and Adam pushed her warning to the back of his mind in case it took over. The only thing to fear is fear itself, he told himself. This time he was going to rub Roger Houston's nose in it real good. As any good food critic knew, revenge is a dish best served cold.

14

'The train on Platform Three goes to Emu Plains. First stop Town Hall, then Central, Ashfield, Strathfield, Parramatta, Westmead then all stations to Emu Plains,' a dignified Indian voice announced over the Public Address System. Justine got on, found an upstairs seat and played with her phone as the train crawled through the underground before emerging into daylight just before Central. It was a stop-start journey and, despite the air-conditioning, the bare skin of her arms and the backs of her knees was soon sweaty against the heavy-duty blue cloth of the seats. Gradually, the Federation era brick cottages of the inner west gave way to houses built of brick veneer and weatherboard. But the clearest sign of her arrival in the real western suburbs was the sight of fibro cottages, the asbestos still contained within them, on the streets abutting the railway line.

Justine got off at Blue Hills, an hour after boarding at Wynyard. It was the first time ever she had gotten off a train between Parramatta and the Blue Mountains. Born and bred on the North Shore, she had only ever experienced the western suburbs in transit, or via sensationalised media accounts of drive-by shootings, gang rapes and racial tension. She was surprised by how normal everything seemed. Mothers with small children were shopping. Old men were sitting on benches and talking. She felt the eyes of men of all ages following her bum. On the southern side a small shopping strip trailed from the station into the suburb. Justine followed the line of shops, a newsagent, a kebab shop, then the Coco Massage Centre which gave way to the Balaclava Café, a Turkish café and sweet shop. Next to it was The Family Jesus Centre, which offered free English lessons and morning tea. It reminded her of the times she'd visited the Hare Krishna

Centre in Darlinghurst as a student, free movies and free meals, at the cost of a chat from a believer on the benefits of mantras and shaved heads. She turned left at the 888 Chinese Restaurant and followed Trick Street up the hill, past the Hush Hush Day Spa, two Indian and Sri Lankan grocery shops with posters commemorating lives lost in the island nation's civil war. The western suburbs were inhabited by the ghosts of many civil wars. Syrian, Sri Lankan, Chilean, Afghan, Lebanese, Vietnamese, Sudanese. There were so many places where just living came at the risk of being bombed, imprisoned, tortured, dispossessed, or disappeared. Justine wondered why she found such places more attractive than her hometown, when for so many people Australia, despite its politicians, was a sanctuary. But only because the kinds of violent corruption that became the norm there, had remained the rare exception. Australia was boring, she thought, but boredom wasn't always the worst thing. Even an adrenaline junkie like herself, had to acknowledge. Even if her own life represented her inability to cope with this. It was weird she thought that this was the first time she was combining her taste for danger, and dislike of power, with the country of her birth. She passed a youth centre with faded newspaper clippings of its students' achievements on a pin board in the window. Beyond that was a doctor's surgery and beyond that – inconspicuously democratic – was a shopfront containing the electoral office for the State Member for Latham, Roger Houston MP.

Justine knocked on the door and went in. Mrs Smith was sitting at the reception desk talking on the phone. There were four empty chairs lined up against the window, which had a large blind pulled down to create privacy. 'I won't be a moment, love,' said Mrs Smith. Justine sat down on one of the chairs and checked her mobile phone for the fiftieth time that day.

Five minutes later, Mrs Smith finished her conversation, which from the snatches Justine overheard, had mainly consisted in organising the menu for a wake. 'What can I do for you, dear?'

'I'm Justine. Roger's assistant in Parliament House. I've come to mind the shop.'

THE GUTS

'Oh, sorry. There was me prattling away thinking you were a constituent.' She came out from behind her desk and extended her hand 'Call me Beryl. Thanks for coming. Not that there's much to do. All the action's in Blacktown, but Roger likes it here. A quiet constituent is a good constituent, he says. If we move to Blacktown they'll be queuing up outside the door for a whinge and a cup of tea.'

'S'pose so,' said Justine, who hadn't quite expected such candour.

'Suits me. You can spend a whole morning here without anyone coming in. Can get a bit busier in the afternoon though.'

'What should I do while I'm here?'

'I wouldn't worry yourself too much, dear. Answer the phone. Collect the mail from the post office box – the key's in the top drawer of my desk – write a few letters, mainly they're annoyed about the M4 and the trains. The developers never really turn up in person. There's a diary on my desk on which you can make appointments for his monthly visit to the office. The days are circled in red. Don't give anyone more than half an hour. Also, there's a list on my desk of a couple of dozen people. If any of them come in, you're to let him know.'

'Who are they?'

'Oh, you know, community leaders, councillors, developers, the chairman of the club and the like. Mostly they just ring him direct, but sometimes they come here fishing, so you have to be a bit careful what you say.'

'Is this all of the office?' Justine was almost dismayed by its unpretentiousness.

'No. I'll show you around.' They went through a door and down a corridor. 'This is Roger's office.' Apart from a series of certificates of gratitude framed on one wall, it was plain, dominated by a dark timber desk. The one window behind the desk was shaded by a timber Venetian blind. The light was standard issue office fluoro. A leather executive chair was behind the desk. Two black plastic chairs were drawn in front of it and several more were stacked in a corner behind the door. On the desk was a photo of Houston and his family, a feature not replicated in his office at Parliament House. The office was extremely orderly. On the desk was an in-tray and an out-tray each with only a slim amount of papers in them, and a computer monitor and keyboard. 'You can work here for the day if you like,' said Beryl.

'Thanks. This is nothing like his other office.'

'I like to run a tight ship. Anything needing attention gets couriered to the Parliament.'

'What else is here?'

'Here's the kitchen,' said Beryl. 'Fridge, kettle, microwave. There's a toasted sandwich maker in the cupboard. Help yourself to the lamingtons by the way. I made them.'

Justine hadn't eaten a lamington in almost ten years. 'Thanks.' She felt warm toward this Beryl, whose Nana charm, she reckoned, would be brilliant for defusing irate constituents.

'And there are packets of Monte Carlos and Iced Vo-Vos in the cupboard next to the cups. Don't ask me why, but they're the ones Roger likes.'

It struck Justine as a curious detail. In town, the Gut was full of fancy restaurant talk and if you made it up to his Parliamentary office, there were Byron Bay Cookies, almond biscotti and an espresso machine. Were these biscuits, however, in the less pressurised climes of outer suburbia his favourites? Vestiges of boyhood taste. He hadn't grown up with money. His father had owned a service station.

'The bathroom's here. There's a shower too, if you want to use it. The last girl he had working for him used it quite a lot. I suppose it's all the yoga and jogging you young people do.'

Justine's neck tensed then released. 'And what's here?' she asked when they came to the final room, whose door was closed.

'Pretty much everything else.' Beryl took a key ring from her pocket and opened the door. The entire room was filled with the detritus of political campaigning. Plastic banners with the Gut's head, Vote 1 Houston for Latham and the Sporty Party's logo were stacked against the wall. There were piles of undelivered newsletters, boxes and boxes and boxes of paper, some of it yellowed with age, some so ancient they still had carbon paper interleafed.

THE GUTS

'I keep offering to clean it up,' said Beryl. 'But he tells me to leave it alone. One day, I tell you, I'll walk into one of these rooms and the blasted boxes will be stacked so high they'll fall and that will be the end of me. Flattened by a box of leftover posters from the campaign of 1991.'

'Hardly ergonomic,' said Justine.

'I've given up. I avoid it, really. Other than to put more boxes in.'

They left the room and went to the back door, which had a security grill, while the window next to it had bars. A Holden Commodore was parked in one of several car spots. 'You can park your car out there.'

'I don't have one,' said Justine.

Beryl frowned at the news. 'I reckon it's about time for a cuppa. And a lamington.'

'Sounds good to me,' said Justine.

Nothing much happened that morning. Justine explored the computer on Houston's desk. She found a database of all the constituents who had come to see him and the reasons why they had with a short summary of the meeting, and another column that contained notes of what if any action had been taken. Because of the multicultural nature of Houston's electorate, much of his constituent work was concerned with migration, mainly help with getting family members visas. Justine imagined it could be a good little earner. Some names appeared with greater regularity than others, and the comments written were somewhat harder to understand: 'Follow up from dinner on 17/06.' 'Agreement on FX3 after Eelam night.' 'Dispensation for Chinese Speaking retirement homes.' 'Blacktown CBD.' None of it seemed controversial. She copied the file onto a pen drive for Paul to compare against any other information he had.

At around midday, Beryl came in and said, 'I'm going to the club for lunch. Here's a spare set of keys if you want to go out. And if you do, just turn the sign on the door so it says back in an hour.'

'Sure.'

Beryl drove off in her Commodore. They didn't make them anymore. It was an opportunity, thought Justine, to have a peek around the rest of the office. The drawers of Beryl's desk were almost empty, except for some stationery. She did run a tight ship. Which left the back room, full of junk, to explore. She was in there when Beryl returned from the club, the sourness of wine on her breath.

'Hello Love.'

'Hi.'

'What are you doing?'

'There's not much to do, and I'm not much good at sitting there twiddling my thumbs, so I thought I might have a go at sorting out this mess.'

'Mmmm,' said Beryl. 'I'm not sure he'd like that. I've tried to tidy it up a zillion times, but he always tells me to leave it alone. If you clean it up, I'll never be able to find anything his lordship reckons. God knows how you can find anything there anyway. But best off leaving it alone.'

The front door opened and Beryl went to see who it was. Justine went back to her office and played scrabble on her phone. She wasn't feeling overly optimistic about her chances of finding anything. And that meant the pressure would be on for Thursday's dinner with the Gut.

Beryl's long lunch was followed by a short afternoon. At three o'clock she came into Houston's office where Justine was catching up on the Gut's correspondence with his constituents. 'I hope you don't mind, but I might give myself a bit of an early mark. I want to beat the peak hour traffic.'

'That's fine.' It was better than fine. This way she had the rest of the afternoon to trawl through the back office just in case.

It really was a shambles and a good part of an hour was spent just unstacking boxes so she could see what lay behind them. By six, she was ready to go home. It would take weeks to sort through all the boxes, most of which had nothing in them but promotional dross. It was all too much. The thought of having to dine with The Gut without having made a breakthrough made her faintly nauseous. The moment of surrender led to serendipity. Glancing around the room in quasi-despair, Justine noticed an old fibreglass Stanley Stamford

THE GUTS

suitcase jutting out of one of the boxes. Her interest piqued and she pulled it down. Locked. She went to Beryl's desk, found a stiletto letter opener and prised the locks open without breaking them. Inside were a series of school exercise books, about a dozen of them. She picked up the first one and flicked through. It was in the form of a diary, but the entries were all about golf, a sport which, in their short acquaintance, the Minister unlike many middle-aged men, was yet to mention.

Saturday, 29th August. Foursome with JT, EO, MA and myself. Discussion on the fourth hole. Par 5, 528m. Had to wait to tee off.

Wednesday, 9th September. Met Mr Titus at the new golf club. He said he had just had a winner on the fourth, a par-four 397m. Normally his drive was about 210. But he really needed to drive 270 to make it possible to pitch onto the green on the second shot. I told him he could probably get away with 250. He thanked me and offered to lend me his lucky putter. I used it on the 14th and made an easy 30m putt. Enjoyed a few schooners on the nineteenth hole.

Tuesday, 29th September. Par 3 at Ermington. Problems with slicing the ball into Parramatta River. HV offered to pay the two-shot penalty for changing the out of bounds

Friday, 16th October. Back nine at Redfern. Problems with GUR. Told HV it could be repaired.

Saturday, 24th October. Played with CC at Moore Park. Told me he played off 16. Eight more like it. Adjusted his handicap for being a burglar.

It went on and on. In another exercise book there were pages and pages of what looked like doctored cricket statistics.

C.E. GRIMES

Player	Match	Inn	NO	Runs	HS	Ave	W	SKILL
HV Smith	12	24	0	1289	154	53.70	23	BAT CHINA
CC Jones	3	6	1	300	150	60.00	70	ARMED
JT Walters	6	10	1	360	68	38.99	121	OFFIE
EO Hole	7	13	4	597	143	63.33		KEEPER
MA Sink	11	20	0	400	52	20.00	65	FMED
BT Mark	2	4	1	145	69	48.33	4	BAT
DR Singh	3	6	0	221	101	36.83	12	AR SLMED
EH Reginals	9	16	6	590	132	59.00	9	LEG
EM Sakura	15	30	2	732	69	26.14	87	CHINA
MB Acton	5	8	1	398	97*	56.86	32	AR OFFIE
MC Gristle	3	5	0	112	69	22.40	154	FAST LH
NA Banks	6	12	7	397	132	79.40		BATKEEP
OP Smokes	2	4	2	301	234	150.50	1	12
RP Ambo	12	18	2	659	106	41.19	11	AR OFFIE
SP Cannon	11	19	4	1233	201	82.20		BAT
PD Matthews	9	18	0	783	143	43.50	43	MYSTERY SPINNER
TH Chins	5	8	1	297	69	42.43	2	BAT LH
WP Cantona	5	9	6	300	100	100.00	6	BAT CHINA

The tables made little sense to Justine, who was not a sports lover. Nor did the pages of notes. All in all, there were several hundred pages across a dozen exercise books. She hoped that if Paul was as smart as he pretended to be, then he'd be able to work it out before she had to go and have dinner then try and drug the Gut. She took the books out and began to scan the contents with the Scanner Pro app on her phone. As she scanned them, she messaged them through to Paul. It was slow going.

Around 9pm, the office phone rang. Soon after so did hers. It was the Gut. 'Someone's just rang to say the lights are on in the electoral office.'

'Sorry, I must have forgotten to turn them off.'

'Ok, then. I'll get someone to pop in and turn them off.'

'By the way, I think I'll need you here tomorrow instead of there.'

'OK.'

'You're wasted out there.'

'Umm, thanks.'

'Goodo. See you tomorrow. Wear something nice.'

The call broke off. She indulged herself with thoughts of punching him. The sound of a key in the door interrupted her reverie. She turned off the backroom light took the suitcase and hid behind a stack of boxes.

The sound of feet came down the corridor.

'Let's smoke a joint,' said a female voice.

'Nah. I don't think he'd like it.'

'How is he ever going to know?'

'You'd be surprised what he knows.'

'What he doesn't know won't hurt him.'

'It's a boring place anyway. Do you like satin sheets?'

One by one the lights went off and Justine breathed a sigh of relief. She waited another 20 minutes before she finished scanning the contents of the suitcase without turning the lights back on. At around 11pm, she slipped out of the back door and walked to the station. What had seemed so benign in the morning suddenly felt creepy. A group of young men dressed in hip hop kit huddled up one end of the station. Justine sat next to an old man, who was the only other person on the platform. The hip hop crew started fighting among themselves. She rang Paul and told him she was coming over.

One of the young warriors swaggered up to her. 'You calling the cops?'

'Nah, why would I want to do that?'

He gave her a smile that wasn't entirely friendly and walked back to join his mates. Soon after the train came. Justine got in the carriage next to the guard. The old man got in with her. He kept staring at her. She plugged in her headphones and listened to The Cure while she watched the suburbs flick past. At Granville she changed for the Bankstown line. The old man got off too, but didn't join her on the city-bound train. The air was cool. The heat of the day had disappeared. At Sydenham, she got off and walked to Paul's.

'Sex, beer, pizza, beer, detection,' she said at the front door which, after calling to order the pizza, was exactly what they did. The sex was like scratching an itch, one that had crept into the day's successes and grown with the hungry eyes of the western suburbs. A distinctly clitoral itch, relieved by the rough-soft rising confusion and dissolution delivered by Paul's flickering tongue.

After orgasms, they cleared a couple of laptops from the table in Paul's dining room, opened the pizza and began to puzzle over the information she had lifted from the office. Their initial hopes of cracking Houston's code soon dwindled and by midnight they were grumpy with each other, a situation not helped by the drinking of half a dozen longnecks, and the consumption of a couple of lines of coke. By three am they knew little more than they had when they'd begun.

'Fuck this,' said Paul. 'I've had enough.'

'Easy for you to give up,' said Justine.

'But what's the point? None of the cricketers actually exist. So the numbers are probably code for some exchange of money, but it doesn't mean anything unless we have the names, and I don't know enough about him or his business associates to be able to figure out any of them. Do you?'

'No.'

'That's the problem with these old school dudes. If he was computer savvy, he probably would have used an algorithm. Which is something I could probably crack. I'll pass some of this onto the journalist. He might be able to work some of it out. That's about all we can do for now.'

'I know. But if Parker goes and the government loses power, what does it matter? Can't we just leave it to natural attrition?'

'No!' Paul's voice was sharply passionate in a manner she hadn't seen before.

She turned to look at him, forcing him to meet her eyes. 'Why?'

'Because this is personal.'

'How come?'

Paul said nothing. 'If we don't crack this code, I'm going to have to seduce this sleazebag. You owe me the reason.'

Paul's eyes slid away. Reluctant.

'If you don't tell me, I'm not going to do it.'

He stared at his screen long enough for Justine to wonder whether he had abandoned the conversation. Her feet scraped back and forth against the carpet, as if building up the requisite static electricity for an exit. The itch to act, it didn't matter that much what, had almost become unbearable by the time he spoke. 'Ok. You know Peter?'

'Yes. That's how I met you.'

'Sure, well, the reason I know him is because he and my sister Sue were good friends at uni. She's a teacher too. She married a guy called John Dykes. A nice dude. He was a muso then, a horn player, but you can't make a living doing that anymore. Not when you've got a family in Sydney. Somehow, he ended up working in the Department of Planning and Development on a temporary contract, and that contract became permanent. They bought a house, had a kid, all the usual stuff. They were just regular people. But after your boss moved into the job, Johnny got wind of some of the dodgy stuff going on. He made a connection with a journalist. Put him onto a big story. The story never broke. Three months later, he was transferred – to Bourke. A job investigating farms the government might buy to help the Darling River flow. They had a beautiful little girl called Corey, my niece. She had a few problems with her health, nothing too serious, she was just a beautiful cheeky little girl. Johnny protested the transfer. He was worried about Corey. About the hospitals out there. Just in case. But they told Johnny that if he didn't take the reassignment, they'd sack him. And with Sue already out of the workforce, he couldn't afford not to work. The order had come from on high. It wasn't hard to put two and two together. Somehow, he'd been compromised. The economy wasn't strong. After applying for other jobs and getting none of them, he took it. Then, around six months later, Corey had an attack. Sue took her to the local hospital, but they didn't have the right equipment. They stuck her in an ambulance and headed for Dubbo. By the time they got there, my three-year-old niece was dead. One chance in 100 000 of it happening, the doctors said. But it happened. And my sister's never been the same again. So, my small compensation to her is to be able to fuck up the life of the cunt who killed Corey. And as far as I've been able to work out, that cunt is your boss. I'd like to kill him, really, but this is as close as I'm going to get.'

Paul's eyes wore a fire she hadn't imagined. He wasn't just some aspie numbers man. 'Don't worry. I'll do it,' she responded without thinking.

He nodded. She moved closer and put the palm of her hand between his shoulders. 'Thank you,' he said. Beneath the tech brilliance and almost brash indifference to the moods of others, Paul suddenly appeared to her as a man moved by brittle passions he couldn't fully control. Her type.

'Let's go to bed,' she said.

They had sex again. Gently.

'I'm not sure that you doing this will fix anything,' said Paul. 'But I feel compelled by Corey to make you try.'

'I've come too far now to turn back,' said Justine.

He held her hand. 'Thank you. Dad ran off when we were kids. Mum did a lot of shit jobs to survive. She was pretty angry about how her life had turned out. Sue and I really only had each other to rely on.' Paul soon fell asleep. Justine had often wished she had a sibling she could rely on. She waited for the cocaine to wear off. Paul's breath rose and fell evenly beside her. She couldn't stop thinking about what it would be like to be naked and touched by her boss. She had never been intimate with someone she despised before. She had never slept with anyone for whom she didn't feel physical attraction. Not even a sympathy fuck. What if her body bucked the directions of her mind and refused to do it? What if the drugs didn't work and she found herself unable to escape? What if he didn't drink the Mickey Finn she planned on slipping him? Lurking on the precipice of sleep, she imagined him on top of her, flubbering like a jellyfish in a hurry. A shiver went up her spine. She tried to catch the whirl of questions rushing through her head and stop them. She failed.

15

Houston's bad mood was getting worse. He had promised the Premier he'd get back to him as soon as he heard anything more. But the fuckwit kept on getting back to him. It was starting to piss him off. Murray was yet to hear from Dorrigo and there was nothing new to say. Still, almost every fifteen minutes a nuisance call came:

'Hardcastle here. The Premier wants to know if there are any developments. Can you ring him back straight away?'

Each time he failed to reply the messages became more insistent until finally it was Pond on the phone himself. 'What's happening? I need to know. We need a solution. Quickly.' The high-pitched crackle in his voice suggested the Premier was on the verge of doing something stupid. The thought of him firing loose cannons alarmed Houston. He wasn't in the mood for political babysitting. Or an emergency cabinet reshuffle. But he was keen to keep the decks clear for tomorrow's rendezvous with Justine. He'd gotten cranky with her this morning. Nothing wrong with a bit of sexual tension. Her pouting face and the way her breasts had seemed independently angry at him were a turn-on. But before that there was work to be done. Pond needed pacification.

He caught a cab to the Premier's office. As he got out of the lift, he could smell the tension in the air. This was not the sleepy afternoon lull environment he'd encountered only days ago. Staffers were gathered in clusters and went silent, waiting for him to pass, before continuing with their whispers. The rumour mills were in motion. Hardcastle, as usual, made him wait before showing him into the Premier's office, where Pond was pacing about, thinning his hair and angsting over the truncation of his unwarranted glory. Despite the air-conditioning, his shirt had sweat patches under the arms. Hardcastle looked on like a mortified schoolmistress brought to a sudden awareness of the flawed character of her favourite student. Houston shooed her out and closed the door behind her. He took a good hard look at the Premier. Pond looked back at him. The panic started to spew forth from his mouth.

'I've got to do something. We've got to do something. Something needs to be done. Now! Reardon's [the Minister for Sport] been on the phone saying that if we lose Parker we're going to have to declare elections and that the jockeying for position has already begun. He reckons if Parker doesn't return, bloody Milton is going to challenge me for the leadership. And that the numbers are going to be tight. What can we do?'

Ninny, thought Houston. Milton Kell MP for Premier was OK with him since he was about the only person who knew that Kell's son was dealing ice. If there was an election Kell's seat was marginal and there was no guarantee he was going to hold it. Houston wasn't sure how much truth there was to the leadership spill rumour, anyway. Reardon was prone to shooting his mouth off. It was a mistake that he was in the parliament at all. Reardon was the beneficiary of a factional deal that had preferred loyal mediocrity over talent. Never destined for the highest office himself, Reardon didn't mind making mischief for those who were. Houston had him marked as a leaker. To the press. He was lazy, and politically careless, and didn't deserve a ministry but the responsibility of a minor portfolio from where he could spread disinformation about the Greens, rather than stir up internal dissent, had helped keep a lid on some of his corrosive ineptitude.

A phone rang and the Premier answered. It was his wife. A problem with a child. If a putsch was being planned, thought Houston, Reardon would know. Like many mediocre people in the upper echelons of organisations, the one area where Reardon shone was in his impeccable instincts for self-preservation.

While the Premier and wife debated the commitments of their calendars, Houston played through the likely scenarios and how they might affect him. Quite a few people would be openly glad to see the back of him. And a lot more would like and be too scared to say it. People often resented his hold over them. His access to their reservoirs of shame. They dreamed of their lost independence and would enjoy seeing him brought down by forces to which they couldn't be linked.

It was also possible they were going around him because they didn't want to be tainted by association. That was the scenario that worried him. Pond wasn't corrupt, nor were most of the Sporty Party's parliamentary members. Many of them, however, were ethically compromised in that they left parliament for jobs with lobbyists, investment banks, gambling companies, miners, insurers, developers and the like. Plum jobs with large salaries and not always a lot of work to do. The public was right to wonder sometimes about how much of those salaries were based on decisions already taken. The overlap between private and public interest. However, if these innocent men and women were completely ignorant of Houston and his ilk, they were arguably too stupid to be tasked with the running of the state. Houston sometimes wondered how he and his ilk managed to get away with what they did, when they were always in the minority. Life's a rort, he thought, and it's only a rort if you're not in it.

'Look, I wouldn't worry about it too much if I were you,' he said. 'Kell is pissing into the wind. No one's really thinks he's leadership material. He's too bloody ugly to begin with. It's the era of television, Winston. Not only does a Premier have to be a leader, he also has to look like one.'

This appeal to his vanity seemed to cheer Pond up a bit, even as a list of the exceptions formed in Houston's mind. The Premier stopped fidgeting, handsomely flicked his fringe off his forehead and straightened his back as Houston continued.

'You see Milton's really only useful as an attack dog. The punters will tolerate him as a necessary evil, but they don't want him running the bloody state. He's like Tony Abbott, only uglier, a beast of negativity, his nickname's the bloody 'troll' for fuck's sake. Do you think the punters are going to be saying to each other, 'I voted for the troll'? Anyone with half a brain knows that. You're sparring at bloody shadows.'

Houston wasn't so sure of his own argument. The public was capable of exceptional stupidity. They fell for the most transparent propaganda all the time, succumbed to the most outrageous beat-ups, and had memories as long as Eddie Obeid on the witness stand. It wouldn't surprise him who they elected. Look who they already had. An Australian Mt Rushmore would be built from termite mounds, called Mt Mediocre, parked next to a service station on some highway and sold as punching above its weight. Political vision usually stopped at the fringes of a politician's self-importance. If you believed in democracy as anything other than a mask for the real power, you were naive. Houston was glad he did not.

'I suppose you're right,' said Pond, flicking his hair again. 'But that doesn't solve the problem of Parker, does it? If we do have to go to an election, the chances are we're going to lose. We haven't been doing well in the polls at all. And if we can't get that development bill through, it's going to cost us in terms of campaign funding, big time. Something must be done.' The reassurance had been brief. Pond slumped forward over his desk and wrung his hands, 'So, what are we going to do?'

The first-person plural pronoun was a dangerous assumption. Houston wanted to tell him that if it came to an election they had Buckley's. Swings and roundabouts. There was bugger all they could do about it except revel in the opportunity for ferocious negativity that being in opposition provided. Of course, if there was an election and they did lose, Winston would have to fall on his sword. But there was no point in him falling on it just now.

'I've got people looking into it, Winston. They're chasing down Parker as we speak. Other people are looking into how the press is finding out about all this. And until they get back to me, we've just got to bluff it out and be confident. OK?'

Winston thought about this for minute. 'I don't know if I can,' he said.

'It's all you can do for the moment. If you try to fix the situation without knowing what it is, chances are it'll only get worse. What's your schedule this afternoon?'

'I'm meant to be touring a nursing home in one of the marginal seats. And then there's a memorial service for Lady Lushley at St Andrews. But I thought I might cancel.'

THE GUTS

'Don't!' said Houston. 'If you go round cancelling things, people will start to believe you're in trouble. And once that starts, it's very hard to stop. You've got to act as if everything is normal. Appearances are crucial. Go out and press the flesh. Look like you're enjoying yourself, show them you're not really worried all. If the media ask you about Parker, tell them you think it's all a bit of a beat-up. As far as you know Parker will be back by the time Parliament resumes. We get through these next few weeks, then we've got almost three months up our sleeves and a whole lot of booze, ham and turkey to be consumed in between, before parliament sits again. Tell them you reckon Parker's been working very hard over the last few months. He's gone bush to recharge his batteries and will be back fresher than ever. The pressures of public life are onerous. Politicians are only human. The reason he can't be contacted is that mobile phone coverage remains inadequate in the remote parts of the state, and that you'll be liaising with the Federal Government as to how that can be fixed. And while you're there, why not publicly chastise the head of Oztel. He's not one of us. That'll deflect some of the heat and it'll please some of those whingers from the bush as well. And if some dumb hack asks you about rumours of a leadership challenge, tell them it's the first you've heard of it, and that if you paid attention to every rumour, you'd never get round to doing what the public has elected you to do.'

'Mmmm. Good. Do you think I can pull it off?'

'Of course you can, Mr Premier. You're the leader of our state.'

'Thank you, Roger. I'm not sure what I'd do without you.' Houston didn't offer his analysis that Pond wouldn't be in this mess in the first place. The Premier had already begun to reinflate.

'Despite what people think, Winston, it's loyalty that makes politics work. Without that essential glue, good government is impossible.'

That much was true thought Houston. But the other thing about politics was that you had to know when loyalty had reached its limit.

Pond brimmed with sentiment. His face was a rictus. For a moment Houston was concerned he'd be hugged. 'Thank you, Roger, I couldn't agree with you more. With your loyal support we've got a good chance of making it. See if you can find out who's behind the Kell rumours. Let's meet again tomorrow. I'll see you out.'

'Can you book Roger in for ten tomorrow morning?' His hand rested on Houston's shoulder. Hardcastle's clear discomfort as she tried to transform a scowl into a compliant smile gave Houston disproportionate pleasure. How galling it must be for her to have all her subtle warnings to her boss about him so easily countered with a few broad strokes of flattery? He shook hands warmly with the Premier. Whispers chased his footsteps to the lift.

His own reading of the situation was it had taken a turn for the worse. Pond's spinelessness was dangerous. It was time to start covering things up. He returned to his office and set up the document shredder. He realised with irritation that he was going to have to visit the electorate office tomorrow too. In the meantime, he set about transferring as much as possible of his dirty lucre offshore. Just in case.

About an hour later, Murray rang. 'I'm coming over with some news.'

'Good, or bad?'

'I'll be there in ten.'

'Sorry boss but the V-team's come a cropper in the search for Parker at Dorrigo,' said Murray. They were sitting on the balcony looking over the parklands of the Domain. A difficult spot to bug.

'What happened?'

'The guy who rang Benny was some goose who owed someone Benny knew money. He was hiding out there himself. On the way to the supermarket for supplies, he thought he saw Parker in the hardware store buying a pair of gumboots,' said Murray. 'Word must have gotten around. He probably thought it was a chance to extricate himself from his own mess, so he rang Benny, hoping to strike a deal. Benny promised him that if the information was good, he'd buy the debt and let the repayment slide. Problem was the guy's fried his brain on magic mushies. You don't have to pay for them if you know where to look. And when you spend too much time alone, everyone starts to look like everyone else.'

THE GUTS

'Yeah, the universe is a single connected entity whose waves we all surf together,' grumbled Houston.

'Until you get on the wrong side of Benny. Then you're all alone and getting chundered. With enough sand down your sluggos to make a batch of cement.'

'Spare me the imagery.'

'Sorry, boss. When Benny and Bruce arrived, they met their source in the local pub. He gave them the address of the house he'd followed Parker to. They drove down a corrugated dirt road. There was a pole house in the remnants of some old-growth forest. They climbed the backstairs and broke down the suspect's door. The suspect was lying on the couch listening to music. He was more than surprised to see them. Apparently, he was a retired mango cultivator or something.'

'Fuck, I was hoping they'd find him.'

'So were they. They were very pissed off. All that driving for nothing.'

'What happened?'

'They warned the guy about going to the cops and slashed a couple of his tires. As for the bloke with the wrong info, they broke his right knee with a hammer. They called me from a roadhouse about half an hour ago.' Houston raised his eyebrows. 'Don't worry. They didn't ring my real phone. They're on the Highway now.'

'Well, there goes that one. If they call again, tell them to wait for further instructions.'

'Sure. I'll keep you posted.' Murray left.

Had Parker really done the bolt and disappeared OS, Houston wondered. It was beginning to seem more likely. If he had left the country, there was little Houston could do to stop him, let alone force him to return to parliament. Even if he managed to get him arrested for some crime and extradited it wasn't going to help the Sporty Party hold onto a majority in the house. And what if it was Parker who was leaking to the food writer? Why? What had he done to Parker to deserve that? Nothing. There were people whose lives he had shortened, others whose lives he had ruined, but not Parker.

C.E. GRIMES

The instinct to start putting his affairs into order was feeling more and more sensible. An extended vacation might be in order. Somewhere with girls in bikinis and no extradition treaty. South America perhaps, or Lebanon, or a Black Sea Resort in Bulgaria. Maybe even Africa, although he did have a thing for blondes. If only there wasn't so much to do. Even he was amazed by the complexity of his finances. When he'd started out, he'd been able to keep all the numbers of his off-the-books business in his head. He had a head for numbers. As a kid, he'd remember all the cricketing averages out of Wisden and spend hours in statistical conversation with his friends. Which is why cricket was one of his codes. He tried to book an urgent appointment with his accountant, but he was holidaying in the Cayman Islands. There were deeds to be gotten from safety deposit boxes and transfers to be made. It wouldn't be that easy accessing his loot if he had to leave. Better to send the money on now. It would guarantee a higher standard of treatment from the local authorities of wherever he landed and a less extortionate exchange rate. He took a stroll to the bank, stopping at the pharmacy to renew his supply of Viagra. At the bank, he emptied two safety deposit boxes of their contents and packed them into a briefcase. The other boxes, located at a range of banks and post offices in the suburbs near his home and electorate office, could wait until tomorrow.

Murray rang with more bad news as Houston returned to the office with a briefcase full of bearer bonds and cash. Dick Mahone had come a cropper at *The Morning Glory*. His attempts to influence editorial policy and to find out the substance of any impending allegations had hit a hastily erected wall of journalistic ethics. Murray was in a bar with Mahone, who was spitting chips. Houston could hear him through the phone.

'They don't know who they're fucking with. I'm not some corporate relations gimp they can bend over and fuck up the arse with their little pinpricks. Do you know how many hitmen I have in my address book? The stupid cunts. Who in the fuck do they think they are?'

'What should I do?' asked Murray, after Mahone had stomped off for a slash. 'People are starting to notice.'

THE GUTS

'I'll give Ken a ring and get back to you in five,' said Houston and hung up.

Ken was Ken Virtue, the owner of Virtue Erections. The swank waterfront penthouse where Houston intended wooing Justine tomorrow tonight was a product of Virtue's largesse, a gesture of appreciation for services rendered to the property industry over the course of his ministerial tenure. Houston had made Virtue millions of dollars: over-riding local council objections, reforming the Land and Environment Court and disposing of surplus government land on secretly favourable terms. He had given Ken advance warning of decisions concerning rezonings and allowed developments to take place where the infrastructure was clearly inadequate without insisting that the developer foot the bill.

Much of the money sitting in his offshore numbered accounts had come from Virtue and his mates. Virtue would know what to do with Mahone, since it was in his capacity as a consultant to Virtue that they'd been able to swing the meeting with Vines at *The Morning Glory*. Houston would usually have suggested Mahone go straight to Julian Circle, who had long ago been paid for and who had the power to pull a story. Or run a political puff-piece for the government. If a minister started sounding too tough, for instance, or if the rumours about someone's whoring got too strong, Circle could be relied on for a feel-good family profile. He remembered Daphne's gritty smile, for the sake of the children, the time it had happened for him. Unfortunately, Sir Julian, a captain's choice for a knighthood in the moment they had come back into vogue, was out of the country. Apparently, he had developed a taste for the private clubs of London.

Mahone had gone in kicking and burnt the fucking bridge by the sounds of it. Ken was unlikely to be happy. Houston put in the call, but Virtue's secretary, after a telling hesitation, told him he wasn't in the office. He tried his mobile. No answer. Fucking caller ID, he thought. Takes all the surprise out of life. When your partners in crime start giving you the silent treatment, trouble.

Five minutes later an email arrived from Hammerhead@yahoo.com:

Dear R, the weather is nice and cool here. Spoke to M. He's a bit too stressed. Maybe time for some deep-sea fishing. Before the cyclone season starts. Time to batten down the hatches for a bit until the storm blows over. They always do.

Relief. Ken was being straight. And as for Mahone going on a fishing trip, well, sometimes sacrifices had to be made. From what he'd heard over the phone, he had gotten too big for his boots at the wrong time. Now they were about to become too big for him. It was hard to imagine that the world would miss him.

He rang Murray back. 'Get yourself a date. You can see him at the wake.'

'Fuck!' exclaimed Murray. 'That's the second time this week. I'll have to dry-clean my suit.' The words didn't make much sense. From the tone of his voice, however, Houston could sense his surprise and displeasure. Mahone, while disliked, was still a colleague, so it was unsurprising that Murray was strongly against such precedents being set.

'Have you heard any more from Bill and Ben?'

'Yeah, they're still on the way back to Sydney. Had a bit of car trouble and had to call the NRMA.

'Keep them out of the way for the moment.'

'There's a delivery needs going to Wollongong.' A bagman drop to a councillor, remembered Houston.

'Sounds good. And get them to check out Parker's South Coast holiday house while they're there.' They had Buckley's of finding him there, but it paid to cover all bases.

The phone went quiet for a moment and Houston could tell Murray was thinking.

'Come on! Out with it! I'm a Minister of the Crown. I haven't got all day.'

'It might be nothing, but Dick said Adam Osborne was in the meeting trying to throw his weight around. Reckons he ended up almost clocking him.'

'It is a bit strange. He's been doing food for the past seven years. I forgot to ask Jack Vines why he's back covering politics.'

'Should I get someone to keep an eye on him?'

'Yeah, maybe. It could just be that they are short-staffed. But if he was in the actual meeting ...'

'I heard that there's another round of retrenchments on the way in preparation for *The Glory* being sold to private equity.' The market's positive response to this rumour alone had earned Circle and Vines almost a million between them in exercised stock options. 'And I've heard that Sir Julian is in need of them.' It was true. His new young wife, Jodie, a former yoga instructor, hadn't married him for his looks, or even for his patrician personality. She had expensive tastes and lacked the brains or family trust to generate the income to satiate them. As Houston well knew, Sir Julian was still paying for the cosmetic surgery and eastern suburbs residences of his previous two wives.

'The more they sack the better,' he said. 'The less of them there are, the freer we are to govern. The only good journalist is the kind you can keep as a pet. Flatter them with exclusives, give them a taste of how it feels to be a player, then press your thumb down hard on the oxygen tube if they ever start to get out of line. The rest of them, Murray, are pests.'

'A bunch of parasites and bottom feeders,' replied Murray. 'And the pay's pretty shit these days too.'

Houston didn't know if he was being ironic or obsequious. 'So what does that make you Murray?'

'Scum rises to the surface.'

'Touche!'

'Righto boss. I better go. The fish is on his way.'

The heat was building up. Houston wondered whether it was wise to take Justine to the penthouse tomorrow night. His desire immediately protested. One more night in the love nest then. A chance to relax. She was looking forward to it. She wouldn't admit it, but he could tell. He wasn't under the illusion that she was in love with him or anything. Some women liked looks, others liked companionship, more and more there were those who would settle for obedience. But despite all the changes in gender relationships that had happened in his time, there were still enough attracted to power and money to keep an ugly bloke like him going till the end. They came in all shapes and sizes. And ages. Justine had an enigmatic quality that was more than just the fact he hadn't shagged her yet. These days he enjoyed the anticipation as much as the deed itself. While his phone was usually attached to the side of his head, his fingers hadn't advanced to the art of sexting. Sending selfies of your bits as a kind of foreplay was for someone of his status (and stature) an invitation to eventual public ridicule. Although he sometimes wished he wasn't, Houston was of the old school and at that moment he wanted nothing more than to rest his hand on her glorious bottom and whisper something smutty into her ear.

16

After the showdown with Mahone, Adam spent a few hours writing an introduction to the next part of the expose:

Sources in the construction industry say some of the state's big players are concerned that a new government would change too many of the rules by which development is done in the state, particularly in the context of a potential economic downturn.

He was going to have to get quotes from the usual suspects to give the impression of all bases covered: the Urban Progress Association, a developer lobby group; someone from the unions; and probably someone whose neighbourhood Houston and his cronies had ridden roughshod over in their enthusiasm to create largesse for their mates. His friend Martin might know someone, he reckoned. It was important, if illusory, to create the impression of neutrality. He was going to hang Houston on the facts alone.

He was too excited to concentrate properly, which made the writing difficult. And he was bursting to tell someone how excited he was.

Most of all he wanted to tell Kate. He rang her work number. No answer. Wrote another sentence. Rang her mobile. Turned off. Wrote another sentence. Deleted it. Repeated the same sequence several times then rang Kate's sister, Gina, who coolly told him she wasn't there, and she didn't know when she'd be back. He asked her to tell Kate he'd rung. It didn't sound promising.

Kate was being unreasonable. Given something to latch on to, his obsessive streak defended it with tunnel vision. If she allowed herself to see what this opportunity was doing for him, she'd probably come round. Instead, she'd buried her head like an ostrich in the sand. Not that ostriches actually did that.

Eventually, Kate's mobile answered.

'Oh! It's you.'

'I've been ringing you all afternoon.'

'I can see. Have you come to your senses yet?'

'You won't believe what just happened.' Adam launched into an account of the meeting and how he had managed to turn Jack Vines around.

'Obviously not!'

'What do you mean? I've never been more full of sense. My whole body is tingling with sense. The sense of excitement. I wish you could understand.'

'Well, I wish you could be as excited about having a life with me.'

'But I am excited about having a life with you. I'm excited about everything.' He thought of telling her that he wanted to start a family but checked himself as an image of her raised eyebrows flashed through his mind.

'You can't always have your cake and eat it too, Adam. You haven't thought about the consequences of this glory hunting at all. It's left me feeling very ambivalent. I'm sorry but I can't give in on this one. I need all the energy I can get without it being drained by worry and anger. I'm at a turning point. I haven't got the time right now to go round and round in circles on the phone. Let me know if you change your mind.'

Adam resisted the urge to throw his iPhone at the wall. Which was just as well. A few minutes later the phone rang. It was an old mate who'd left the city for a laidback lifestyle and a job on the *Coffs Courier*. Apparently in Dorrigo, some thugs had been roughing people up thinking they were Alexander Parker. Parker's unlucky doppelganger was furious. He'd marched in the Anti-Vietnam War rallies of the early seventies and was a world-class cultivator of tropical fruit. He'd met Parker once and no one had remarked how similar they were then. 'This is what happens when animals are running the state,' was the quote.

It changed what he was going to write considerably. He left the office and took a walk around the block, fought the crowd rushing from their offices, then came back and wrote the article. It proved a good escape from worrying about Kate. He filed the story and began writing his next piece. Then he went to the pub himself. Another farewell. For one of the younger journalists who had seen the writing on the wall and decided to defect to the financial security of the law. Beer changed to wine and Adam joined a splinter group that left the pub to eat tapas. Adam switched to tequila soda and allowed his triumph to radiate. At some point he became part of an even smaller splinter group that found themselves drinking nightcaps at a small dark downstairs joint called Lower the Bar.

'You're Adam Osborne, the restaurant reviewer, aren't you?' He was sitting on a couch. Tango music was piping through the house speakers. He was still drinking tequila and had reached that odd point of inebriated equilibrium where he felt clear-headed and conversationally lucid, as if he had drunk himself sober.

'Yes, and who are you?'

'I'm Pippa.' Pippa was in her late twenties and had dark olive skin. Her face glowed in the soft lighting and her eyes were sharp with curiosity. Her voice was playful. 'I write food reviews too. And I'm a little bit drunk.'

'Then that makes two of us.'

'What's your favourite food?' she asked.

'Chinese BBQ duck.

What about you?'

THE GUTS

'I had it for dinner. Why don't you kiss me and guess?'

Maybe I am Mikhail Blomqvist thought Adam as he looked Pippa in the eye. This sort of thing never happened. 'Go on! I dare you!'

The mischief in her eyes was hard to argue with. Her head inched closer to his. Their lips brushed then moved back again. Their necks stretched so their mouths were at a good angle for docking. Their lips brushed again and formed a seal. Pippa's tongue was the first to voyage out and as it brushed against the tops of his teeth, Adam tasted fish sauce, lemongrass and pork. His tongue pushed back against hers to discover chunks of peanut in her mouth, and a freshening hint of mint.

Adam pulled his mouth away. 'Grilled Vietnamese lemongrass pork.'

'Very good. And you are chorizo, patatas bravas and garlic prawns.' All of which was true. 'Now let's see if you can taste the dessert.' She leaned into him again, her hand now gripping his thigh. Adam's head moved forward to meet Pippa's, but when their lips met for the third time, he suddenly pulled away.

'No! I'm sorry. I can't do this,' he said.

Pippa looked at him. A flicker of disagreement crossed her face. She let go of Adam's leg. 'Too drunk to fuck?' The playfulness returned to her eyes.

'No. Not that. I could do it, but I can't.'

'Well, if that's the case Mr Chorizo, Spuds and Garlic prawns, I think it's time you went home.'

It was good advice and Adam took it. He had verged on a point of no return. He would rue the missed opportunity to spend a night with the bold and impressive Pippa, but not as much as he would have regretted it if he'd woken up naked in her bed. With his marriage already rocky, it would have made rapprochement with Kate almost impossible. And even if he didn't tell her, the guilt would have stifled his ability to work through the predicament they were in.

These were not the thoughts, however, that accompanied him in the taxi home. In the taxi, his tongue probed his own mouth for the last of Pippa's lemongrass kiss. The other stuff only came when he woke up still half-drunk and full of remorse at four o'clock in the morning. Too much sugar remained in his system from the alcohol he had drunk to be able to get back to sleep. Nascent justifications tangled uncomfortably with the still drunk animality of his unsatisfied lust. He tossed and turned, masturbated, but was unable to come and release the tension keeping him from sleep. A bit after five he heard the slap of the paper being dumped at his door and decided he might as well get up. His own byline greeted him again.

THE GUTS

WALKABOUT OR WALKOUT?

While the Government continues to assert that Alexander Parker is taking a breather in a remote wilderness area, evidence is building to the contrary. The whereabouts of Parker, whose presence is crucial to the passing of key legislation when parliament resumes sitting in four days' time, clearly has some people worried. Yesterday in Dorrigo the house of a retired horticulturalist, Arthur Coach, was broken into by two men, who were under the impression he was Parker.

'They threatened me and slapped my face,' he said. 'I'm still in shock. They refused to believe I wasn't a politician. It took me three photo IDs and an old wedding photo to convince them. They turned the house over. It looks like it's been hit by a tornado.'

The Morning Glory has reason to believe that Mr Coach's visitors were emissaries from elements of the construction industry. According to secret documents received by this reporter, the forthcoming Development Bill is an integral part of a long-term financial arrangement between prominent figures in the Sporty Party and certain leaders in the construction industry. *The Morning Glory* suspects that Mr Parker is aware of these allegations and that his disappearance at this crucial time is in some way a comment upon them.

According to Dr Anna Ng, Senior Lecturer in Political Science at the University of Sydney, 'if there is substance to the rumours, the Pond government faces the strong possibility of going down in disgrace.' With its majority reduced to one, Pond's tenure as Premier is looking more precarious than ever. The big question is, if Pond goes what truths will emerge from the rubble of his tired and unpopular government?

Along with Adam's piece was an inset article by one of the paper's junior political reporters on how Winston Pond was continuing to claim Parker was merely on holidays in some remote part of the state. Further in on page four was another article, headed POND BLAMES OZTEL, where it was claimed that inadequate mobile phone coverage in remote parts of the state was the reason why Parker was currently uncontactable. A spokesman for Oztel had replied by arguing that since over 98% of the state was in the mobile network, chances were if you were in an area where you couldn't be reached by mobile phone, it was probably because you didn't want to be. According to Oztel, apart from several large far-western landholdings, most no-phone zones were in the thickly vegetated valleys of the state's national parks. A coda to the article reported that Alexander Parker was a known fan of bushwalking. A small file photo of Parker wearing a beanie and a rucksack, about to go walking in the Barrington Tops National Park abutted the text.

Adam wondered what the Premier was really thinking. Pond was a cleanskin as far as he knew but it was common wisdom that this was more a product of ignorance than virtue. The likes of Houston had been running rings around him. Pond wouldn't know the half of all the deals going down. His political nous was probably just sharp enough to realise if he paid too much attention, they were likely to get rid of him of him and bring in someone more compliant. Houston and his allies were responsible for large slabs of the Sporty Party's funding. Pond was a constitutional Premier, but such arrangements are doomed to end in tears. Someone gets ambitious, or greedy for posterity. Someone gets discovered. The Premier was screwed, reckoned Adam. Houston would be taking preventative action already. Perhaps the kerfuffle in Dorrigo was part of it. Adam hoped he wouldn't have the time to sweep everything under the carpet.

At 6am, Adam took himself down for a swim and felt immediately better. On the way home, he bought a takeaway coffee and a bacon and egg roll with barbecue sauce. He turned on the computer and worked as he ate. First, he checked the opposition, *the Chronicle*'s website to

THE GUTS

see if they had picked up on his story. So far nothing, only a brief mention of the government explaining the whereabouts of 'missing' MP. Alexander Parker. He then checked his email. Nothing much. Except a brief email from his old source John Dykes, from whom he hadn't heard anything since the brass had nobbled his story. 'Kill the fucker. Make him suffer!' That was the subject. The message was empty. It steeled his resolve inside the discombobulation of his hangover. Dykes had a right to be angry. His public conscience in going against these people last time had cost him the life of his first child and subsequently his marriage. He lived in Thailand now.

Half an hour later, there was a knock at the door. It was a courier with a pen drive. Adam plugged it in to his computer and began to pore over the lists Justine had found in the Stanley Stamford suitcase out at Blue Hills. The last page was a note: *more info coming tonight*. For a couple of hours Adam sat there going through the stuff. He let it filter through his head for a bit while he tried to contact Kate. The kiss guilt bothered him, and he hoped that talking to her would negate it. No answer.

He returned to the files. Obviously, it was code. The people weren't real cricketers. But who were they? It was time to go fishing.

Adam got dressed and took a taxi to the office. The message button was blinking on his work phone. The first was an attempt at a bribe.

'Silence is golden. Talk is cheap. Unless you talk to us,' said a smooth voice before reading out a phone number. No one serious left messages like that on answering machines. Still, it was a lead. When Adam dialled, an old lady answered the phone. Probably kids.

Radio had picked the story up too and there were messages from producers looking to interview him on their shows. It would be on the TV news tonight too and there was a call from *Newskew*, a current affairs debate program wanting to set up a discussion between Adam and a government representative. He wasn't quite ready for that yet. He wanted to able to figure out the stuff on the pen drive before he battled the government on TV. There was also his first threat.

'How much do you like the taste of cement?' a rough voice said.

Chloe had warned him at the meeting with Mahone. But he brushed it off as someone who had over-enjoyed *The Sopranos*.

Unable to crack the cricketing code, he headed into work. At about eleven Jim Sway paid a visit to Adam's cubicle. 'Morning Adam. Nice piece today. Looking forward to seeing the follow-up tomorrow.'

'Thanks Jim,' he replied, hoping not to have to say much more.

'Listen, have you got five minutes? Jack wants to have a coffee and talk tactics for keeping the story as a scoop.'

Adam rolled his eyes.

'He's come full circle. He's claiming that your return to investigative journalism was a managerial masterstroke. Ten bucks he calls you mate.'

'Wanker! I'll be down in a couple of minutes.'

The outdoor café next to the lobby of *The Morning Glory's* building was full of the morning meeting crowd. Journalists fishing for stories. Salespeople fishing for ads. Executives fishing for heads that had long since been lost up their arses. Sway was sitting at a table in the shade smoking a ciggie. They ordered coffees. Adam some vegemite toast. While they waited for Vines, he outlined his plan of attack.

'For tomorrow I'm thinking of running a catalogue of all the types of dodginess that have been going on. I can probably string it out over a couple of days. Then I need to find a source to corroborate my stuff, so we can start divulging names without the lawyers wetting their pants. I've got a few leads already and hopefully the details will provoke people to talk.' He held back on the information that had arrived by courier that morning. Given the threats he was already receiving, he didn't want anyone to get too excited.

'Sounds kosher to me,' said Sway, whose subtle twitching implied his ongoing battle with the DTs. Conversation switched to the cricket. A Jack Vines underling arrived to say he was with an important client and would they mind waiting. And they did. Not that they had a choice. Another latte only added to Sway's tremors. The cricket talk petered out on reminiscences of the Ashes before last, the end of a golden era for the game. Heat began to fill the day. Sway filled the conversational void:

THE GUTS

'You know, Adam, this is a cunt of a business. I can't wait till I get the chance to retire. I don't care if the internet is driving newspapers into the dirt. I'm tired of being the meat in the sandwich, hated by nearly everyone because of it. Tired of trying to maintain the quality of something with constantly dwindling resources. A decade ago, a paper was a thing an editor could stamp their vision on. Now it's just the management of costs. As soon as they offer me a redundancy, I'm done. I've bought a nice little acreage out of Lithgow and I'm going to grow grapes. Cool climate pinot noir. I'm going to make the best bloody burgundy in the country and I'm going to sit there drinking it while I listen to Johnny Cash on the porch. And the world, and all these dickheads who reckon they're making it spin, can go and get fucked. I've written and read so many fucking newspaper stories, I've come to see the world in column inches. It's flat, black and white. Thirty years I've been doing this. One day it's alarming, the next it's wrapping chips.'

Adam nodded his head and raised it. He looked at Sway, uncomfortable with the intimacy of this confession.

'My instinct tells me the stuff you're getting is red-hot,' continued Sway. 'But if you start getting the heat, and that heat starts getting too hot for you, I wouldn't blame you if you wanted to pull up stumps. There are far worse things than having to do lunch for a living.'

Through the haze of his hangover, Adam saw that Sway was another half-smart, dream-prone muddler the world had gotten big on. But there was a difference. Adam was still trying; Sway had chucked in the towel. Sway had decided that the world was rotten, and the knowledge had marooned him. He wasn't going to retire to Lithgow and make the best pinot noir in Australia, he was going to make the wine so he could pace himself as he drank himself to death. Still, his candour, conspicuously absent the last time, affected Adam, who needed someone to talk to. Only Jack Vines bounced in like a vitamin and the confidence was broken.

'Great stuff, Adam! Great stuff, old boy!' he bellowed, giving him a thunderous clap on the shoulder that almost spilled Adam's coffee.

'It's going to put the circulation up and I've been getting some very favourable reactions from some very important people. It's got the potential to become as big as the Queensland story of the 1980s. Keep this up and we might be able to see you through to a pay rise. How's 'chief state political reporter' sound to you?'

It sounded fine. 'Sure.'

'So what's happening for tomorrow?' he asked. Adam had intended to brush Vines off with a few sketchy details but his desire to show off got the better of him.

'I've got some new stuff to release over the next few days. For the moment more the kinds of things that have been going on. A bit of 'Guess Who, Don't Sue' while I'm waiting for sources to be confirmed and the lawyers to tie everything together. I can't tell you yet, but I should have something to upload to the internet tonight.'

'Good stuff!' enthused Vines. 'I'm pleased to see *The Morning Glory* getting its teeth into the way government corrupts the natural efficiencies of markets. Make sure you nail the bastards but watch out for collateral damage. We don't want to throw the baby out with the bath water, do we?'

Adam didn't understand what he meant. Vines didn't register Adam's puzzlement. Nor did he elaborate.

'Keep up the good work! Oh, and I need to ask you a small favour. Is it possible to keep up the restaurant stuff until we can roll you over into your new position? The board's been complaining about staff costs.'

'I suppose so,' said Adam, lacking the energy to argue.

'Good on you. You can always take your laptop with you and write things up as you work your way through the menu, eh?'

Vines strutted off to another table where Blake House, the paper's property editor, was sitting with a couple of suits. One of them gave Adam a venomous look.

'What's his problem?' he asked Sway.

'That's Shane Vickery. He sells the display ads for NEST. The big colour ones with the spiffy artist's impressions of boutique developments. There are a few developers threatening to pull their advertising

THE GUTS

because of you,' he said. 'Virtue is Vickery's biggest account. If it happens, it'll cost him forty grand a year in commissions. And if he loses that he might have to downsize his house.'

'Fuck! How do you know all that?'

'Call me old school, but it's amazing what you can learn in the pub. I've even seen middle-aged men, hardly in peak physical shape, get hit on by young food writers,' Sway grinned.

Adam swallowed his embarrassment and let the remark go through to the keeper. 'What do you think Vines was crapping on about?'

'I think he meant that when it comes to doling out the blame, try to keep it focused on Houston. He's the evil mandarin that property developers in the pursuit of an honest buck must subsidise merely to survive.'

'If I bring Houston down, he's the kind of scumbag who'll take everyone with him. I'm happy to let him do the dirty work.'

'Don't bet on it! He'll go to court and say that he can't remember anything. The thing about someone like Houston is that he's so convinced he's running the show he's incapable of recognising when he's being played. He thinks he's the king of all this, but he's really just a well-paid serf. When this balloon bursts, it's going to come as a shock for him to realise how fragile his authority actually is.

'If he's smart, he'll keep schtumm. If he goes to jail, he'll want friends inside. That way he won't have to worry about bending over in the showers. Not that all the horny ice-addicts of the world will be queuing up for his fat arse. But if he keeps his trap shut and plays the game, he'll get protection and there'll be a nice little nest egg waiting for him on his release. There always is. It won't quite be a seat on the board of a bank, but there'll be something. Things are more sophisticated than the old days when crook politicians ended up running hot dog stands when they got out of jail. If people aren't rewarded for carrying the can, the system doesn't survive. And Houston should know that if he doesn't play by the rules, someone might economically rationalise that his permanent silence is the optimum risk management strategy.

That can easily be arranged in jail. But if he clams up and does his time, I can't imagine him having to spend more than three years of an eight-year sentence, reduced to five on appeal, minimum security too, growing potatoes on a prison farm or something, given the bullshit way how judges when sentencing rich people always take into consideration the shame and social embarrassment of their fall from grace. What shame! Any money he'll be developing some serious ailments too.

'Fuck that. He won't get off that easy. Not if I can help it.'

'If you want to catch all the fish in the pond, you need to use dynamite. Try and blow them all up at the same time with one big hit. They're more likely to lash out at each other if they're paranoid and confused. As soon as they've organised someone like Houston to take the fall, they'll be safe. You need to make it seem like their only hope is every man for himself.'

Sway looked round quickly to see if Vines was within earshot, but he was busy bonding with his salesmen. 'You'll also have to convince our friend Jack Vines that implicating some of the paper's major clients is the only way to go. Some friends in the DPP [Department of Public Prosecutions] will come in handy too. Give Jane Murphy a ring. She's senior, straight and doesn't play politics. She's got a strong sense of justice, and a grudge against the mates' network as a result of bruising her head on the glass ceiling one too many times.'

'Thanks Jim.' Adam said.

Sway shifted uneasily in his chair and swallowed some coffee, while he weighed up whether to say what was on his mind. 'No problems, Adam. I owe you. Last time I dudded you. I didn't really have a choice. I could have put my head on the chopping block over interference in the editorial by the board, but my contract was up for renewal and they would have just terminated it and told my replacement not to publish. Even if they hadn't sacked me, they could have sent me off to some health farm on stress leave while Vines quietly swept things under the carpet. This time, though, the cards are falling in the right places. Mahone got nobbled in the meeting, and Vines' self-preservation instinct has come down in favour of running the story. Circle's still away and the story has already gone too far for him to directly intervene. But be careful. The more reason you give them to be worried the more likely they are to resort to extra-judicial tactics. If I were you, I'd be getting myself a room under a false name in a hotel. That goes for Kate as well. And use taxis instead of your car, just in case your brakes decide they're going to fail. The paper will spring for the expenses.'

'Thanks for the concern, Jim,' replied Adam. He felt big in himself. Thin with hangover but ballooning, though at risk of becoming sentimental. 'I appreciate it. But it should be OK. The flat's got deadlocks on the doors and windows, and we had a sensor alarm put in after some punk came in and nicked the home theatre. Kate's got the shits with me and has moved to her sisters. She's taken the car with her, so I'm on a bus and taxi regimen anyway.'

'Just be careful,' he said. 'By the way it's 12.30. You look like you need a hair of the dog. Shall we nick across the road to the pub?'

It was a tempting proposition. Adam knew how good a beer would feel. He also felt a certain obligation to Sway. Partly because of the generosity of his advice, but also because he had badly underestimated the man. He might be a high-functioning alcoholic caught in the unenviable position of having to compromise his editorial judgement to the whims of the corporate fat cats who employed him, but he was aware of this and of the need to play for small victories when the opportunity presented itself. The fact that his staff demonised him as a gutless yes-man whose only form of protest consisted in throwing his dreams into the bottom of a beer glass can't have made it any easier.

'OK, Jim. Just the one though. I've still got a lot of work to do.'

Three beers later, Adam refused the offer of a fourth and went back to work, feeling stabilised if not refreshed. Back at his desk, he puzzled over the pile of notes on his desk. On a whim, he decided to send some of them to John Dykes, who had emailed him that morning. Unable to confirm the initials, he put together an article designed to provoke a response.

C.E. GRIMES

Cryptic Corruption

Tuesday, 29th September. Par 3 at Ermington. Problems with slicing the ball into Parramatta River. HV offered to pay the two-shot penalty for changing the out of bounds.

Friday, 16th October. Back nine at Redfern. Problems with GUR. Told HV it could be repaired.

Saturday, 24th October. Played with CC at Moore Park. Told me he played off 16. Eight more like it. Adjusted his handicap for being a burglar.

With code like this you could be forgiven for thinking that the state is being run by golfers and for all we know it is. However, recent documents that have fallen into the hands of the political investigations section of *The Morning Glory* suggest these cryptic remarks are essentially a map of some of the highest-level corruption in the state. We came across these riddles without the assistance of WikiLeaks, but we are relying on our readers to help decode them for us. All plausible solutions will be in line to win an Apple iPad.

Adam added a few more coded entries for the initials he thought he could put to names. A write-off came to him: 'Uncover these bad apples and we'll send you a good one.' The convergence of hard-nosed investigative journalism and product placement might please Jack Vines. By the time he sent the story to the sub-editors he was completely knackered. The lunchtime beers had faded to a headache. He saved copies of his work and the files that had come by courier to a number of password protected pen drives, one for home, one for the car and one which he mailed to his own post office box. He was about to turn off his computer when the phone rang. He was tempted not to answer it, but curiosity got the better of him. It was a restaurant called Babyface confirming a booking for 7pm. In all the hangover and excitement, he'd completely forgotten about his other job, the one that

THE GUTS

Vines had reminded him he was still meant to be doing. For the past week or so, he'd been living on stories already written, but by now he was pretty much out of stock.

'I'm very sorry but I'm afraid I'm going to have to cancel.'

He checked his email one more time. His inbox was full of PR junk from the people who promoted restaurants. Before he could hit the off button a message appeared from Ingrid.

I: I need Babyface.

She'd been listening.

A: I'll do it next week.

I: I need it this week.

A: Why?

She was looking at him from three booths away.

I: Jack said you were still going to do the job.

A: Yes, but what's the hurry.

There wasn't an emoticon invented to encapsulate the weary vexation that had materialised on Ingrid's face.

I: We've got 'goodies for oldies' as a section cover story next week and I need this for a spin-off.

A: I'm sorry. I've been really busy. I'm bushed. I don't think I'd be able to do it justice. Besides I'm not feeling too well.

I: Nothing a Bloody Mary won't fix.

Ingrid had been in the pub the night before. At least she drank, thought Adam. As opposed to Phoebe, his previous editor, whose favourite way to wind down had been colonic irrigation.

Ingrid looked at him again. She was still a journalist. And part of her was impressed by his scoop.

I: Please.

Adam swore he could hear her eyebrows arch. He knew the cause was lost.

I: All you need is a nice dinner and an early night. I'll ring and rebook the table. OK?

A: OK. I suppose I won't be the only one nodding off at the table.

I: Good.

C.E. GRIMES

Getting a grip on the AB retiree market had figured importantly in Ingrid's latest key performance indicators. As the baby boomers started retiring, there were more and more cashed-up people in their sixties, seventies and eighties, looking to enjoy their prosperity, even as their health began to wane. They were also the rusted-on readers of the physical version of the paper and *The Glory*, and its advertisers were, in the words of Jack Vines, searching for new ways to 'monetise' them. While Ingrid probably didn't give a shit about how old fogies got their kicks, she did give a shit about her KPIs, so unless Adam wanted to be complained about in senior editor's meetings by a woman he sometimes ached to call 'Bubbles', there was no escape.

Adam dug out the press release for Babyface from the bottom of his in-tray while his computer copied the file he'd forgotten. Babyface was a culinary marketing gimmick if ever there was one. It promised the utmost in 'soft food sophistication'. The release claimed that soft food was the newest thing in America, specifically designed to cater to the rapidly ageing population, many of whom no longer had their original teeth and found the mastication of great chunks of meat and crunchy vegetables a bit of an ordeal. Soft food was:

... a revolution in culinary texture. All your favourite tastes combined in a way that is uniquely smooth. Instead of just a regular meal in a food processor, Babyface has specially researched foods that will melt in your mouth, presented in an array of striking combinations that refined palates will find difficult to ignore. At Babyface the customer no longer has to sacrifice quality of taste and texture merely because they find things difficult to chew.

Suffice to say he was going to have to go alone. One of the perks of restaurant reviewing was that you could usually bring a friend. But the only person he could usually drag to these sorts of places was Kate, whose professional curiosity was powerful. Friends were more than happy to keep him company in return for a free feed in most restaurants, but the idea of eating jelly designed for the gerontocracy was an exception.

THE GUTS

Adam set off on foot for Darling Harbour. He followed the foreshore, dodging the clusters of families and tourists to where a neon image of a *Baby's Face* beckoned. A waitress showed him to a solo table, thankfully set outside where a cool breeze was blowing off the water, and away from a crowded inside populated by large groups of loud and gaudy senior citizens, some of them in wheelchairs, many wearing bibs. He ordered a mineral water and perused the menu. Soups, pates and oysters dominated the entrees. The mains were a bit more esoteric: bone marrow softly stir-fried with Japanese aubergine and topped with pummelled puy lentils; micro-minced lamb with a mint sauce and parsnip puree served in a parfait bowl with a straw and spoon; flakes of hiramasa kingfish stewed in coconut milk and smattered over a sweet potato jelly; steamed sliced trepang stuck to a caviar mousse; liquefied chicken drizzled over truffle infused soft polenta. There was even a nostalgia dish of the 1969 space paste Neil Armstrong and co. had eaten on their voyage to the moon, temporarily off the menu, according to the waitress, in deference to the victims of the latest space station disaster. The dessert list was long and included ice creams, sorbets, soft fruits with mascarpone, a variety of jellies, exotically flavoured custards and pannacotta.

On paper, Adam thought the food didn't look as bad as the sight of the two ancient drooling epicures sitting next to him in their bibs and leisurewear finery. A cruise shipped was docked over the other side of the bay and these people with their loud American accents and bird of paradise outfits almost certainly belonged to it. The old man complained about hooligans on a train they'd caught, the woman reminded him how he'd been a hooligan in his time, to which he'd responded by telling her to shut up and eat her oysters, to which she'd responded by saying what's the point, to which he'd responded by slicing an enormous chunk of pate and stuffing into his mouth. Adam turned away from the man's open-mouthed and gummy mastication.

The old man distressed Adam. When you get old, he thought, somewhat idealistically, your appetites should taper off, life should be more in the mind. The man's proximity to death made his gluttony seem decadent and somehow cruel. He would eat like that even if everyone around him was in famine. Adam put his napkin on the table and went inside to find the bathroom. On the way he found his wife. She was at a table with half a dozen oldies. Adam watched her pick small amounts of food off her plate and spoon them into her mouth. She rolled them around with her tongue, one cheek bulging then the next, a gesture of conspicuous tasting; her head was arched back like a petite pelican so her palate could gain a full appreciation of the taste and texture before she swallowed. It looked like she was eating the tahini and beetroot jelly trifle. Between mouthfuls, she stopped to listen to her fellow diners who seemed to be competing for her attention. When he returned from the bathroom, lavender scented, extra-wide cubicles with handrails, and nappy bins, Adam wanted to interrupt but couldn't think of anything to interrupt with. Hello, didn't seem enough, so he stood there watching. The cool breeze off the water was delicious after a muggy day, a full moon was rising further up the harbour, and his wife, in profile, was looking even more beautiful for him not having seen her for a while. She'd had a haircut and her newly exposed neck as it engaged in the business of eating seemed both vulnerable and noble. He wanted to run his fingers along its soft skin and even softer, barely visible, down. He wanted to nuzzle in and kiss it.

    Although her back was to him, Kate turned around, probably feeling the heat of his gaze. Adam waved then sat down again and began talking his review into his phone. Kate seemed more beautiful, more precious, for the fact he had narrowly escaped cheating on her. He watched her through the window, her fine brown hair, bright eyes, the nose which she hated but had learned to live with, her mutable lips, the newly exposed elegant curves of her slender throat sweeping down to those parts unavailable to public view. She was amazing. He remembered the hand-sized heft of her breasts, the creamy skin of her soft tummy which wobbled like pannacotta when tickled, the soft brush of her pubic hair, the delicate folds of her cunt lips and her creamy-salty one in a million taste. It was more than a month since they'd last had sex and Adam's unresolved lust clamoured for expression.

THE GUTS

The entrée's arrival disrupted his reverie. It was an assortment of pastes from the specials board fetchingly spiralled onto a large white plate. There was fresh anchovy paste spotted with caviar, a green olive tapenade striped with capsicum jelly, and a stilton cheese softened with walnut oil and infused with a granny smith apple puree. The food was surprisingly tasty but lacking in substance for someone in Adam's hungover state. He asked for some bread to mop up the paste. The waiter, an older man with a comb-over hairdo and a moustache replied that it was against the soft food philosophy to taint their delicate textures with the coarse necessity of chewing. Adam muttered a note into his phone: waitstaff prone to wankery. Not that it would make the pages of *The Glory*. When he looked up from his food, Kate was standing before him.

'Hello', she said, 'What are you doing here? I thought you were too much of a hotshot for this sort of caper these days. Aren't you too busy getting your byline on the front page? Or is it just that you couldn't be bothered cooking for yourself?' She waited, but not for long. 'Or have you decided to start stalking me?' She was in the peppery mood that often came when she drank red wine.

'Where are your dining companions?'

'Gone home.'

'I suppose it is late for them,' he said.

'It's late for lots of things.'

Adam felt the heat of her stare. 'Do you want to sit down?'

'Should I?'

Adam shrugged. Kate stared at him. 'Please,' he said.

She sat down. 'What are you doing here?'

'I'm planning a Grey Power convention,' she said.

'Very exciting.'

'Very lucrative. You seem to have been busy.' Her voice softened into a strictly patrolled concern. 'Have the threats started coming in yet?'

'Nothing serious.'

'Well, be careful then. Just because I'm furious with you, doesn't mean I want you dead.'

'That's very kind of you,' he said half-jokingly. 'What do you think of the food?'

'Not bad, but I won't be coming here for my birthday.'

The waiter arrived with Adam's main, a fruit of the sea special: flaked lobster served in the shell with a truffled sea urchin sauce and dotted with salmon roe. 'Look,' said Adam after the waiter had retreated. 'I really need to talk to you.'

Kate looked down at her hands then back at Adam. Her eyes were glistening. She wanted to make up. He knew it.

'I'm sorry. I can't talk to you now. I'm working. And I'm not sure that at the moment we've got much to talk about anyway. It's all over the papers now, so the situation's even worse. I know you. You're not going to pull out now. There's too much momentum. But that doesn't change anything. I told you what I thought, and you ignored me. Your ambition was more important to you than us. When you get whatever it is that's bugging you out of your system, let me know. Then, maybe, we can talk.'

'Can't we reach some sort of a compromise?' he pleaded.

'Apparently not.'

'Come on, Kate ...' a hint of angry frustration in his tone.

'Be careful,' she said and before he had time to answer she was gone. Even a pannacotta with a Moscato d'asti and cherry sauce failed to take the bitter taste of her departure out his mouth.

Adam finished his meal as fast as the service allowed him and hailed a cab for home. It must have been about 10.30pm when he put the key in the door. But he never quite got through it. As he pushed it open, there was a presence at his back. He tried to turn round but, before he could, a large hand pulled on his shoulder and a wet cloth, smelling sickly sweet, smothered his face. 'Kate, I'm sorry!' he muttered into the cloth as his mind began to fade.

17

After a hot shower, Justine put on a black pair of lace knickers and a matching bra. She pulled a little black dress over her head and smoothed it over her curves. A touch of mascara, eyeliner and a dark red, carnivorous lipstick. Her hair was unclipped and flowing over her shoulders. She wrestled on a pair of Spanish fuck-me boots, then swapped them for Chelsea boots in preparation for a rapid departure. She put on her favourite leather jacket. Armour. A quick check in the mirror, a small line of coke and she was ready for battle. A horn honked on the street below. Her taxi.

Around the same time Adam arrived for his dinner at Babyface, Justine was on the other side of Darling Harbour being shown to her table by the maître d' of Fetish. If they'd had binoculars they could have waved. A waiter came. The 'Madam' in his greeting carried a faint sneer, a false obsequiousness comprised of a delicate balance of misogyny and the desire to make customers wonder about the adequacy of their taste. Halfway through his description of the cocktail of the day, Justine cut him off and ordered a glass of shiraz. She sat there wired, with fear, anticipation and a couple of lines of coke. The vials of SP-117 and Rohypnol clinked in her jacket pocket as her leg tremored beneath the table. This was it.

Justine played with her napkin and studied the menu. The Gut was late. He wasn't answering his phone. Had something gone wrong? Had it all been for nothing? He texted. *Held up in a meeting. Be there in 1* . Relief competed with trepidation. She went outside for a cigarette and had two, only going back in when some well-preserved guy in his fifties with a smile like a real estate agent's string of adjectives started to chat her up. When people like that called her beautiful, she wanted to punch them. Inside again, she sat and started up a list of the top ten places she would rather be: diving in the Maldives, punk rock in Berlin, walking in Nepal, researching Penguins in the Antarctic.

'I hope you're thinking about me,' said the Gut.

'Yes, I was.'

'What were you thinking?'

'I was thinking you were going to stand me up.'

'Why would I do that?'

'Where have you been?'

'Placating the Premier.'

'Successfully?'

He gave her an appraising look. 'What do you reckon?' The Gut filled his chair and immersed himself in the menu. 'The Coffin Bay oysters sound good,' he said with a slight leer. 'Let's get a dozen each.'

The Gut was one of those men who liked to order for the table. Justine sighed inwardly, not that she was really thinking of the food. 'What with red wine?' she said, pointing to her glass of shiraz.

'OK smartypants. I'll get some Riesling as well.'

Justine didn't really feel like oysters. There was enough stuff sliding down the back of her throat already. 'Do you mind if I have the smoked duck instead?'

'Last time I checked, we were still living in a democracy!' he replied.

'And I'll have the lamb tenderloin with anchovy sauce for a main.'

'I'm saving that for dessert,' he said, but without the energy that could add charisma to his dirty old man routine. 'Suckling pig for me.'

Justine kept a tight hold on a wave of disgust. How did sex workers manage it, she wondered to herself. Perhaps the build-up was worse that the thing itself. The food was ordered. Now what. An awkward moment across the table. Houston turned on the charm and filled the void. He began to ask her about her childhood, her work, her dreams. Justine sipped her wine slowly in case she tangled herself up in lies. He knew how to read between the lines. It was part of the reason, she supposed, that he had been successful. She played with the vials in her pocket. She hadn't expected to answer so many questions. Men like the Gut mostly talked about themselves.

'What about you?' she asked. Two glasses of wine had disappeared by then. 'What was your childhood like?' He told the story well, from the summit of his success back to the stern Methodist Minister father committed to his parishioners, indifferent to his family. The self-denying mother who held it all together living out her dreams and disappointments through her two sons, one now sadly a drug addict. So many of these politicians were inadequately fathered men, scared little boys carrying their mothers' dreams, who accumulated impressive armours, but were spiritual invertebrates. Justine didn't need to know this, though. The boy Houston, no matter how touchingly rendered, was dead, replaced by adult drives and their consequences. She wondered briefly about his mother, sex with one man, no career or adventures of her own, how grim it must have been, then forced herself to concentrate. She needed to know what this oddly compelling amalgam of charm and evil, the poor woman's son, was thinking about now. What was he hiding? How far was she going to have to go to try and find out?

'What's the story with Alexander Parker all about?'

He looked her with penetrating focus. 'It's all a storm in a teacup,' he said. 'The over-active imaginations of people with not enough to do. I don't know where he is.' He checked his phone and put it down on the table. 'But surely we've got more interesting things to talk about than that.'

The phone rang. He looked at the caller ID and turned it off.

'Who was that?' she asked.

'Just someone who's not doing their job very well.' He looked at her sharply. Was she pushing too hard? Asking too many questions. The entrée arrived and she was grateful.

The duck was very good. The Gut put several of his oysters on her plate. Her fear of gagging on them was unfounded. He ate quickly. She wondered how he managed to enjoy it at that speed. When you had seen people who were starving eating their first meals in days, it was strange to watch someone eat with such unthinking greed, with so little sense of the enormous effort that went into feeding his privilege. He might as well have been eating tinned spaghetti and perhaps there was a part of him, the same part of him that hankered after iced vo-vos, that would have preferred it. How many people, Justine wondered, ate at these restaurants not because they liked the food, but because they believed it was a necessary performance of taste as part of the acquisition and maintenance of their social status. Houston washed his unconsidered food down with gulps of wine and Justine had to stamp on the urge to keep up.

'What do you think of politics?' he asked. An oyster filled the chewing space inside one of his cheeks.

'I don't mind it. It's interesting being so close to the decisions. It makes you feel kind of special.' That much was true. She liked for her actions to have effect. It was one reason for her previous addiction to aid work, the visible evidence that the work you did saved lives.

'Yes, it does, doesn't it? It's even better when those decisions are yours,' he smiled omitting the compromised truths of factions and committees, lobbyists and donors, of the necessity always to make sure you had the numbers.

'I agree,' she said. If she were serious about politics sleeping with the boss was the wrong way to climb. The sexual double standard was still in play. The Sporty Party's love affair with nepotism embraced mates, sons, brothers, sisters, husbands and even wives but rarely stretched to shags on the side. They were public liabilities as Joe Rosti's girlfriend had recently found out to her disgust.

When the pork arrived, Houston sent it back complaining it was overcooked. The waiter wasn't convinced but torn between the abuse of the chef and the loss of a possibly sizeable tip he demurred and returned it to the kitchen.

Houston enjoyed sending things back. It was all about exercising power.

'They need to be reminded the customer is always right.' he said. Justine's lamb was going cold on the plate, which was fine. She wasn't hungry. The smell of the anchovy sauce had turned her off. The waiter returned some ten minutes later with a pork that was pink instead of white. Probably spat upon too, she thought. She thought of a friend who had once gotten so sick of being abused in the restaurant kitchen he worked in that he had masturbated into a bowl of tartare sauce. It had been a lonely triumph, he said. Nobody had even noticed. The Gut attacked the pork with relish while Justine toyed with her lamb. They both passed on dessert.

Other than the usual stream of innuendo, Justine was getting anxious. The Gut was yet to hit on her. His phone rang. He looked at it again.

'How about I turn this thing off?'

'I don't mind.' Justine had had a mobile phone for most of her life.

'But I'd like to talk to you. I'd like to get to know you better.' Justine felt his eyes blazing into hers, the charm of before but this time with intent. This was it. Butterflies dissolved the weight of the food in her stomach. She felt herself blush. The Gut's eyes were shining, power's confidence in its own charisma. She looked back at him. It was like she was in a movie. No, it was like she was watching herself in a movie. His hand moved under the table and landed gently on her knee. Justine didn't move.

She felt ashamed. She battled herself and made the lie, eyes blinking, voice trembling, 'I'd like to get to know you better too.'

The waiter returned with the bill. Houston removed his hand from under the table. He pulled his wallet from his trousers and put his credit card on the plate. He offered Justine one of the after-dinner mints that had come with the bill. She twiddled with its wrapper and forced herself to take a deep breath. Then another. She wanted to run. She put the mint in her mouth and swallowed it almost whole. His hand returned to her leg and began to knead her thigh. Justine fingered the vials in her coat pocket.

'A friend of mine has an apartment round the corner. I have the key. The view's amazing. You can see through the Harbour Bridge and all the way up to Manly. There's champagne in the fridge. How about we go up there and get to know each other a little bit better.'

'I'm not sure.' She didn't want it to seem too easy. She didn't want him to think she would simply undress and lie down like a starfish on the bed. She needed to make him work to seduce her if her plan was going to work.

He took his hand off her thigh. It felt sticky. 'Just for a nightcap. As part of your professional development.'

Her eyes tested his face for veracity and found only charm. 'Ok then. But just the one.'

They left the restaurant and walked to the Stevedore Apartments several hundred metres away. Houston huffed with the exercise. Justine kept her hands in her jacket pockets. Their bodies bumped together. They went up a lane and Houston swiped the door into the building. They climbed several floors in the lift, then entered the apartment with a further swipe.

'This is the loungeroom,' said Houston. A large white leather lounge occupied the centre of the room and faced out towards a loggia veranda that looked north across the Harbour to Luna Park.

'Nice view,' said Justine. She wondered who else had received this same tour.

'Wait till you see the view from the bedroom.'

'Let's have a drink.'

'What do you feel like?'

'Champagne?'

Houston went to the kitchen and returned with two glasses and a bottle of Veuve Clicquot.

They went out onto the veranda, where Houston popped open the champagne. He filled their glasses and Justine thought about how to spike his drink.

'Here's to the mixing of work and pleasure,' said Houston by way of a toast. They clinked glasses and drank. Justine leaned against the railings of the verandah's glass fence and stared out over the harbour. Houston sidled up to her. She felt the heat of his body against hers. She felt the need to urinate.

'I've got to go to the toilet.'

THE GUTS

'It's past the first bedroom on the left.'

When she finished, she opened both vials and took a sniff. There was a knock on the door. 'Can I come in?'

'Just a minute.'

She put the lids back on the vials and washed her face. She unlocked the door and slid past the Gut as his arms swept round to embrace her. She blew him a kiss. He continued into the bathroom. She returned to the balcony where she put some of the SP 117 into the Gut's champagne.

He returned. 'Just had to take my medicine,' he said, winking, a reference she presumed to pill fuelled virility.

'How is your health?' she asked.

'Better than it needs to be.'

Their stares turned again to the harbour, leaning against the railing they admired the lights, marking time.

'What would you be if you could be anything?' asked Justine, forcing herself not to flinch as his hand cupped her bum.

'I don't know. I like this life. But if I could be anything, I'd do the same job in a more important place.'

'Where?'

'I don't know. Somewhere like New York, or Shanghai, or Mumbai; somewhere that feels like it's the centre of things rather than an afterthought of civilisation plonked at the bottom of the world.'

Justine shivered inside. She had thought the same thing. It was awful to discover that they had things in common.

'Don't you like Sydney?'

'I love it but ...'

'It could be worse, surely.'

'Sure. It could be Adelaide, Auckland or the Falkland Islands.'

'I like Adelaide,' said Justine, who had never been to the other two.

'You can keep it. It's a place that's running out of reasons to exist. And they still think they're special. No convicts. Everything's sown up there by the time you're born. At least in Sydney people get to create themselves.'

Houston sculled the rest of his glass of champagne. To Justine's great relief, he seemed to be opening up. But surely it was too soon for the SP-117 to be having its effect. 'What I like is doing deals. But what about you?' he asked. 'What's your dream job?'

'I dunno. Playing piano in a bar.'

'You'll get over it.' His hand slid up her bottom, fingers briefly tracing the crack between her cheeks, and stopped at the small of her back. His arm slid around her waist and turned her to face him.

'And what are you doing, a beautiful young woman like you, standing here with an old man like me?' The humility was false. Suddenly, she felt like prey. Did he know?

'I don't know, I've always found older men more interesting to talk to. Young men are beautiful but they're usually much too self-absorbed.'

The Gut's pulled her closer. She was surprised at how gentle his fingers were. Firm but not forcing her to yield. Their eyes met again, as if they were in a movie. 'Do you find me interesting?'

To answer in the affirmative was an invitation. But what else could she do? 'Yes,' she said. Her voice did not feel like it was her own. The Gut's head moved down and in. They kissed. Cognitive dissonance. Even if it was a better, somehow less sleazy kiss than she had anticipated. Another name perhaps for her (short) list of bad men who were tender in bed. His tongue slid over her teeth. Then she remembered what he had done and wondered what would happen if she vomited in his mouth.

'I'm a whole lot more than who you think I am,' he said. Justine sighed with relief. The drugs seemed to be working. The Gut misinterpreted her sigh as a sign of lust. He pressed her against the railing with his body, his hands on her hips. He was getting hard.

'I can tell.'

He kissed her again. It was easier the second time.

'Let's go and make ourselves comfortable in the bedroom. You can see the whole of the Harbour Bridge while you're lying down.'

'But first, let's finish this lovely champagne.' Justine charged their glasses. They went inside and sat down on the white leather lounge.

THE GUTS

His fingers traced behind her ears, down the nape of her neck and rested on her clavicle. 'Why did you choose to become a politician?'

'I wanted the feeling of knowing what it is like for my actions to change the world.'

'Does it feel good?'

'Yes and no. It's great to see things happen, but the constant compromise drives me nuts.'

Houston reached around behind Justine's back, slid his hand up the back of her dress and expertly unclipped her bra.

'And how do you adapt?' asked Justine as another hand slid to her thigh. It was getting hard to keep track of them. She twisted to face him and placed her palm firmly on his chest, pushing him back into the sofa.

'How did I adapt? I adapted by making a stack of money. In the end it's the only real measure of your achievement.' The boast was out, the drugs were working.

'How?'

'I facilitate things.'

'Like what?' Houston's hand reached around and cupped her breast. It was too much. She wanted to punch him in the face, but she resisted. Her body was stiff with tension. She was arguing with herself. This was war. People get killed in war, children starve, whole families are ripped to bits and all you have to do is wank off a rich old pervert, she told herself.

'Like most of the largest property deals in the state.'

'Really?' His fingers tweaked her nipple, moved down over her belly, circled her navel and flicked the elastic on her knickers before resting back on her thigh. 'What for Harry Virtue and the like?'

'Yes. And he's just one of many. Did you know he owns the apartment we're sitting in right now? And I can use it, we can use it, whenever we want?'

His mouth moved into hers for another kiss.

Justine allowed it then broke away on the edge of gagging. She took a hold of his belt and pulled the short strip of overhang back through the loop of his trousers. She smiled. He smiled. The SP-117 had diminished his ego in favour of his id, his childish pleasure seeking self. He was the star of a story that was going to have a happy ending. That was all he needed to know.

'I don't want you to think that I'm being nosy,' said Justine. 'It's just that when I was in the electoral office the other day, I saw all this weird code, stuff about cricketers and schooners.'

'Ahh yes,' said the Gut. 'My secret accounting.' Justine undid the buckle of his belt and in doing so her hand brushed against his erection. 'I am glad to have been born in an age ruled by accountants rather than artists or statesmen.'

'What does it all mean?'

'Who wants to know?' Had she pushed too hard? She felt the need to placate him. Rested her palm on the fly of his pants and moved it up and down against him.

'I'm just curious. It was like a cryptic cricket crossword.'

'Well, the initials are real people. Except the last ones don't mean anything. Same with the sheet of averages.'

'Like who?

Is HVS the same as HV Smith?'

'Yes.' The Gut let out a sigh. 'That feels really good.'

His stubby index finger traced her breasts. Again, the surprising delicacy. If she could just concentrate on the sensation and forget the person administering it ... is that how the sex workers did it? But that wasn't why she was here.

'If the last initial doesn't count, does that mean HV is Harry Virtue?'

'Go to the top of the class.'

'But what does the rest mean?' Her hand moved up and down along his erection again. She released the clasp at the top of his fly. His stomach spilled over and blocked her hand as she reached to unzip the rest. Her father's pot belly had been hard, a beer-built Buddha on bandy legs, but this stomach was a mass of rolling skin.

The Gut moved his hands upwards gathering Justine's dress as he did. He pulled it up and she raised her arms. He stood up to pull it off and in doing so his own trousers fell to a puddle on the floor.

THE GUTS

'Nice boxer shorts.' They were blue with pink elephants gambolling across them.

The Gut stepped out of his trousers and flicked the bra straps off her shoulder. The bra fell to the floor. 'Even nicer breasts.' His hands cupped them as if they were scales. Things were moving a bit too quickly. She stood up, using for the first time the lessons from a burlesque course she had once taken, which would necessitate an edit of her list of useless things I have done.

'And what about the cricket stuff. What does all that mean?' she asked when she felt she had wobbled her breasts enough.

'It's quite clever really. The total is how much they've paid to me; except for those with an average of 69. That means a currency of sexual or other non-monetary favours.'

'Do you mean you sleep with them?' She hadn't meant to say it.

'No, silly girl, it's more that I facilitate introductions to people who can satisfy their appetites.' He gave her a puzzled look. 'I probably shouldn't be saying all this should I?' She put her arms out from her sides, palms upwards and shrugged.

'You look like a can-can dancer,' he said. 'Anyway, where was I?'

'What about the beverages next to the averages?'

'The booze is where the money goes to. Gluhwein goes to Switzerland; Red Stripe to the Cayman Islands; Champagne is Monte Carlo; schooners is favours for favours; Tsing Tao, Hong Kong and Macau; Kingfisher, India. The bowlers are people I can blackmail. The other stuff is just notes to myself. The addresses in the other book are the account numbers. (02) Swiss, (03) Cayman (07) Tonga etc. The phone number and postcode together make up the twelve.' He gave her another puzzled look. 'Why am I telling you all this?'

Justine worried that he was falling out of his reverie. Had she spiked his drink enough? 'You tell me.' She went to him and pulled his boxer shorts down. An average sized cock followed the curve of his stomach as if it were a strut on a Chinese lantern.

The Gut's confusion at his confession was quickly replaced by lust. 'I've been thinking about you since the day you walked into my office.

Come here so I can take those knickers off and smell you.'

Justine reckoned she had enough information. It was time to leave the party. 'What's the hurry?' she smiled. 'I need some more champagne. Do you want some?' She refilled their glasses, took a gulp from hers and playfully squirted it at his face. His hand reached out to grab her but she danced away.

'What you need is a bloody good spanking.'

'Probably.' She was trying to remember where her jacket was, because the vials were in its pocket. 'But you're going to have to catch me first.'

The Gut was into the spirit. Justine evaded a second attempt to grab her and headed for the balcony in search of her jacket. She found it sitting on the chair. He was waiting for her with his belt folded in his hand when she came back in.

'What do you need that for?' he asked.

'I was worried it would get rained on.'

'It's not raining.'

He flicked at her bottom with his belt. 'Ouch!'

His third attempt to grab her was successful. In the force of his grip, her jacket slipped from her grasp and fell to the coffee table in front of the couch. To her horror, the vials slipped out of the pocket and landed on the floor.

'Well, well, well. What do we have here?' She wasn't sure if his smile was curious or suspicious. She thought of stripping off her knickers and doing another dance. But deflection of the question would be too obvious. The longer she waited to answer him, the more intense his look became. At some point if she didn't come up with something convincing, his drug fugue would stop protecting her. And if he decided to stop being nice, she wasn't sure that escape would be that easy.

'This one's liquid ecstasy and this one's an aphrodisiac. It makes your orgasm more intense. A bit like Amyl Nitrate. Sometimes it makes me see colours. Do you want to try?'

'You first.'

She picked up the vials from the coffee table. Fortunately, they weren't labelled. The SP-117 had a green lid, and the Rohypnol had

THE GUTS

a blue one. She opened the SP-117 first, sucked up some of the fluid with the dropper and took a couple of drops. She hoped she could knock the Gut out with the barbiturate before she started telling the truth herself. She passed it onto Houston. 'This one's the ecstasy.'

Houston took a couple more drops. 'I want the fuck colours too.'

Justine opened the lid and filled the dropper with Rohypnol. She passed it to the Gut. 'Don't take too much, just a couple of drops – it can get quite heavy.'

'You kids think you invented drugs.' He took the dropper and ostentatiously administered the drug. One drop, two drops. Three drops. Four drops. Twice the dose Paul had recommended. 'I'm already heavy. In almost every sense of the word. Open your mouth.'

Justine hoped there wasn't anything left in the dropper. She opened her mouth and stuck out her tongue. A drop landed and she tried to slide it off against her lips as she returned her tongue to her mouth. But she could taste the liquid and knew she hadn't been fully successful.

'One more for the road,' ordered the Gut.

'That's more than enough happiness for me,' said Justine.

'Doctor's orders. Or else, I'm going to have to spank you.'

Would it be better to be spanked while conscious rather than take the risk of falling unconscious? The Gut looked like he had the potential to get carried away. And she had no intention of letting him treat her like her namesake had been treated by the Marquis de Sade. 'Ok then.' She took the dropper and put another drop on her tongue and again slid as much as possible of the liquid off against her lips.

'I just need to go to the bathroom.' She felt his eyes on her back as she walked wearing only her undies across the carpet.

In the bathroom, Justine rinsed her mouth, hoping it might negate the effects of the drugs. She snorted another line of coke. The champagne on top of the red wine was making her woozy already. She washed her face and took a sachet of hand lotion back to the lounge room. Better to wank him off than have his tongue in her mouth again.

The Gut was lying on the couch staring at the ceiling. 'I can see what you mean by the colours.' His voice was a little slurred.

She knelt on the floor and rubbed the lotion into her hands then took a grip of his penis and began to stroke it.

'I feel purple,' said the Gut.

'I feel blue,' said Justine

'I suppose that makes us a bruise.'

She reached with her other hand and scrunched his balls until he gave a small yelp.

'Pain is green.' She stroked his penis harder.

'Yes.' His hand reached across to grab her breast but fell off it. The drugs were beginning to work.

'Yes. Oh yes, oh yes.'

She gripped his penis harder and moved her hands repeatedly over its circumcised head.

'Fuck me. Get on top of me and fuck me!'

'Don't you worry. You'll be fucked by the time I'm finished with you.' The SP-117 was affecting her level of candour, but the Gut was too far gone to question the remark.

His head was purple and his breathing laboured. He looked as if he was about to explode. Justine wondered if she was going to kill him by making him come. But then he relaxed a little. A faraway look entered his eyes and a thin spurt of semen trickled onto Justine's pumping fist.

'Amazing. Amazing. All the colours of ... all the colours of the rainbow ...' His mouth went slack and he collapsed back into the couch.

She wiped her hand on the carpet. Watched him snoring for a minute or so. He wasn't pretending. She tried to stand up. It wasn't easy. But she did it. She steadied herself by holding onto the armrest of the couch. Time to go. She stumbled around the lounge room in search of her clothes. She managed to put most of them on. She didn't quite make the door.

18

When Adam came to, he was groggy, gagged and blindfolded. His arms were tied behind the back of a metal chair. His legs tied to its legs. The cord was cutting into his skin. The air was cool and smelt of oil and brine. An object pinged metallically and was followed by a flap of wings. A warehouse of some sort, or a workshop. Big, tinny, empty.

'Fucking sky rats,' someone cursed. 'Shat on my fucking jacket.'

'Lucky it wasn't your head.' said another.

A rough hand ripped out the piece of cloth that was wedged between his teeth.

'Where am I?' he asked.

'Wag your tongue and you'll lose it, dickhead,' said the first voice.

Adam's thinking had the consistency of scrambled eggs. Whatever they'd knocked him out with had mushed his mind. He felt nauseous and his throat was parched. 'Can I have some water?'

'If you tell us what we need to know.'

'Can I go to the toilet?'

'If you're going to ask a question, put your hand up first,' his tormentor chuckled.

'Please? I'm busting.'

'No-one's stopping you, are they? So shut up before I get angry,' said the voice.

'Come on. Can't you at least get me a bucket?'

Adam felt a sharp slap to his head. His right ear rang furiously. The pain restored some clarity. He concentrated on controlling his bladder.

'Who are you working for and why am I here?' he asked.

'I'm asking the questions here and I want to know where you are getting your porkie pies from prickface.'

An enormous hand ringed Adam's neck and squeezed it till there was no hope of answering at all.

'Easy does it Bruce,' said another voice. 'Wait till we find out what they want with him. Then you can beat the shit out of him.' The second guy sounded second generation Australian. Lebanese or Greek perhaps. Bruce, however, had the accent of an original Aussie moron, the descendant of some fool, thought Adam, dumb enough to have been transported for stealing a rotten cabbage.

'Hey Benny, this is the same guy who had the cat, isn't it?' he said.

'Oh yeah! I'd forgotten about that.'

'You fucking arseholes,' Adam hissed. Another slap in the head.

'Some people never learn, do they? Sitting up there in your tower beating off into your computer, thinking you're a big cheese and all that. Bet you don't feel like a hero now, Mr Big-time newspaperman, eh?' said Bruce, with a sharp prod to his chest.

He was right. Adam didn't. He was dead-tired, groggy and angry with himself. If only he'd taken more heed of the warnings. He'd taken his middle-class comfort and professional security for granted. Too late. He couldn't afford to give up, though. Where had they taken him? The air smelt like the harbour. It still had the coolness of night. A number was punched into a mobile phone. Benny spoke.

'Yeah mate, we picked up the delivery. What do you want us to do? ... Righto ... Get him to ring before he gets here.'

The phone rang again. Benny answered. He walked away from Adam. 'I'm tied up right now ... How urgent is it? ... Where? ... The Bondi Hotel? Ok. I'll be there in half an hour.'

The Bondi Hotel shut at five a.m. Adam had left Babyface just after nine.

'Fuck me,' said Benny, 'when it rains it bloody pours. First the trip to Dorrigo, then we have to pick up this prick, now I've got to go and pick up Dick and find him a bed.

Can you look after this clown for a while by yourself?'

'Piece of cake, he's a ballerina. You aren't going to cause me any trouble are you, my pretty,' said Bruce and landed an unfriendly slap on Adam's shoulder that almost broke his collarbone.

THE GUTS

Adam cried out in pain.

'Go easy Bruce. Give him something to drink. And help him to take a piss. They want him to talk, so you don't want to fuck him up too much before they get here. OK?' The old good cop, bad cop routine, only the cops were thugs and the good thug was about to go.

'Don't want to give him the idea he's getting room service,' grumbled Bruce.

'I suppose not. But I don't want you getting too much satisfaction from your job. You're getting paid for this. Save the random violence for the weekend.'

'OK boss. And give our mate a good night kiss from me. Reckoned his shit didn't stink, the cunt. Just as well, 'cos he'll be shitting himself soon,' he chuckled. 'When will you be back?'

'As soon as I can. Now remember, be nice to our friend here, or he might start writing nasty things about you in his paper. But don't let him get too vocal. If he starts complaining, gag him. The morning shift next door starts in an hour, and we might have to keep him here for a while.'

The words gave Adam hope. He just had to hold on and maybe someone would come and rescue him. Maybe not. People tuned out whatever it was that had nothing to do with them. A guy shouting in an industrial unit was probably just an argument between two workers. Easily filtered. Whoever was next door would be unlikely to notice anything at all. Benny and Bruce's footsteps walked across the concrete floor. He heard them whispering. A door opened. Adam smelled the breeze. A door closed. A car started then drove away.

Adam homed in on his surroundings. An industrial area, somewhere near the water from the salty smell of the air. Less than half an hour from Bondi, and since there were no industrial areas left on the harbour, he reckoned he was probably somewhere near Botany Bay. Bruce came back. Boots heavy on the deck. Adam asked him again for a drink.

'First you piss and then you drink,' said Bruce. He unzipped Adams' fly and yanked out his penis. 'Shit! I didn't know they made them that small.' Adam felt something plastic, like a milk container, cover his penis.

It was better than nothing. Better than pissing his pants. He breathed in deeply and tried to urinate. Although his bladder was full, he couldn't.

'Got stage fright, have you? You might talk big in that fancy paper of yours, but when it comes to the crunch you ain't got no balls.' Bruce was the basic school bully type. Very basic. And he wasn't going to leave Adam alone. But in every bully was an insecurity. A button to push. If only he could find it. Adam's penis flopped back inside his pants.

'Give me a fucking drink!'

'Watch your fucking language!' Bruce slapped Adam across the face. His blindfold slipped with the blow, leaving his left eye covered by a single piece of cloth. Through the small holes in the material, he could make out things. Two enormous fluoro tubes hung from the ceiling. The light they cast disappeared into ink. The room was big. Definitely a factory or a warehouse. A skylight in the roof suggested the sky was turning from black to blue. The sun was on its way. He must have been out to it for hours.

Against the light was a silhouette of his captor. Bruce was built like a brick shithouse. Perhaps he should just go back to being submissive. Wait it out. But then this was probably his only chance of one on one. Even if the others who came were reasonable, he would be entirely at their mercy and by the sounds of what Benny had gone off to do, mercy wasn't in their repertoire. Adam's embarrassment at his urge, then inability to piss, made him angry. He tried to remember the moves he'd learned twenty years ago during a brief foray into karate. He imagined sticking his fingers into the hard jelly of Bruce's eyeballs. This was still his one big chance to turn his life around. He wasn't going to let this moron dictate the terms.

'You heard the boss. Get me a drink!' he shouted.

'He's not my boss. Shut the fuck up!' Bruce slapped him again then punched him in the gut. The pain trumped his stage fright. The spread of warmth down his legs was a magnificent relief soon checked by a clammy shame.

It didn't take long for Bruce to notice. 'Pissed your pants, have you? You know what happens to boys who piss their pants, don't you?' he aped. Scenarios involving urine as a conductor of electricity entered Adam's mind and he regretted all those hungover afternoons reading crime fiction on the couch.

Fortunately, Bruce wasn't a reader. The ensuing slap in the head was almost a relief. The blindfold shifted a bit more and Adam could see his assailant's face quite clearly through the gauze now only just covering his left eye. Bruce was the kind of person who made democracy seem like a backward civilisation. Adam puffed himself up with elitist contempt. The more he was convinced this guy was an animal, the better.

'Look,' he said. 'Get me a fucking drink.' Another slap. Bruce was enjoying it. Stupidity was no barrier to sadism; it merely came with a lack of imagination.

'Pleease!' he said, just to see how he'd deal with politeness.

'OK. If you want to drink something, then drink this.' Adam heard a plastic bottle being filled with liquid. Soon after, his face was drenched in piss. It stung his eyes; the acrid stench filled his nostrils. All the sophisticated soft food in his stomach surged into a projectile vomit. He covered Bruce in spew.

The red mist descended. Bruce was a fastidious idiot. 'You dirty, dirty, dirty, dirty ...' The following smack in the head was the hardest Adam had ever been hit. 'Who do you fucking think you are?' The next was even harder. Something gave way in his nose. He tasted blood where his cheeks had been slapped into his teeth. Through his stinging eyes, he saw Bruce draw his arm back and clench his fist. He wasn't going to stop, Adam reckoned. This wasn't just his last chance to turn his life around. It was his only chance. He leaned forward and ducked the blow. The unspoken rules were off. Bruce pushed Adam's head up so he could try and smash it in again, Adam moved sharply forward into Bruce's lap. He got his mouth around Bruce's dick, which had remained dangling after pissing into the bottle, and clamped down with his teeth. It was a big one. Bruce's enormous hands gripped Adam's head and tried to rip him off, but Adam kept biting down.

'Get off you cunt. Get the fuck off. I'm going to fucking kill you. Get off!' He released his grip on Adam's head and started furiously punching it. Adam had trouble holding on, but he did. Bruce kept on screaming. Adam thought of black pudding. 'Fuck! Fuck! Fuck! Fuck! Fuck!' screamed Bruce. One punch landed so hard, Adam felt his jaw had dislocated. Then a fist came down and smashed two of his teeth. Another fist. Another tooth. His bite was broken.

There was a brief lull. Adam prayed that the screaming had attracted attention. He started screaming out 'Help!'

'You cunt. You've ruined my chances of having kids.'

I'll collect my Order of Australia for services to evolution at the gate, thought Adam, surprised at his inner steel. He screamed again for help. The glint of a knife appeared in Bruce's hand. Adam screamed again. There was steel and there was steel.

'I'll fucking shut you up.' And that was the last thing he knew.

19

Justine woke up with her face in the carpet. She was lying across the hallway, a metre away from the front door. Where am I? It didn't take long to remember. Shit! She stood up and looked around to see if anyone was still there. Yes. She could hear the Gut snoring. She followed the sound into the lounge room. Her shoes and handbag were there. The sky was lightening through the balcony doors. The Gut was lying on his side, naked, fat, vulnerable. His large face was slack, its jowls had spilled into the carpet. The snores more snuffle than roar. Who was he when he was dreaming, she wondered? Flashbacks came from the night before. She wondered how it would feel to put a pillow over his head and press down. What if she squeezed the remaining barbiturate via the dropper into his anus? Maybe the snoring would stop. She remembered taking the drops on her own tongue, but it was hard to get a fix on what had happened after that. 'Had they fucked?' She put one hand between her thighs to check for residue. Nothing obvious. But the outside of her hand felt sticky. Carpet fibres had adhered to it. She looked at him on the floor, the folds of his gut and man boobs shuddered with his breath. His skin was pale and blemished with pimples and moles. How deeply unappealing. Deprived of charisma, she almost felt sorry for him. Almost. Her memory was returning. Phew! It wasn't the kind of sperm you wanted making its evolutionary gamble inside you. Mission successful! She wasn't dancing a jig, but she was looking forward to telling Paul. Her head was still woozy and she was glad she had recorded the evening's proceedings on her phone. Or she hoped she had. When she found it on the floor, its battery was dead.

Justine went to the kitchen and washed the Gut's dried come off her hands. Then it was time to leave. The front door was deadlocked though. Arsehole! She thought about climbing over the balcony to the floor below, then saw her Rohypnol assisted clumsiness splashed across the front page of *The Morning Glory* as a tragic suicide, the highly-strung political staffer who had flung herself to the ground after a night with her older lover like some troubled, young, power-dazzled Monica Lewinsky. All this ugly effort would be wasted if her crucial information didn't make it back to Paul. She tiptoed up to the Gut who was asleep on the puddle of his pants. She took one leg and began to tug. His head lifted. Her heart thumped. His eyes opened, looked around. She nodded at him. He grunted and went back to sleep. Another tug and she had his pants. The key, of the credit card variety, was in his pocket. She took it, draped her bra over his belly, and walked out the door, closing it behind her. She wanted him to wake up thinking he'd fucked her brains out. It would buy her time.

Justine found a cab at the Casino, several hundred metres down the road. It was five in the morning and there were only a few people around. She got in a taxi and directed the driver to Paul's. He came to the door in his boxer shorts and a T-Shirt with an elephant on it. 'I did it,' she told him when she was safely inside. 'I fucking did it.'

'Where is he?' asked Paul

'Sleeping it off.'

Paul's arms reached around her and drew her into a hug. Justine disengaged. 'I'm sorry, I don't feel like being touched at the moment.'

'I don't blame you. Come into the dining room and show me what you got.'

'I ended up drinking some of the drugs. My head's a bit of a blur. But it should be in the phone. Have you got a charger?'

She followed Paul down the hall to where the laptops sat banked on the dining room table. A can of baked beans with a spoon sticking out of it and a plastic bottle of coke were at one end. Paul plugged the phone into one of the computers and they waited nervously until there was sufficient charge for the screen to light up.

'Have you got the files I found at his electoral office?' asked Justine.

'Yes, they're on the table somewhere.'

THE GUTS

The phone lit up. She looked through her voice memos. The Gut's voice barked out from the phone. Justine felt dirty. Paul looked hard at his computer as the sleaze unfolded. When the talk turned to business, his fingers flew across the keyboard in transcription.

Justine busied herself with the files she had got from the suitcase. Her memory had sharpened with the sound of the Gut's voice.

When the Gut had finished his confession, Justine showed Paul how the coded cricket charts worked. As she did, Paul typed furiously into his computer. When she finished, he sent an email off.

'Actually, that's not all,' she said.

'What else, then?'

'The numbers to a series of bank accounts.'

'Awesome. Show me.'

Justine sifted through the photocopies until she found the appropriate pages. Phone numbers, plus postcodes. 'These ones convert to bank accounts.'

'Cool.'

'And now I need to take a shower,' she said.

'Of course. You know where it is.' Paul didn't look up.

She found a towel lying on his bedroom floor. It felt dry enough. The shower felt fantastic. She stayed in there until the hot water began to cool. She dried herself and rifled through Paul's clothes until she found a T-shirt that smelt almost fresh.

'What's up?' she said when she returned to the dining room. Paul was looking very pleased with himself.

'For a minute, you were a very rich woman. Until you made an offer on 100 000 hectares of Brazilian rainforest. I was thinking you might like to turn it into a conservation zone.'

'He's not going to like that.'

'No, he's not.'

'That's why you probably need these.' He handed her a passport, an air ticket, and a fat wad of traveller's cheques in US dollars.

'You're probably right.'

'I've booked you an e-ticket to Santiago with a connecting flight via Sao Paulo to Manaus. Thought you might like to explore your new dominion. There'll be someone to meet you at the airport there.'

Justine nodded her head. It seemed as good an idea as any. 'I also took the liberty of getting you some things together. It's probably not a good idea to go home. Check out the suitcase in my bedroom.'

She went and opened a small carry-on suitcase. In it were a pair of jeans, a couple of T-shirts, some swimmers, a summer dress, a cardigan and some underwear. She put the jeans on surprised at how well they fitted. Even the bra was OK. It was the first time a man had successfully bought clothes for her. She hadn't picked him as the type.

She returned to Paul. 'It might be lonely there. Do you want to come with me?'

'I'd like to ...'

Perhaps he hadn't done the shopping.

'But?'

'I can't. There's still too much to do here and I've got responsibilities to my sister's family.'

'Fair enough. Then I suppose it's **Hasta la Vista**.'

'One for the road?'

''Fraid that fat man's put me off.'

'**Hasta la Vista**, then. Thanks for putting yourself on the line. I hope you're OK.'

'It was my decision. I'll let you know whether or not I hate you when I get to Brazil.'

She looked at the ticket. 'I better go.'

'Take care,' he said. He put his hand on her shoulder and looked into her eyes.

'You too. Hope you find a way to stop being angry.'

'I hope the lovers of Latin America aren't as good as they pretend to be,' he said.

'I'll let you know.' This time they hugged. She put her hand on his cheek, looked into his eyes and kissed him on the lips goodbye.

20

Houston woke up on the lounge room floor of Harry Virtue's pad with a furry mouth and little memory of where the night had gone. He couldn't even remember the fucking. He looked at his body, blotched from the carpet. He rolled over onto his back and felt for his penis, limp below his belly. Either slugs had been crawling over it in his sleep or at some stage during the evening he had come. It was decades since his last wet dream. Then how? He sat up to inspect himself and saw the tell-tale flecks in his pubic hair. So he had. Only he couldn't remember it. But why? He hadn't drunk that much. Maybe it was the stress. Whatever it was, he couldn't remember what it had been like to be inside her for the first time. And that was a terrible shame.

His head felt like he'd been drinking for a week. Slowly he got up. His skin was itchy where it had rubbed against the shag pile. He sniffed Justine's bra where it rested on the floor. Was she still here? In a bedroom somewhere? He went to the bathroom and pissed. Checked the bedrooms. She must have already gone. He took a shower. It helped a little to freshen his head. He dried himself impatiently and returned to the living room, leaving a trail of water behind him on the carpet. It didn't matter. The cleaners would be coming. He gathered his clothes from the couch, got dressed, then checked the rooms to see if he had left anything behind. He rang Murray, who didn't answer. 'Ring me when you get this,' was the message. It was almost nine o'clock.

Having checked himself in the hall mirror and adjusted his tie, Houston left the apartment and took a lift down to the side entrance.

In the interests of discretion, he hadn't ordered the ministerial car. But there wasn't a taxi in sight. Out of desperation, he jumped on a bus that was filling with commuters at a stop. It was the first time he had been on public transport in years. Trains and buses were for people who were unable to drive, too poor to own a car, or insufficiently important to have someone drive them. He moved down towards the back of the bus and found himself a seat. The woman beside him shrank into the window side as his arse and thighs colonised the surface. She looked at him, he gave her a death-ray stare. He spread his legs, partly for steadiness but more to assert his imperialism over the warm rough cloth. His phone began to vibrate in his pocket. Murray.

'Morning boss.'

'Have you seen the paper yet?'

'No.'

'I think you better take a look. And that's not all the bad news I've got for you.'

A young woman in her twenties came down the aisle of the bus. It was Justine's friend, Sarah, who'd received a call from the airport and had waited for him to exit the building. 'Hey Minister, how's your love life?'

'As occasional as most middle-aged men who've been married for twenty-five years.'

'Not what I've heard. Was your wife with you at the Stevedore Apartments last night?'

'Who says I was there?'

'I saw you coming out this morning.'

'Breakfast meeting.'

'My friend saw you going in last night.'

'What are you trying to say?'

'That you've been using your connections with the property industry to prosecute your love life?'

The bus rounded a bend and slammed on its brakes. It lurched to a violent stop just before it rear-ended a garbage truck. Sarah grabbed a pole for support, but the sudden momentum swung her round and threw her face forward onto the Minister's lap.'

The adrenaline erased the vestiges of Houston's drug haze.

THE GUTS

'Come to my office at seven o'clock tonight and we can talk about my love life then,' he said with a sleazy smile. 'I like the cut of your blouse.'

'That's on the record.'

'Then it won't make any difference whether or not I tell you to fuck off,' he snapped.

Sarah searched for a community of outrage from her fellow commuters, but they all pretended to be busy with their phones.

'Did you hear all that?' Houston said to Murray, hoping he was still at the other end of the phone.

'Yes, I did. I don't know what to tell you Roger. It's going to get worse. The V-team have gone and done something very silly.'

'How silly?'

'I'll tell you when I see you.'

'Shit!'

'Something wrong, Minister?' asked Sarah, standing upright again as the bus moved off slowly. He ignored her.

It took him another fifteen minutes in peak hour traffic to get to town. The young journalist stood there glowering at him without attempting to interview him again. When the bus reached the QVB, he pushed past her to get off.

'If I come to your office tonight, Minister, will I get to see your boxers with the pink elephants?'

Houston turned to look at her. Said nothing. She snapped a photo of him with her phone.

He got into a vacant taxi and gave the directions to parliament. How had she known what kind of underpants he was wearing? He looked down at his trousers to find his fly undone.

The taxi drove him to the parliament Houston. He texted Murray. *I'm in the office. Come!*

While he waited for Murray, he read the paper. Osborne was smelling the smoke, but Houston didn't think he'd found the fire. Not yet. That's why he'd got them to scare him off. But what had happened last night? Benny and Bruce had only been supposed to frighten him. It had worked last time. No reason for it not to work again. From the sounds of Murray's voice, he wasn't sure he wanted to know what had happened. But here he was waiting to find out. Unable to plot his best course of action until he did. Houston hated waiting. How much easier life would be if you didn't have to deal with idiots, he thought. His years as a parliamentary representative in a democratic system had only hardened the belief. His night with Justine was puzzling him too. Something wasn't right. It wasn't just the holes in his memory. Alcohol had done that before. It was more that he wasn't feeling the afterglow. He couldn't remember the sex and his body couldn't remember it either. Which was bizarre considering how much mental effort had been consumed in its anticipation.

And what was that journalist doing on the bus? One he didn't even recognise. Of course, it was a risk to have taken Justine to dinner in the current climate. She was probably some young chancer with no job looking to impress her way to employment by breaking a big story. She must have stalked him and Justine all the way from the restaurant to the penthouse. He thought of Justine, of the sway of her hips and the lush shape of her breasts. He wasn't feeling good, but he should be, a man of his age getting it on with a girl like that. He rang her. Seeking confirmation. No answer.

Murray arrived in Lycra looking like some kind of circus seal. He was carrying two coffees, probably hoping he wasn't going to be wearing one by the time he finished talking to his boss. Houston took one. 'Thanks.' Anything to get some clarity back into his head. They went out on to the balcony to talk. 'Fucked headline,' said Murray.

'He's onto something.' Houston sipped from his coffee and gave Murray a get on with the bad news look.

'He's in intensive care.'

'Fuck! What happened?'

'Benny's been working for Ken as well. He got a call to go and pick up Mahone, who was talking too loudly at the Bondi Hotel. He left Osborne with Bruce. Bruce fucked up!'

'Big time.'

'Has it hit the press yet?'

'No, but it will.'
'Is anyone aware of our connection to these clowns?'
'I don't think so. Only us and Ken. And Dick.
'Where is Dick?'
'You don't want to know.'
'Well Ken's not going to care what happens to these idiots, is he?'
'I suppose not.'
'What's the best way to get rid of them?'

Murray hesitated. His lips pressed firmly together. Benny was his friend. Without him Murray's service offering was considerably weaker.

'It was Bruce's fuck-up. What if I get Benny to get rid of him, then make himself scarce?'

'But Osborne knows who he is.'

'I'll tell him to do it quickly.'

'Well, it's never been easy to find a careful contract killer at short notice. I suppose that's the best option we have.'

Murray looked relieved. 'I'll make the call.'

Houston's phone had been buzzing non-stop in his pocket, an unerotic insistence. The office phone was also ringing. It reminded him of the absence of Justine. Where was she? If he could only see her …

The thought was interrupted by Winston Pond barging into his office.

'Stay here, Murray.'

Pond was waving a copy of *The Morning Glory* in front of him with considerable agitation.

'I want you to tell me, Roger, that you'll be suing these bastards for defamation.'

Houston looked at him and said nothing.

Pond took a breath and lost some of the anger that had temporarily inflated him. 'Shit,' he said. 'How bad is it going to get?'

Houston looked at Pond again. He wasn't sure he could stop the story anymore. And once the news about Osborne broke, it was going to go ballistic. The best thing he could do was get the hell out of the country before the police got involved.

'Winston, I don't think you need to worry ...'

Pond looked at him with an incomprehension that segued into furious hope. They differed only in their methods, Houston thought. In an unchecked world Pond would rather execute people than stop being Premier.

'But perhaps it's time we took some precautionary measures. I know it's not ideal, but how about I stand down as Minister while there's an inquiry? There's a meeting on high-rise construction in Dubai I'd like to go to.'

'I think that's a good idea,' said the Premier.

He picked up the paper. A bad feeling was creeping up on him. He calmed the Premier with the automatic part of his mind.

'They're just fishing around. Somebody's obviously fed them a load of bullshit and they're trying to provoke a story by getting us to react. Which is why it's better if I went overseas. And if you stand me down from Cabinet, it shows you're in control.'

'I still don't like it. It worries me.'

'Winston. You and I both know you worry too much.'

The Premier gave his Minister a long look. Houston looked back. They were measuring looks, a ritual of willpower that masked the fact that the power struggle between them had been resolved long ago. Eventually Pond nodded at his technical subordinate, who nodded back.

'Thank you, Mr Premier.'

'I don't care what you have to do. Just fix it!' said Pond, who turned and left.

Houston rolled his eyes and returned to Murray on the balcony.

'Time to start packing,' he said.

'It won't be long though before your enemies are seeking him out,' said Murray.

'True. Have you seen Justine?'

'No,' said Murray, 'but she sent a text saying she wasn't feeling well, food poisoning, so she probably wasn't going to come in.'

So that was it, thought Houston. Maybe that was why he'd woken up feeling so out of it. He had a cast-iron stomach, so maybe it had affected her more than him. He made a mental note to call Fetish and abuse them.

He thought again. He'd been to the toilet this morning and his stool had been solid. Not even a hint of the squirts. He texted Justine: *You shouldn't have eaten the duck.* But maybe it was just that she was too embarrassed to show her face. It had happened before. A one-night stand closely followed by a resignation. Houston hoped not. 'I better ring Ken,' he said to Murray

Virtue's mobile didn't answer and when Houston rang Virtue's office his secretary told him that he wasn't there. Only Houston was sure that she had put him on hold and asked someone before she came back with her answer. It was the second time this had happened in a row.

After all the business they'd done together, was Ken setting him up for the fall? Was it he who had leaked Houston's whereabouts to the try-hard young journo who had accosted him on the bus.

Whatever was going on, at least he still had his money. Enough for several lifetimes in style. It was time he represented the state on some important overseas business.

'You know that Business Class ticket to Thailand you bought the other day, Murray.'

'Yeah.'

'I reckon you might want to book yourself on it today.'

'Already done, boss. Need a lift to the airport?'

Murray changed from his bicycle kit into a summer-weight suit. It was cheaper to buy clothes in Bangkok. Everything was cheaper in Bangkok. Houston had an overnight bag that he kept permanently in his office. It had come in handy after nights in Virtue's love nest. Now it was in the back of a taxi on the way to the airport. A change of clothes and a wad of cash to last him until he could access his transferred monies in Dubai. At the airport the two men separated. Murray ran to the check-in for his flight to Thailand. Houston was early for his flight. He checked in and retired to the Chairman's Lounge where he received a disturbing text from Murray: *Is Justine flying with you?*

Not that I know of. Why? But there was no reply. Presumably Murray had been told to turn off his phone for take-off. He rang Justine, but it went through to voicemail. He rang his wife. That went through to voicemail too. He told her he had gone to Dubai and would be back by the end of the week. He wondered if she might be relieved when she discovered this wasn't the case. Would he ever be able to come back? He loved Sydney. It was his city. Calls kept coming in from undisplayed numbers. He answered one. A journalist. 'Have you any comment on the story in this morning's *Glory*?'

'I will be holding a press conference later this afternoon,' he lied then hung up. He turned his phone off, ordered a wagyu burger. A cricket test from somewhere else in the world was on the television. As he watched it, he began to feel sentimental. He ordered a beer to settle the unease in his stomach. At least there weren't any pesky journalists in the Chairman's Lounge. It was relatively quiet. He nodded hello to the CEO of a mining company that had borrowed too much money. He waved at a Supreme Court Judge who was talking to a beautiful supermodel, the latest to emerge from the quarter acre blocks of Australian suburbia and add their lustre to a range of international products. Houston couldn't remember her name. Those women were a little too manufactured for his taste. There were a couple of Asian businessmen, the rest were staff, patiently waiting to serve the uber-important. Usually the cricket bored him, but as he reclined in one of the club chairs, he was reminded of the long-ago days of his childhood when his father, a Methodist Minister, and he would sometimes sit on the back verandah of the family home and listen to the cricket on the radio. It was one of the sounds of his past, like cicadas and the bell next to their front door, which constantly rang with parishioners who'd be seen by his mother into the study where his father would listen to their crises and offer whatever sagacity he had. They were dead now. His father had died when he was 24. They were never close. He was building his first block of units and his mother had come to the site to tell him. Once the shock had worn off, the feeling he remembered was freedom. His father had been like some kind

THE GUTS

of moral abacus, he looked at you and measured the quality of your soul; it was hard to get into the swing of the way things were really done when you were burdened with a constraint like that. His mother was different. She'd gotten dementia 15 years later. She was a grandmother by then. Blissfully ignorant of her son's approach to public life. His success was her most prized possession. Houston had some money and was able to put her into the best care there was. He hated seeing her decline to the extent where they had to put thickener in her water just so she could drink it without choking. When she died, it had been a relief too. He thought about his mother often. She'd spent her life being good, but she hadn't really lived. Unlike her son. He had lived with enough appetite for all of them. Still, he was glad she wasn't around to read this latest instalment in his career.

He was thinking about his mother and watching off-spin bowling when they came for him, just before the lunchbreak and a mere fifteen minutes before he was due to board his flight. A discreet and beautiful concierge approached him first. 'Excuse me, sir. There's a lady and a gentleman to see you outside.'

'Who are they? If they're journalists, tell them I'm not commenting upon anything at this point in time.'

'They're not journalists, sir.'

'Then who are they? Tell them to go away.'

'They're police.'

Houston looked at her and couldn't help peeking through to the black bra between the buttons on her blouse. She smelt of musk. He shrugged his shoulders and prepared himself for the bluff. 'Tell them, I'll be right with them.'

He wheeled his case with his suit jacket folded over his arm towards the door to the lounge. At the concierge desk were a woman and a man. Houston was relieved they weren't in uniform.

'Sir, I'm afraid you'll have to come with us. We need to ask you some questions.'

21

Adam woke up in hospital in the company of machines. He was high on morphine. His face was bandaged everywhere except for his eyes and the holes that made way for the tubes. The dope blocked out most of the pain. But as the grogginess wore off, he became increasingly aware of an absence. A clumsiness in his mouth, as if he'd been in a dentist's chair for a week. It took him a while to work out what it was. And he didn't like when he did. When the nurse came in and he tried to speak, the gargle that followed confirmed his suspicion that he no longer had all of his tongue.

Kate came several hours later and when he saw her, he cried. She stroked his head and told him everything was going to be OK. She was crying too. When she left, he curled up into a ball and prayed for the chance to die.

If someone's conscience hadn't got the better of them, he may well have. At 5am, a 000 call from a worker at the Lucky Shell Seafood Import/Export Pty Ltd had reported hearing screaming in a Matraville warehouse. When the police arrived, siren blazing, they found Adam tied to a toppled chair and lying in a pool of blood. A suspect was hobbling from the premises, but the cops were too concerned about giving first aid to Adam to give chase. A minute or so later they heard a car start and drive off at pace. They weren't to know that the blood Adam was lying in was largely not his own. Nor were they to know that the veins in the tongue are peripheral. Unless you are a haemophiliac, having your tongue chopped off is unlikely to kill you. It was Bruce who was at greater risk of bleeding to death. But he had run away, if running was what you could call it. The police called an ambulance and staunched

Adam's wound by filling his mouth with a bandage and getting him to breathe through his nose.

Twenty minutes later Adam had arrived in the emergency ward of the Prince of Wales Hospital, which was just as well since Bruce's kicks and punches had ruptured his spleen, dislocated his right collarbone, broken three of his ribs and given him a dangerous case of concussion. The doctors knocked him out while they went about their business of making emergency repairs.

The forensic squad had located his missing tongue and a chunk of penis on the warehouse floor. They had packed the excised organ parts in an esky and taken it to the hospital. The microsurgeons did their best but were unable to sew the tongue back on. It had been too long in the wild. Bruce never showed up to collect his missing bit.

He had managed to sever a third of Adam's tongue. No mean feat according to the surgeons, since only the front third was visible to the naked eye. They had reconstructed it as best as they could, which meant that with the right therapy he would be able to swallow safely and eat through his mouth rather than through a tube into his stomach. With intensive speech therapy, it would mean he would be able to talk too, although it was going to take time. In the first weeks after, as Adam lay in hospital recuperating, a stream of doctors came through with paddlepop sticks that they poked in Adam's mouth.

Of course it was in the papers. And on the television news. Adam had been in an induced coma when Houston was arrested at the airport. But he was awake when he was remanded in custody as a flight risk. Colleagues dropped in to congratulate him. But they mostly only came once. The talk was as awkward as the silence. Only his cartoonist mate Bob remained constant, every second day or so he'd rock up with the cryptic crossword and they'd sit there and do it together. On the weekends, he dropped in too to watch some sport and drink an illicit beer or two. Fluids he could mostly cope with.

Kate was in and out each day too. Her worst fears had come true. She dealt with the doctors who seemed to think that Adam's sudden inability to speak was a kind of retardation. She managed the stream of visitors so that Adam got the chance to rest. She primed him for the enormous effort of the speech therapy.

Her work remained busy, however, and Adam was often left alone to think upon his fate. Like anyone, he had taken his tongue for granted until he lost it. He now knew what a difficult thing it was to lose. It was difficult to move food from the front to the back of his mouth. After chewing, he found it hard to swallow. When the food got to the back of his mouth, there was a risk of the gagging reflex being activated and he was in danger of choking himself to death. His nutrition now came to him through a stomach tube. But the doctors thought that this might change.

Where people who lost their arms and legs got phantom limbs, Adam got phantom tastes. Lying in his hospital bed reading a crime novel he'd be assailed by the memory of his favourite dishes: Lamb Rogan Josh, Miso Ramen, or Salt and Pepper Squid.

When the stream of surgeons was replaced by psychiatrists gently mouthing slogans such as adapting to change, and speech therapists who sat there patiently while he mangled the English language, Adam knew it was time to go home. But what was going to happen between him and Kate when he did? Frightened by the idea of it and unable to express himself in the way he was used to, he stalled his departure from the hospital until he was physically strong enough to swim. Getting back into the water was the one thing he thought he could look forward to.

Jack Vines had been in to offer his support. The story had been taken up by others in his absence. Someone called Sarah Bishop had picked up the story for *The Chronicle*. But it was *The Glory* who had broken it. Circulation was up as a result. Vines had gambled right. And now he was munificent in his victory. 'Don't worry Adam, we've got you covered. We'll work something out when you get well.'

The house hadn't changed. All his notes were sprawled across the study. Kate arranged for someone from the police to pick them up. Everything was evidence now. But there was no need to be scared. Benny had been arrested and Bruce seemed to have vanished into thin air. Houston was on remand. Dick Mahone had been found floating in Botany Bay. Sir Julian Circle had chosen that moment to retire from the Chairmanship of the company that published *The Morning Glory* and move to the Bahamas.

At first it was good to be home. To lie on the couch and watch the cricket or listen to music. Or walk down to the beach on a summer's morning and go for a swim. As long as he didn't have to open his mouth, no one would notice he was damaged. He shopped in the supermarket, bought a coffee machine for home. Kate even made love to him. She kissed his wounded mouth and encouraged him to kiss her back then she climbed on top of him and rode him gently until he came.

But before long though the goodwill of glad to be home began to wear off. He fell into a deep funk. It was foolish, but only natural that he started to take it out on Kate. While the Crown put together its case against Houston and the V-team, the media moved onto other stories. Adam became a demanding convalescent, complaining when his meals weren't blended, sulking when she went to work. If she went out in the evening, he would send her jealous texts. *Who are you with? When will you be home?*

Kate tolerated it in the beginning, but inevitably things came to a head. Placating Adam's anger only provoked him to greater obnoxity as the growing awareness of the permanence of his loss caused him to slide into the depths of self-pity. The nicer she was, the worse he behaved. 'Maake meee shome shoup,' he'd shout, as she walked in the door after a long day at work. He would fly into incoherent rage when she couldn't understand what he was saying. Despite his efforts with the speech therapist and Kate's attempts to understand, it wasn't easy and their conversations increasingly occurred via text even when they were sitting in the same room.

About the only time Adam didn't complain was when he was asleep, something he did a lot of as a means of avoiding reality. Occasionally she'd ask him to do things for her while she was at work. He never did. *My arm was hurting,* he'd text her, when asked where the dry-cleaning was. One Sunday afternoon, with a Rugby League pre-season game on

THE GUTS

the telly, she emerged from the bedroom for the second time in a year with a suitcase.

'Whearere aare ouu 'oing?' he asked. Consonants were more difficult than vowels.

'I'm leaving.'

'Why?'

'Because this is impossible.'

'Youu jusht want to ummmp mee cause aiiim a cwipple,' he said, gesticulating furiously as she read the text.

'If you hadn't gotten injured, I would have been long gone by now.' she replied, bristling at the accusation of selfishness. 'I've been thinking of doing it ever since you got yourself into this stupid mess. I warned you about all this. But you couldn't see it. You were blind because of your ego and suckered because of it.'

''hat's no fhair,' he said.

She ignored him. 'I didn't just go to Gina's because I was afraid. I went because I needed somewhere to think where my judgement wouldn't be clouded by habit.'

'Youu 'an't 'eave me,' he said. 'I 'eed youu

'No you don't. I can't help you anymore. You're just using me as an excuse not to get better.'

It was true. ''ere are youu 'oing?'

'I'm flying to Italy tomorrow. For two months. I can't bear it anymore.' She was crying. 'You can stay in the flat until I come back, and we can sort something out after that.'

''ut youu can't oo iss oo mee.'

'I didn't. You did this to yourself.'

22

'Don't you know who I am?' barked the Gut at the two policemen who had escorted him out of the airport.

He was sitting in the back of a Commodore headed into town. Lucky, he supposed, not to be in the back of a paddy wagon. 'Of course, we do, sir,' replied the male policeman, while his colleague drove the car.

'What are your names again?'

'Constable Lloyd,' said the male. 'And she's Senior Constable Beresford.'

'Well then you better be sure what you're doing, don't you reckon? It's very hot in Wilcannia at this time of year.'

Houston looked into the mirror and saw the worry on their faces.

'Just obeying orders, sir.'

'We could have cuffed you, but we didn't,' said the driver. That much was true. Perhaps he'd get them transferred to Molong instead.

The rest of the trip was silent except for the sound of the static coming from the police radio. As they drove towards the Goulburn Street complex that housed Police Headquarters, Senior Constable Beresford said 'You might want to put that jacket over your head. The media are waiting.'

And there they were. A scrum of the nosy scum. Waiting to surround the car and take his picture. Fuck that! Putting the jacket over his head was the gambit of a guilty man and he didn't give a shit. He met the flashes of the photographers as if he was in the ministerial vehicle on the way to meet the queen.

They drove into the Goulburn St police complex and parked underground. Houston followed the two officers to a lift. The door opened and he was ushered down a corridor and into a room and invited to sit down.

'What am I doing here?' he asked the tall man in a suit who was sitting at the other side of the table from him.

'Detective Chief Superintendent McCook. I'm sorry, Mr Houston, but we have some questions for you.'

Houston took the measure of his adversary. Were they on a fishing expedition or did they already know? Superintendent McCook looked a little too relaxed for his liking. 'Where's the Minister? Where's Darren Bailey?' he said to McCook. Houston knew that Bailey's son Gill had a drug problem.

'As far away from here as he can get, I would imagine,' replied McCook with the weariness of the underling used to dealing with the caprices of incompetent superiors. And he was probably right, thought Houston. Bailey had been in the Upper House for too many years to have a work ethic.

'I'm not going to answer any questions until my lawyer gets here.'

Superintendent McCook picked up the phone that was sitting on his side of the table. 'Why don't you make that call?'

'Don't worry I'll use my own.' He pulled his phone from his jacket pocket and scrolled through his address book until he found the number for Harry Phillips then dialled.

'Hello, Roger. I've just seen you on the television. I was wondering if you'd call.'

'I'm down at Goulburn Street. Can you come?'

'Be there in twenty minutes. You know the drill. Don't say anything until I get there.'

'Sure. Bye.'

'He'll be here in 20 minutes,' said Houston to McCook, who nodded in response. Harry would sort it out. He knew both sides of the law equally well. The best that money could buy. Harry knew how to buy things that weren't supposed to be bought.

Houston took the opportunity to play with his phone. He surfed the newspaper websites to see what was being reported. There was the news of the attack on Osborne. There were the pictures of him just thirty minutes ago arriving at the police station. *Minister taken in for questioning over development corruption – more to come.*

Harry arrived and the questioning began. McCook showed Houston the sheets of paper he had kept in the Stanley Stamford in the electoral office. His face went red when he saw them. 'How did you get your hands on that?'

'I'll be asking the questions, thank you, Minister.'

It all began to make a bit more sense. Justine at the airport, the sex he couldn't remember. No fool like an old fool.

'Do you mind if I confer with my legal advisor?' he asked McCook.

'Interview suspended at 3.05pm. Fine with me. Looks like you'll be overnighting with us anyway. Bit late now to get a bail hearing for the day.'

'You've got to be joking,' said Harry, with his best feigned exasperation. 'This is a Minister of the Crown you're talking about. Don't tell me you're going to refuse bail.'

'A Minister we've just picked up as he was about to flee the country.'

'I was going to Dubai on government business,' said Houston. 'You can check it out with the Premier. He's the one who asked me to go.'

'We did,' replied McCook. 'He said he didn't know anything about it.'

Fuck! thought Houston. Pond was a rat. He was a ship. Who else?

'Are you going to charge him?'

'Yes, we are going to charge him. With misconduct in public office and conspiracy. We're also going to charge him as an accessory after the fact to grievous bodily harm and murder.'

'Who got murdered?'

'For the murder of Richard Mahone.'

'I don't know anything about that.'

'We're refusing bail. You can sort it out with the magistrate.'

McCook left the room.

'Do you think they're listening?'

'No. It's illegal. But they're probably watching,' said Phillips, pointing to a camera in the ceiling. 'Not least to make sure you don't try and top yourself. If we turn around this way and whisper, they won't be able to work out what we're saying even if they do decide to eavesdrop.'

'How bad do you reckon it is?' asked Houston.

'Not good.'

'How much bail do you think they'll want?'

'Maybe a mill.'

'Shit!'

'Problem?'

'No, but I'm going to have to move stuff back from offshore.'

'So, you had some idea this was going to happen.'

'I knew it was a risk.'

'You should have told me earlier.'

It was true, thought Houston. Why hadn't he? 'You can get the money from the following accounts. Can I trust you to do that?'

'Sure.'

Houston took out his phone and scrolled through his contacts. He stopped at a number. 'This one. And this one. Take my phone with you. That should do the trick.'

'Are they serious about keeping me in tonight?'

'I'm afraid so. Nonetheless, I'm going to insist on an immediate bail hearing.'

Phillips went to the door of the interview room and knocked. Superintendent McCook returned. He conferred briefly with Phillips who left the room. McCook said to Houston, 'You're proving very cagey for someone who doesn't have anything to hide.'

'You're being very bold for someone whose career has just gone down the toilet.'

'I can tell you Minister, there are places I would rather be. I imagine you might be thinking the same. Long Bay and Silverwater are two of the only places left in Sydney where they don't serve espresso. Now, do you know these people at all?' McCook showed him a picture of Murray, Benny and Bruce. 'That's my advisor, Murray Lime.'

'Do you know the other two?'

'Not sure. One might be a friend of Murray's, the other I'm not sure.'

'Are you sure you're not sure?'

It was time, Houston realised, to shut up. 'I don't recall.'

THE GUTS

'You don't recall what?'
'I can't remember.'
'What is it you can't remember?'
'I don't recall.'

Nothing further was said. Around an hour later, there was a knock on the door. It was Phillips. 'Gentlemen! Bail hearing in two hours. I need to confer with my client.'

McCook shook his head. He and his confederate left the room.

'We've got a problem,' said Harry.

'Tell me the bleeding obvious, won't you Harry.'

'Those accounts you gave me are empty.'

'Bullshit. I only put the money in them the other day.'

'It seems there was a transfer around five am this morning. To Brazil.'

'Fuck!' Houston was really worried now. The awful idea came to him that Brazil might have been Justine's destination. What had happened last night? A honey trap and grand larceny. It was Justine they should be charging. Not only had she stolen from him, but she'd dobbed him in as well. He should have known it. Why would a young woman that spectacular be interested in him? He'd let himself become the Geoffrey Edelsten of Australian politics. Only Justine was smart. She'd taken his money without having to swan around on his arm with her tits busting out of her dress. Bitch! Less than 24 hours ago he was naked in a penthouse apartment, champagne in hand and a belly fully of haute cuisine about to sleep with someone who *Penthouse* would have put on its cover. And now here he was. In a windowless room in a police station contemplating the end of life as he knew it.

'This is going to be expensive, Roger.' said Phillips. 'Can you afford it? You need to think of what is going to happen after ...'

'After what?'

'After your troubles have passed. You need to think about how you are going to make a living.'

'But there are millions stashed away.' Or were there? Houston saw his own doubt reflected in Phillips's face. 'You can take the money in my luggage for starters.'

'Evidence I'm afraid.'
'Have you spoken to Murray?'
'Briefly. He won't be coming back.'
'Where is he?'
'He made his plane.'
'Lucky prick!'
'Don't worry about the money Harry. It will be OK. You will be looked after as long as you don't remember who your friends are.'

'Sure.' He hoped it wasn't going to come to that. If he got bail, he could fly to Darwin in a light plane then sneak across to Indonesia by boat. And once he got there, with his Dominican Republic passport, he could go anywhere. Put a posse together and try and track down that little strumpet in Brazil. And if they tracked him down, he could always buy a doctor to keep him sick enough to declare him too ill to travel. Just like Christopher Skase had. The only problem was that his Dominican Republic passport was with his cash in the carry-on bag that had been retained for evidence. Fuck!

McCook and another policeman arrived and said they were going to formally charge him before they took him to court. They went upstairs to the reception area. They took his wallet and keys and made him empty his pockets

'Where's the phone?' asked McCook.
'It's with me,' said Phillips. 'I took it back to my office.'
'We'll need that back I'm afraid. For evidence.'

'I'll drop it in tomorrow,' said Phillips. He gave Houston a barely perceptible nod. Thank Christ for dodgy lawyers thought Houston. They took his fingerprints and photo. Asked if they could swab for DNA. With Harry beside him, Houston complied. He didn't like this powerlessness. He wanted to break out and abuse them. He would punish them when he got the chance. Badly. Just as he had punished anyone who had crossed him in the past. For a man unable to recall anything, he had a very long memory. You didn't mess with Roger Houston and get away with it. McCook produced a set of handcuffs and motioned for him to put out his arms.

THE GUTS

'Surely that won't be necessary,' said Phillips.

'Boss's orders.'

'I'll see you there Roger,' said Harry.

The police led Houston to the lift and down to the carpark. They put him in a car. Some photographers were waiting at the exit. But not nearly as many as were milling around the court when they arrived some ten minutes later. They drove around the waiting throng and went in the back way.

He waited for half an hour in a cell with a man who had beaten his wife to death before two different police came and brought him into the court. The police made their case for refusing bail. He was a flight risk and likely to interfere with witnesses. Harry made his case. An important member of the community, who would be vigorously fighting the charges, the damage already done to his public reputation. The magistrate seemed sympathetic. A member of the elite with empathy for his own. Until the police played their trump card and produced the passport to the Dominican Republic. At which point the magistrate began to think of how his own career would look if he allowed the minister bail against the strong protestations of the police, and Houston did skip the country.

'These are very serious charges and have consequences for the public trust in the governance of this state. Given the evidence provided by the police, it would seem that you are at serious risk of absconding from this jurisdiction. I remand you in custody until your hearing to be determined at a later date.'

'Don't worry Roger, I'll appeal it. Just sit tight and we should be able to get you home with a bracelet around your leg.'

It was then that he remembered. He had forgotten to ring his wife.

23

The man at Immigration looked at her passport photo, then looked at her, then handed her passport back. 'Welcome home!'

'Thanks.' It had been almost two years. She passed through the Customs 'nothing to declare line', strolled through the door and down the ramp to the arrivals hall.

Sarah was coming to meet her. Thanks to Justine, and her information about the Gut, Sarah now had a job on *The Chronicle*. She was late. Justine soaked in the air. A sea breeze spiced with Avgas was blowing in off Botany Bay. She took in the diversity of all the people gathered in anticipation of their reconnections. Was it possible that society could even cater to the needs of all of them? Airports always heightened her sense of humanity.

Two years ago, she had caught a taxi from Paul's to the airport and checked in. Still groggy from the Rohypnol the night before, her anxiety levels had peaked when she spotted Houston's advisor, Murray Lime, on the travelator in front of her. She had just misappropriated about 10 million dollars of the Gut's ill-gotten gains. In South American, they wouldn't bother with the niceties of arrest.

While she waited for the plane, she had logged in and seen the news of Houston's arrest. There was a text from Paul confirming it. Sarah had picked up the story. It was horrible to read what had happened to Adam Osborne. Giving a hand job to a sleazy old man was nothing compared to losing your tongue. Maybe she had been lucky. Lucky not to have fallen from the balcony perhaps. *Tragic End to Highly Strung Political Staffer.* She had boarded the plane half-expecting to be hauled off it. When it finally departed, and the seatbelt signs were off, she ordered a glass of champagne.

In Santiago, she learned that Houston had been denied bail. She took the connecting flight Paul had booked for her to Sao Paulo. From there she took another flight to Manaus. A surprise awaited her when she landed. Parker. In a T-shirt, jeans and thongs, handsome in a slightly gawky way, holding a sign with her name written on it. She looked around for signs of the police. Only a couple of sleepy Brazilians with their machine guns slung over their shoulders. Her fears of an Interpol intervention and extradition subsided. She approached him cautiously nonetheless. What was he doing here? What did he want with her? Was he an emissary from the lost tribe of NSW politics, some modern refiguring of the Paraguayan experiment coming to claim her.

'Welcome to Amazonas,' he said. The penny dropped. Paul hadn't been working alone. Parker's disappearance had been a deliberate trigger. The hair on the back of her neck stood up. A fierce alertness trumped her jetlag. What did they want her to do next? Who did they want her to do next? Did they want her to become a swallow? They could think again. She wanted nothing more to do with these party animals. She had done her bit. Her role in the Gut's demise was an episode in her life she didn't want to be defined by. Parker was stubbled and his skin was creased by the sun. His hair was an unparliamentary struggle. The crinkles on the sides of his eyes made her think of wisdom. He looked younger than his 48 years. Almost good looking.

'Why are you here?' she asked.

'I've come to pick you up and show you to your new estate. I think you'll be impressed.'

Justine struggled to comprehend how all this had happened so quickly, but then it dawned on her. Paul and Parker and whoever else they worked with had been planning this for some time. Parker had been in parliament for more than a decade. It was ten years since Paul's sister had lost her child after her husband was transferred by the Gut to Bourke. Her role with the Gut was the end game of a much longer project.

Outside the airport the heat and humidity hit. Parker hailed a taxi and gave the driver directions in Portuguese. Manaus was larger than

THE GUTS

she expected. More concrete than tropical jungle. Skyscrapers competed with Portuguese colonial architecture from the golden days of rubber. About 20 minutes later they arrived at the port. It wasn't the Amazon but its tributary the Rio Negro, a black river from the tree tannins it picked up on its way from the Andes. The river was huge, for an Australian it was almost unbelievable so much water could exist this far from the coast. Along the banks there were cranes loading Panamax cargo ships. Large cruise liners waited for complements of Americans in loud shirts to arrive. Smaller wooden cruise boats, colourful and stocky, sat on the water like large multi-layered cakes. They drove along the docks for several minutes weaving through cars and lorries.

'It's busy. The river is still the main means of transportation here,' said Parker as if he had guessed her thinking.

They parked near a smaller dock. Parker took Justine's bag and she followed him down to a jetty to where several boats were moored. They boarded a timber cruiser. Parker led her down through the galley to the front of the boat where there were several cabins. He opened a door and showed her in.

'You must be tired.'

'Where are we going?'

'First to the meeting of the waters, then we'll leave this river and take the Amazon upstream as far as the Purus. There's plenty of time for sightseeing. We'll be on the boat for about three days.'

'You're not going to feed me to the piranhas while I'm sleeping, are you?'

'No, but if Paolo has any say in it, we'll be eating them for dinner.'

She had so many questions to ask. But she had been operating on hyper-alert for almost 72 hours and now she could hardly keep her eyes open. She nodded and Parker left the cabin. She lay down on the bed and was gone before she knew it.

When she woke up it was dark. In Sydney it was ten in the morning, a sleep in. Here it was seven in the evening. She smelled barbecue, changed her clothes and went upstairs. Parker and Paolo, who she presumed was the captain, were waiting for her on deck and handed her a glass of red wine. Steaks were cooking and there were vegetables and rice. She was hungry.

They ate in silence and when Paolo drew up the anchor and returned to the helm, Justine and Parker sat in the moonlight.

'You didn't just come to chaperone me. Why are you really here?' she asked, emboldened by the wine.

'Because I choose to be.'

'Houston was raving and ranting about you. He didn't understand why.'

'Sometimes you have to make a stand. I was never a particularly ambitious politician. Believe or not I got involved in politics because I wanted to make a difference. And you can. In all sorts of small ways mostly. Getting government funding for the community. Trying to preserve the environment. Solving problems for people. But then it got to the point where our government got so bad that anything good I did seemed irrelevant. The greatest good was for our government to lose and for its inner workings to become public. When it was suggested that I could help achieve that simply by disappearing and doing what I love, it was a no-brainer.'

'What do you mean, doing what you love?'

'It's a long story, but my real passion is not so much for people but for butterflies and the Amazon is full of them.'

Justine cocked an eye and examined Parker for veracity. He wasn't joking.

'I studied entomology at uni, but my family had no money, and I wasn't confident it could supply me with a living, so I became a lawyer instead.' He shrugged his shoulders as if in acknowledgement of his folly. 'I've been coming here for a few years now. Every chance I get. It's where I met Oruga. She's Brazilian Japanese.'

'Is she interested in butterflies too?'

'No, she prefers the grubs.'

'How do you know Paul?' She thought of him with his computers and processed food, his house under the flight path. He would have hated the Amazon.

THE GUTS

'I can't say. That secrecy kept us safe. There's no need to undermine it now. I suggest you do the same. Remember what happened to Monica Lewinsky?'

Justine wondered how she would be portrayed if the press did find out what happened. She breathed in a sigh of relief. He wasn't going to try and convince her to do it again.

They travelled up the yellow waters of the Amazon then down one of its tributaries, the Purus. More than two days later they turned again into a smaller river and soon after that they anchored then went ashore in a tinny.

'This is it,' said Parker. 'Thanks to our mutual friend's kind donation we've liberated it from some cattle ranchers, who never quite made a go of it. We're going through the process of registering it as an ecological reserve.'

A few huts were clustered around a larger hut. 'How big is it?' she asked.

'Enormous,' said Parker. 'We're going on an expedition tomorrow and it will take us a few weeks. You're welcome to come with us if you like.'

Chasing butterflies through the jungle wasn't her kind of adventure. 'I might stay here and chill.'

And so she did. Off grid. Offline. Nothing very much to do. Nowhere for her to escape to. There were fish, turtles and dolphins in the river and half of the world's remaining biodiversity in the jungle, but unless she became some kind of scientist there was nothing for her to do. She didn't have the patience for science. She stayed until Parker and his Oruga returned. There was tension. Oruga was leaving to do a Ph.D. in Japan. Justine liked looking at Parker with his shirt off, his body brown and a little scrawny, his eyes alive with fascination for the contents of the jungle. She realised she was looking at a man who had found his home. But the more she saw that, the more she knew she hadn't. The Amazon Basin, for all its vastness, was claustrophobic, too far away from the sea. She left with Oruga for Manaus, then took a boat up the Amazon to Iquitos in Peru, a city of 400 000 people that couldn't be reached by road.

Thousands of emails were waiting in her inbox, the most interesting ones from Paul. She learned that Houston's arrest and Parker's continued absence had flipped the balance in parliament. A vote of no confidence had brought the Pond government down. The opposition had won in a landslide while Houston was still on remand. There were speeches about reforming the way that government was done in New South Wales. Two months later a Minister in the new government had resigned because of work he had done on behalf of a property developer. None of the businessmen Houston had been involved with were ever charged.

The prosecution had subpoenaed her as a witness. But they hadn't known where she was. There were emails detailing her obligations under the law and emails from Paul recommending she stay away.

She was in Buenos Aires, a place where you could find grace in sadness, when Houston went on trial. They hadn't needed her. One of the thugs had rolled and implicated him in the kidnapping and assault of Osborne. The guilty verdict was unanimous. There was surprise when Houston was sentenced to 12 years. His refusal to name his confederates went against him, as did the severity of public feeling. They were sick of politicians treating public life as a buffet. At the sentencing hearing his defence had talked of the fall from grace, the shame, the fact that it would be harder for him in jail than it was for normal people, but the judge invoked the importance of deterrence in her decision to impose a sentence at the upper limit. It was essential that justice was done and seen to be done, especially when it came to the abuse of public position. His reputation as a sleaze didn't help him. His chances of rehabilitation were poor given the Minister was unlikely ever to hold a position of public office again and he had refused to cooperate with the authorities. Nor had he offered any restitution of his ill-gotten gains. No one believed his claim that he had been robbed of them.

Justine travelled. Argentina, Colombia, Cuba, Mexico, The United States, where she was amazed to see how many poor people lived in the richest country in the world.

THE GUTS

It was where Australia was heading and it made her sad. The erosion of the egalitarian ideal. It might only ever have been a fiction, but it was a fiction capable of shaping the way people treated each other. A goal.

She spilled her coffee all over the table of a New York diner when she opened the online *Glory* to see the headline: *Houston does a Hutchence*, how he'd died as the suspected consequence of an over-enthusiastic pursuit of auto-erotic asphyxiation in Cessnock Jail.

According to Paul, there were rumours Houston had tried to truncate his sentence by becoming an informer. That the knowledge which served him so well for so long had made him too great a liability. Or perhaps he was simply a man who came as he went. Justine knew the insistence of his libido. And unlike some of the South American countries she'd been in, where prisoners of a certain standing could 'rent' an apartment-cell and install their mistresses, the opportunities for its expression in Cessnock Jail were limited.

The coronial inquiry was inconclusive. It didn't matter to her that much. With the Gut gone, it was safe to go back.

Sarah arrived flustered and apologetic. They battled the Sydney traffic back to Manly where Sarah was now living. It was a beautiful day and Justine headed straight down to the beach for a ritual cleansing in the surf. Sydney, she loved it, and she hated it, but however she felt about it, it was under her skin. Every time she left it, she ended up coming back. The beach was one of the best parts of it. In the water it felt like time was melting. Out the back, floating between the sets, an idea began to form of how she would spend the rest of Houston's money. This time, she hoped, she wasn't going to get bored.

24

He had been a dickhead and Kate had the right to be angry with him. She'd stuck by him in the hospital and stayed around to help him get back on his feet and he'd been a dickhead. Now she was gone.

Adam's injury finished his career as a food critic. What tasted good to him, no longer corresponded with what tasted good to other people. The injury also meant the end of his career as an investigative journalist. It was hard to get information out of people if they no longer understood the questions you were asking. Email was no substitute for the nuanced interrogative pressure of conversation, in person or on the phone. And people with their reputations or freedom on the line were usually indifferent to the disability provisions of the Anti-Discrimination Act.

In the lonely nights after her departure Adam sometimes wished he was more like Kate, a pragmatist, able to live in the world and enjoy it for what it was. Sydney's ethics were epicurean, based on the senses. If Adam could have accepted that, then he could have slotted into a comfortable niche and led a good life, a privileged life marked by the luck of being born Australian with his intelligence and level of education. But he had a bee in his bonnet, as his mother might have said, or was it ants in his pants, and no matter how much and how often he tried to tranquilise himself, some insect was always bothering away at him. Perhaps happiness was not for him. In the long aftermath of his great scoop, Adam fantasised about the glory that had never really arrived. But perhaps it had, and he'd missed it because he'd anticipated it would be so much more.

Even the satisfaction of discovering how the puzzle had been put together felt anti-climactic. A month or so after his return from hospital, he received a visit from Sarah Bishop, the journalist who'd been running stories about the case in *The Chronicle*. Off the record and for the vault, she told him, it was one of Houston's staffers who had leaked to her and that the staffer was in league with a hacker. They'd ganged up on Houston and done him like a dinner. He described the young woman who'd been lunching with Houston at Dosh. His type, Sarah had said, but the way she moved her eyes told him it was more than that. The headline *Houston Honey-Trapped* flashed across his brain. But he wasn't going to be able to write the story.

The paper, needing heroes in a time of declining fortunes, was good to him. He came back to work to find himself the recipient of a two-grade pay rise. They let him work from home. The workload was so light he was forced to describe himself as a columnist on his tax return. In addition to a weekly column on politics he did bits of TV, book and music reviewing too.

It was inevitable though that Jack Vines would find some way to monetise him. And given the largesse, he couldn't really refuse when he was asked to appear in a series of TV commercials for the paper.

"ometimes 'er 'ruth is ard oo unnerand,' Adam muttered in his unique dialect assisted by sub-titles against a mugshot of Houston and footage of him at work in the parliament's bearpit. 'ut oo can 'rust *The Morning Glory* oo bwing er har' news oo you ... and everything you need to make the most of Sydney life,' interrupted the voice of a bright young fashionable woman, thankfully not Ingrid, as the ad moved into selling the paper's lifestyle sections. He'd gotten his moment of TV fame in the end. But Kate was away and there was no one else with whom to share the irony of it all.

Work colleagues with whom he'd been having easy-going conversations for years avoided him in the corridors now, embarrassed by the mangled sounds coming out of his mouth, ashamed because they were. More and more Adam preferred staying home alone, communicating by email and text where he was still able to make his point with poise. If he submitted his work, the paper didn't really care where he was.

THE GUTS

As his solitude grew, it became harder and harder to move. He abandoned the marital bed and slept on the day bed in the lounge room. It became his office too, reading books, watching TV shows, typing on his laptop. The bathroom, lounge room and kitchen became the only three rooms he used. The TV came on earlier and earlier, as were his trips to the beer fridge. With the curtains closed to cut the reflection on the idiot box, Adam bunkered down in semi-darkness binging on Netflix and chasing sporting events from round the globe. Most of the time he could tell himself it was work. He stopped his swims. He drove to the Gap and watched. He googled the fatal doses of pills.

The more his life became an interaction with the screen, the more his dreams invaded his days. Flashbacks came without warning, bursts of narrative that overruled his thoughts and boiled his blood as he segued from memory to intense fantasies of violent recrimination. His grief and anger were so horribly intertwined that it was impossible to have one without the other. One minute, he'd be eating dinner with Kate, talking easily about the day, then she'd be weeping at his grave, then he'd be hacking Roger Houston into pieces with an axe and nailing his bits to the door, Kate shouting over the top, 'I told you so, I told you so, I told you so.' Adam pulled out of his fantasies with a pounding heart, his jaw clenched, adrenaline pumping. These fantasies of vigilante justice might express the urge for moral equilibrium, but it was an illusion. They made him paranoid and edgy, half terrified when he braved his way to the shops to stock up on beer and milk. Every time he put the key in the front door he felt as if he was about to be mugged.

Kate was gone. Jim Sway had taken the opportunity to retire on a high note and sent occasional emails from his new life as a vigneron. Wine confused Adam now. He drank beer for the bubbles, and vodka for the effect. Like many middle-aged men, his friends were mostly acquaintances. His real friends had dwindled over the years through families, careers, the social dominance of wives and male laziness. His social life consisted of work colleagues and 'their' friends, but when Kate left, their friends went with her, except for the odd group email like when the Hendersons returned from South America with an adopted child. He began to explore social media for the first time. Only Bob, recovering from the train wreck of his own personal life, was happy enough to spend time with an angry-eyed man whose glum talk came out of his mouth in a garble. 'At least you weren't working in radio.' he said.

It was Bob who suggested that Adam might like to try Vipassana, a ten-day silent retreat at Blackheath in the Blue Mountains. Bob had done the course once. The food was shit and some of the dharma talks a bit hard to take, but it had helped his brain declutter and had put some of the humour back into his cynicism, which was in the habit of slipping into Gothic futility.

Adam poo-poohed the idea. But then he lost a bet over a cricket match with his friend and there he was on the train to Blackheath, ten days of silence ahead of him. On the first afternoon they were shown around. The rules were explained. A gruelling schedule of meditation that started at 4am and didn't finish until 9.30pm. No talk, no reading, no writing, no phones, no touching, no coffee, no jogging.

The first dharma talk was from an Asian monk whose English was difficult to understand. Adam didn't really pay much attention. His mind was locked into its own obsessions. The talk was followed by the first of the meditations they would be doing at least four times a day for the next ten days. At first, he found it weird. Sitting there with his legs crossed silently marking from a point on his abdomen the rise and fall of his breath. Adam was a stimulation junkie. He found it hard to sit still without a magazine, book, television or stereo to anchor him. The initial feeling was one of overwhelming boredom and restlessness. He twiddled his thumbs. Thoughts buzzed around his brain like flies about a sheep, and were just as impossible to catch. Unremembered childhood grievances came super-imposed upon forgotten clashes with work colleagues and lusty regrets about women he had only met once. His obsessions remained on high rotation, like a chief sponsor's ad during the telecast of a major sporting event.

THE GUTS

He dreamed of all the things he could do with a tongue. He only managed to counter the urge to leave by imagining the shit he'd cop from Bob, who wasn't a fan of people who welshed on their bets.

The days passed, the noise of his mind intensified in proportion to the silence outside it. A flock of Myna birds at dawn, screeching into the soft edges of an insomniac's hard-won dreams. A fragmenting burble; arguing, chattering, interrupting. The opinions of all the bit-part actors that made up his mind. Moral diatribes, bursts of abuse, tempting rationalisations aimed with delicious smoothness at character weaknesses, schizoid mimicry – the borrowed voices of parents, bosses, wives – blazing arguments, vain resistances, the ghosts of all his forgotten great ideas whispered their laments. Fragile moderate voices were branded as cowardly and hauled back into silence by unforgiving will. The parliament of his mind had been unseated, replaced by a rule of cliques. He was structurally corrupt. In all the cacophony, there was nothing he could rely on. After all, which of the voices was actually him?

On day five, this mental noise began to abate. Dark thoughts surged into the new emptiness. He obsessed over the choices that had led to the loss of Kate and his tongue. The events rolled through him like the chundering sets of a big surf. His skin was itchy electric. His legs twitched. Involuntary shudders bolted up his spine and rattled his neck. His eyes leaked tears and his head ached from the clenching of his jaw. Nausea concentrated in the pit of his stomach, as if his intestines were a tug-o-war rope. Every thought was a potential brain aneurysm, whatever they were meant to feel like.

On the sixth evening in the meditation hall, he keeled over and spewed up a litre of lentil soup. He went to bed and slept. When he woke, Adam knew he had crossed a threshold. For the next few days, a feeling of stillness came and went. It was respite from the past and the future. At the end of the course, he caught the train down the mountain sheltered by a new tranquillity. It survived the change to the Eastern Suburbs line at Central and the walk down the hill from Bondi Junction to his apartment.

When he opened the front door, however, the old fears assailed him. He wasn't alone. Now that Houston was gone, and Mahone, were they cleaning up all the loose ends? He stood still, listening closely, ready to run. A noise came from the kitchen. Footsteps.

It was Kate! 'Hi!'

'Hi. How was I'ary?'

'Bellissimo.'

'Good.'

'How are you?'

'A bit berrer.' Tee was one of the hardest sounds to say. 'Coffee?'

It was strange. She was already there, yet he was playing the host. Kate patted her stomach and paused before answering. 'No thanks.'

''ea?'

'I've just had a glass of water. Adam I've got something I need to tell you.'

The last of his tranquillity drained. He felt sick. He looked at her. She looked at him. Her hands were crossed in front of her and her right thumb was rubbing her left wrist. She shifted her weight between her feet. He waited.

'Adam! O shit! I don't know how to say this.'

He stared at her. Waiting. Wondering who it was that she had met.

'I'm pregnant.'

He took a deep breath.

'Is i' mine?'

Kate looked at him. Was it love or pity he saw in her eyes?

'It is if you want it to be.'

His heart thumped. Was he too ruined to go through with it? He looked at Kate. What did she think? The answer came. What else was there? He smiled and nodded his head, 'Yes!'

Later that night when they had finished talking and Kate, still jet-lagged, was asleep, Adam lay in bed and thought of his child and the world it would have to live in. Maybe what he had done was worth it, that the battle for a fair and honest society was ongoing, and always

THE GUTS

would be. He had played his part and paid a heavy price, but when he was gone, perhaps he'd be remembered with pride.